## Lonely Road

Nevil Shute was born in 1899 and educated at Shrewsbury School and Balliol College, Oxford. Having decided early on an aeronautical career, he went to work for the de Havilland Aircraft Company as an engineer, where he played a large part in the construction of the airship R100. His first novel, *Marazan* (1926), was written at this time, After the disaster to the R101, he turned his attention to aeroplane construction and founded his own firm, Airspeed Ltd, in 1931. In the war Nevil Shute served in the Navy, doing secret work for the Admiralty. He still found time to write, however, and during this time produced several novels including *Pied Piper*, *Pastoral* and *Most Secret*. These were followed in 1947 by *The Chequer Board* and, in 1948, *No Highway*, which became a great best-seller and an extremely popular film. In 1948 he went to Australia for two months, a trip that inspired his most popular novel, *A Town Like Alice*. He returned there for good with his family, and remained until his death in 1960. His later novels include *In the Wet*, *Requiem for a Wren*, *On the Beach* and *Trustee from the Toolroom*.

Nevil Shute
# Lonely Road

**Pan Books** in association with
**William Heinemann**

First published 1932 by William Heinemann Ltd
This edition published 1962 by Pan Books Ltd,
Cavaye Place, London SW10 9PG,
in association with William Heinemann Ltd
13th printing 1978
All rights reserved
ISBN 0 330 20268 5
Made and printed in Great Britain by
Hunt Barnard Printing Ltd, Aylesbury, Bucks

# AUTHOR'S NOTE

THIS was the third of my books to be published, in 1932, when I was thirty-three years old. It took me about a year to write it, in the evenings after a day spent on other work, and it was written twice through from start to finish. I was evidently still obsessed with police action as a source of drama, but with the growth of experience in writing, the character studies and the love story appear to have smothered the plot a bit, and these aspects of the book now seem to me to be the best.

The first chapter was quite frankly an experiment, and one which pleases me still. It was a dangerous experiment, however, for a young writer to make in the first pages of a book, for it defeated a good many readers who might have enjoyed the story if they had been able to read on. In spite of this the book did moderately well in this country and in America. In 1936 a film was made from it at the Ealing Studios, starring Clive Brook and Victoria Hopper.

NEVIL SHUTE

*When thy story long time hence shall be perused,*
*Let the blemish of thy rule be thus excused—*
*None ever lived more just, none more abused.*

THOMAS CAMPION

# PREFACE

THE writer of this book, Malcolm Logan Stevenson, was born in the year 1891. On the death of his father, in 1895, the boy came under the care of his uncle, Sir Lionel Cope, the greater part of his boyhood being spent at Courton Hall in West Sussex. He was educated at Winchester and New College. Throughout his life his financial position was such as to cause him no anxiety; he was, in fact, a man of very considerable estate.

As a young man he displayed little enthusiasm for any form of regular occupation, in marked distinction to his later life. His interests at that time were essentially in things adventurous rather than academic. From Oxford he joined the ill-fated Catter-Delina expedition to the Amazon, leaving this country for Para in the autumn of 1911. He returned to England with the survivors of that party in the spring of 1913 and devoted himself with some energy to the sport of yacht cruising, an exercise to which he was much attached. In the winter of 1913 he commenced a desultory study of the economic factors affecting commercial ships and shipping, spending some months upon the Clyde. Previous to the war, however, he made no venture in this business.

In September, 1914, he was granted a commission as Sub-Lieutenant in the RNVR, and served upon minesweepers until the summer of 1917, principally in the Channel and the Irish Sea. During this period his vessel was twice mined; in the second of these explosions he lost the third and fourth fingers of his left hand.

In September, 1917, he was promoted to Lieutenant and was posted to a so-called mystery ship, the *Jane Ellen*, of Bideford, under Commander D. A. Faulkner, RN. This vessel was a coastal schooner of some one hundred and fifty tons, normally trading in china clay and coal between the southern ports of Cornwall and the north-east coast. Under Commander Faulkner she was employed as a submarine decoy.

The action of the *Jane Ellen* (HMS Q 83) will be found

described in a supplement to the *London Gazette* published shortly after the Armistice, together with the list of awards. Sir Arthur Mortimer, in the second volume of his 'Naval History of the Great War', gives a reliable account of the engagement, which he refers to as 'one of the bloodiest naval actions ever fought'. Briefly, the *Jane Ellen* engaged the U187 at dawn, on April 18th, 1918, at a point some forty miles west of the Scillies. Casualties on the British vessel were extremely heavy and included the Commander, the ship's company of forty-seven being reduced eventually to three in number Finally the U187 was sunk by gunfire at about noon, the gun being manned by Lieutenant Stevenson and a midshipman. No survivors were rescued from the German vessel.

As a result of this action Stevenson was promoted to Lieutenant-Commander; he was then about twenty-seven years of age. Injuries to his lungs, aggravated by exposure, necessitated a prolonged period in hospital subsequent to the action. It would not be beyond the truth to say that these injuries were ultimately responsible for his early death.

In the spring of 1919 Commander Stevenson commenced to build up a fleet of schooners and small ketches which had carried the bulk of the coastwise traffic of this country before the war. At that time these vessels had disappeared almost entirely from British waters. A certain number of them were sold abroad during the war; the remainder were sunk as they carried on their business.

In the years following the war Commander Stevenson repurchased a number of these vessels from their Scandinavian owners and, establishing himself in a shipyard on the River Dart, commenced to operate them in their ancient trade. At the time of his death he was the owner of no less than seventeen of these ships. At the outset this speculation involved him in a financial loss which was severe even for a man of his resources; in later years the losses decreased, and at the time of his death the business was in a fair way to show a profit.

In the settlement of his estate the fleet was broken up, the majority of the vessels being sold abroad again. It is doubtful whether this form of coastwise trading can be regarded as an economic business in these days. It is at least doubtful whether Commander Stevenson cared if it were so or not.

From the year 1919 until his death, ten years later, he lived in the Port House above Dartmouth Harbour, alone but for a housekeeper and a few servants. As the business of his fleet became stereotyped, demanding less of his attention, he showed some inclination to develop his shipyard as a building centre for yachts and small sailing craft of various kinds.

In the winter of last year he died, after a comparatively short illness, at the early age of thirty-nine.

In person, Malcolm Stevenson was a man of medium height; his hair, from the war onwards, was almost completely grey. He walked with a slight limp; he was sensitive to the injury to his left hand, for which reason he usually wore a glove. In temperament he was very taciturn, perhaps bitter. He was popular with his acquaintances but admitted few to friendship; with women he was diffident and shy. He had few interests beyond the sea. For recreation he was accustomed to cruise single-handed, or with at most one friend, in his ten-ton cutter *Runagate*; he was a regular competitor in the Ocean Race. He was a member of the Squadron. He held both Master's and Extra Master's certificates, and on occasions when he was short of a skipper would sometimes act as Master in one of his own little ships upon a coastal cruise.

He had few relatives, and those few he neglected. His closest tie was with his cousin, Lady Stenning. In the later years of his life he seldom left Dartmouth except to stay at her house in Golders Green, and he became on terms of considerable friendship, if not intimacy, with her husband, Sir Philip Stenning. To Sir Philip he left a very considerable legacy; for the remainder, his testament was eccentric and beyond the scope of this preface.

The book which is now published was written by Commander Stevenson shortly before the illness which terminated in his death. The MS is written in pencil in a foolscap ledger freely interspersed with memoranda of a personal nature; it would seem from internal evidence that the compilation of this book was a relaxation for his leisure hours over a period of about two months.

In the settlement of his estate the MS was read first by the writer of this preface, and later by Sir Philip and Lady

Stenning, who confirmed the truth of the account. It seemed desirable, and even necessary, that the facts contained therein should be made public at an early date, for which reason it was first proposed that a condensed and impersonal edition of the narrative should be prepared. Upon a closer investigation, however, it became evident that the task of expurgation would prove to be a most formidable one, and that a great mass of extraneous matter would require to be inserted in explanation of motives which were wholly personal and therefore to be omitted from the book. In these circumstances it has seemed better to publish the MS substantially in the form in which it was discovered, only modifying those names and places which bear too close a relation to the world as it is lived in today.

With this course the relatives of Commander Stevenson are in agreement. I am indebted to Sir Lionel Cope for advice upon matters pertaining to the family, and to Lady Stenning for much assistance in the preparation of the narrative. If the effect of publication in this form should be to indicate a quality of greatness in a man of singular reserve, then the intrusion into his privacy may not be quite unjustified.

T. A. JENKINSON

*Messrs. Louden, Jenkinson, and Priestly,*
*Lincoln's Inn Fields,*
*London.*

# CHAPTER 1

I THINK that as a man pursues his life he sometimes comes to a point, just once and again, when he must realise that for the last three weeks or six he has been living as a stranger to himself. That has happened to me on two or three occasions, generally in connection with some girl; I cherish these vignettes, only a few weeks each, in which I have been kind and true, thought clearly and acted generously. I cherish them as an old lady cherishes her love-letters—things unreal, almost unbelievable in their tenderness, and yet which actually happened. For this reason I want to write down something about the weeks I lived last summer, so that if I live to be old I may have this notebook with me to look over. It is the details, the silly little things that meant so much to me, that I want to remember; I should be very willing to forget the major incidents.

I crashed my car one night last spring, driving home along the shore road in the dark. That is what they told me in the nursing home, when I recovered consciousness on the evening of the following day. But I think I must begin my story before that, and try if I can put down all that I have ever been able to remember of the earlier portion of the night, before my accident.

What I have to write about that evening will appear confused. Bachelor evenings sometimes are like that, and I had much that day that I would willingly have drowned in gin. Looking back now upon that evening I think I must have had some measure of success, and that is what made the elucidation of my accident a little difficult when I came to my senses in the nursing home. But I had better start by putting down exactly what I can remember of that night.

I was in Plymouth. I don't know exactly when it was that I left the club; it was after midnight. I must have been the last to leave, or one of the last. I remember we had dinner in the club and went on to the Empire; we had a box there. Then we went back to the club for a game of snooker. I won that, not because I can play snooker, but because I was practically stone sober. Nothing seemed to sink me that night, which was a pity.

I was the last to leave, or one of the last. Our three cars were drawn up together outside the club, and because I could see that the others might want help I waited till they got away. Kennet was the first to go; he got in to second all right, but third defeated him, and so he went home like that. It was Jim's turn next, and I put him into his saloon and pressed the starter for him, and shut the door, and pushed him off back home. I was left by myself on the pavement, then, thirty miles from my own place. And I was alone, or I supposed I was. I don't remember anyone else.

I stood there for a bit looking round, and the moon was very round and plain and the sky was deep blue, so that the moon hung in it like a great shilling. Behind me and to the left there were lights in the downstairs of the house; I stood there nursing my apples and wondering what they would do if they knew that I was there. By standing on my toes I could rest my arms on the top of the wall and see into the paddock. I had to rest my arm like that because the faggots hurt my bare feet, and the roughness of the bricks rasped my arms and chest through the woolly stuff of my pyjamas. And where I pressed my chest against the wall the apple crammed into the pocket of my jacket stuck into me and hurt, and I think perhaps I may have bruised it because there was a great scent of apples in the brilliant silence of the night.

I saw an owl fly out from somewhere into the trees on the other side of the paddock; I heard him hoot and I wondered if that meant that he had caught a mouse. I knew that was what he came out for, to catch mice. And I wondered, as I stood there shifting from foot to foot, how he could manage to see such a little thing as a mouse in the darkness or whether it was just a sort of story like they tell you when they think it's something that you ought not to know.

I could hear the pony chumping away over on the other side of the field, but he was in the dark shadow of the trees and I couldn't see where he was, but only hear him chumping. I wondered if I could catch him with an apple, because I could spare one of my apples to catch him and have a ride on his back. I could get another one as I went back through the garden to the house. I'd probably have to leave one apple behind anyway, because I didn't see how I was going to climb up to my bedroom window carrying three of them, because you want two hands to carry three apples and I had to have one left to climb with.

I thought he might come for an apple, but it wasn't so good as a bit of sugar, because I knew he'd come for that, because I'd tried it. And they said I must hold my hand quite flat, and not be afraid. And then I wondered if I caught him whether he would let me get on to his back, or whether I could, because he was much too high for me to get up on to unless he would let me lead him up to the gate and get on him from that. I wondered whether he would stand still and let me climb up his front leg. I thought that I could get on his back that way if he'd stand still and let me, and I wondered if people ever tried that way of getting on to a pony's back. Because I'd never heard of it being done.

I stood there for a long time in the bright moonlight, shifting from one foot to the other on the crinkly woodpile, resting my folded arms on the wall and looking over. I had three apples in my hands and another in my pyjama jacket that was digging into me as it rubbed against the wall. And I stood there till I was sleepy for my bed, and cold in my pyjamas, and stiff with standing on my toes and with the pain in my feet.

And presently somebody touched me on the shoulder. "Beg pardon, sir," he said, "but was you wanting . . . anything?"

Very slowly I raised myself and turned my head; then I dropped my arms from the saloon top of my car and stood erect upon the kerb. The moon was very round and plain and the sky was deep blue, so that the moon hung in it like a great shilling. It was Nicholson, the grey-haired, infinitely discreet, head waiter at the club. He was in a soft hat and a raincoat; on his way home, I suppose. And I had something in my hand, and I said to him: "What's this I've got, Nicholson?"

I think I remember that the old man chuckled, and he said: "Why, sir, that's the apple what you took away with you from the dinner table, and you've been carrying about with you all evening."

And I stared at him, and I said: "Is it an eating apple?"

13

And he said: "Yes, sir, they're very good apples, those."

"Then I'll eat it," I said, conscious of having reached a true decision after wading through a tangled mass of evidence. "I'll eat it, Nicholson. And I'm bloody sorry to have kept you up so late."

"Oh, that's all right, sir," he said. I think I must have got away then, because the next thing that I remember is that I was sliding through the outskirts of the town at fifty or sixty, raucous on the horn at every corner that I passed.

Some time that night I passed through a village, the street brilliant in the yellow light of the acetylenes. I remember that very clearly. I swung her round by the school and opened her out as we dropped down the hill into the country, and as we went I looked at my watch and calculated that we had averaged twenty-eight miles an hour for the run. With open country and clear roads ahead it ought to be possible to do better; with luck I might push that up to an average thirty for the journey. I thought that there were very few cars in England that could do that speed at night. And full of this I leaned over to Jardine beside me in the bucket seat and shouted against the roaring of the engine that I would bet him a sovereign that we should be in Oxford by eleven.

He pulled out his watch, snapped it open, leaned forward to study it in the dim light reflected from the road, and shook his head. "You can't do seventeen miles in thirty-one minutes," he shouted.

I laughed. "I can. She'll go up to fifty if I let her out."

He went fumbling round the back of his seat as the great car pitched and dithered. "Have an apple," he said, and held one out to me. "What's she doing now?"

I peered at the square box of the speedometer, but it was too dark to see the flickering needle. "I bet we were doing forty-five along that straight," I said, crunched my teeth into the apple, and dropped it on my lap to clutch the jerking wheel before we left the road. And as I drove I can remember that the scent of apples rose all around me in the draughty stuffiness beneath the hood.

I don't know what time it was when we drew up before the new motor garage in Longwall Street, but I remember chucking the sovereign to Jardine for him to catch as we stood upon the pavement waiting for the young manager to come and open up. In that place there was a light in the offices upstairs to all hours of the night. I think he used to design cars up there by night after the work of the garage was over for the day; I remember going up there one night when I was late and drinking coffee with him and listening as he told me of the cars he had in mind to build. Cars for everybody; the cars of a dream. He was very lean and restless; he brushed his hair straight back from his forehead and he worked all night.

We walked on down Holywell to the digs; the moon was round and bright and the sky deep blue, and it was very still. There was whisky and a siphon left out for us on the table in the digs. I had driven the car too hard upon the run from London; that and perhaps the whisky filled my night with dreams, the nightmares of the road. Once a white donkey walked out of a gate into the road in the brilliance of my headlights not thirty yards ahead of me. I must have been doing sixty and I flung the car sideways beneath its nose, and missed it, and took the grass by the roadside with a lurch and a tremendous skid, and I awoke clutching the blankets in a sweat of terror. And once, sitting quiet in the saloon, driving with one hand and with the other fingering the apple in my pocket because it seemed to be that that was the only thing worth having that remained, I came round a bend in the road at a great speed to find myself faced by a plain brick wall and a shop front, where the road made a **T**-turn in a little town. In such a case the movements are entirely automatic. I remember the ringing grind of the brakes, the scream of the tyres, and a series of swift accelerations and rotations, and the Bentley came to a standstill ten yards up the top right-hand arm of the **T**, broadside across the road with the front and rear wheels in the gutter on each side.

And there was a man standing by the corner of the pavement. It was very quiet in the little street, and I said to him: "I didn't drop my apple." Because when we had broadsided to a standstill I found I had it undamaged in my hand, and it was fragrant in the stuffiness of the saloon.

He said: "What's that?"

And I said: "I didn't drop my apple."

In the dim light he walked slowly towards the window at my elbow. "You didn't ought to drive like that," he said heavily. "Where d'you want to go to?"

I sat there staring at him for a minute. I could go anywhere I liked, because I had had the car filled up in Plymouth. Three hundred miles. I could go on the run and get right away, if that was any good.

"London," I said at last. "I should be there by dawn."

He said: "You want to go through Totnes for that. That way." And he pointed to the other road.

I jerked my head towards the road that I was on. "Where does this go?" But I knew. It went home. And I knew that if I went the other way that night it would only be because I was afraid to go back and be alone.

"Slapton," he said.

I nodded. "That's right," I said. "That's where I want to go." I backed the car a little and then swung her forward over the pavement of that narrow street and went gently up between the houses for fear that I should wake the sleeping people of the town, and over a bridge across a river and so out into the moonlit country where I was alone again.

I shall always be alone. It seemed to me then that I was back in the little town that I had left that afternoon, and although I suppose that these things must have happened earlier in the day I cannot expunge them from the sequence of my memories of the night. I think they may have happened to me that afternoon. I only know they happened to me that night.

There was a sunset in the room. There must have been, because there is no other light that could have given to her face and throat the warm glow, translucent, that was spreading slowly downwards as she leaned forward to scrape the ashes from the grate. It was early in April, and it was a Wednesday, because that was her free day. It was just after tea. I remember that because she had given me tea in her little room; the teapot and the large, blue-rimmed cups with oranges on them were still upon the table. I don't know why there was a fire, or how there could have been a sunset at tea-time on that day. But there was. No other light could have given to her the warm colours that I remember, and I remember them so well.

We stayed there like that for a long time in silence. I had said all that I had to say; I leaned back in my chair and watched her playing with the poker till the fire glowed in the bars with a fierce, destructive efficiency that was foreign to that room. I knew what was coming to me, and as I sat there I can remember thinking that one should just take what little pleasures one can get and let the big ones go, the policy of small profits. And so I sat quiet in her room while she would let me, watching the play of the light upon the soft, straight hair that ended at her neck, and the grace of her movements. I have these things still, so that I saved something after all from the disaster of that afternoon.

And presently she looked up at me. "I'm so frightfully sorry," she said quietly. "You do know that, don't you? I never knew you cared for me like that a bit. Or not so much. I thought we were—just friends."

My time was getting short, and at the thought I stirred a little in my chair. "Well, we weren't," I said. "That was just my cunning. You ought to have seen through that."

She shook her head. "I didn't. You've been so quiet about it. Honestly, I never knew that you were thinking about me in that way. Or I'd have let you know before—that it wasn't any good."

I nodded. "I know you would."

She laid the poker down and turned to me. "It's been a wonderful thing to hear you say this," she said simply. "For me. It means a lot to a girl to hear what you've said to me. I'm only so frightfully sorry that I can't play up." She paused, and turned again towards the fire so that she gave me back her profile. "Of course, I know that you could make things different for me—with all your money. I suppose you'd be able to give me all the little bits of things I've wanted all my life"—her voice dropped a little—"things that I'll never be able to afford. But that's not everything—is it? You wouldn't want me to marry you for that?"

I roused myself. "No," I said quietly. "I wouldn't want you to marry me for that." It wasn't true, but it sounded as if it was the right thing to say.

"And there's nothing more to it than that," she said.

I winced a bit at that one. I suppose everyone likes to picture himself as a Lancelot, though God knows I ought to have outgrown that by now. And while I was recovering I said:

"You're quite sure about it? You know you can have as long as you like, to think it over."

She shook her head. "It wouldn't be any good. I'm most frightfully sorry—for myself as well as you. But if it was ever going to be different, I think one'd know."

"I suppose you would," I said.

I would willingly have spun out the Indian summer that remained to us. I would have liked to have sat on for a little longer in the room with her, but there was nothing left to stay for. And so:

"I expect it's time I went away," I said.

She came with me to the door. "There's such lots of other girls," she said quietly. "Malcolm, you won't go worrying about this? It's not worth it. You'll find somebody else"— she did not say 'with all your money'—'and then you'll probably be glad it wasn't me.'

I turned to her and laughed. "You don't want to worry about that," I said. "This happens to me every eighteen months. There's only another seven or eight months to go before I start again. I run pretty regularly to schedule."

She eyed me a little wistfully. "I wish you didn't live alone."

I laughed. "I'm not going to—not next winter, anyway. I'll pay some sweet young thing a salary to come and live with me." I think that reassured her a little, because she was smiling when I went away. We succeeded in making a joke out of what might have been a most embarrassing affair, and so it is that my last memory of her is of her laughter.

All that night her laughter followed me along the winding roads that stretched brilliantly in front of me and eddied into dust behind. I remember that there was a bridge. I stood there for a moment staring down the stream, and as I stood there listening to the rippling of the water it seemed to me that here was a pause in my journey, a little time when I might be alone. I had left my hat somewhere, and a wind came down the river lifting the hair upon my forehead and blowing coolly in my face. My mouth was dry and parched. And so I went down the bank a little way until I reached the gravel spit where the cattle went down to drink. I had an apple with me in my hand, and as I stooped to drink I thrust it deep into the pocket of my ulster to be safe. I can remember that the water was very cool and sweet upon my face, dipping it up and drinking from my hands, and the moon most infinitely clear. Beyond the bridge the Bentley loomed silent by the roadside, a dark mass pierced by the brilliance of the red tail light. It was very quiet by the stream.

I left the water and went and sat down upon a hummock of grass on the bank, and as I went I shivered. And I remember that I was concerned about myself because I was feeling cold; I wrapped my coat more closely round me and thought I must get back to the car. I thought that I must be very careful now and look after myself very well, or I should be ill again. That, I suppose, is one of the last tenets of the bachelor, but for three months I had forgotten it. But now, from now onwards, I said that I must be very careful and look after myself, because there'd be nobody to do it for me. And that amused me a little, and I remembered being amused by it before.

And so I went back to the car upon the bridge, fingering the apple as I went; I swung the door open and got in and we moved away down the lane. And as we went the lights by the roadside loomed and swung, so that each standard as we passed it threw a beam of light into the car, gleaming upon the white and silver of the young woman's dress beside me. I forget her name now, but she was a wombat, a little brown furry animal that Joan had wished on to me because she thought I ought to have a wife.

In the front seat Joan sat impassive by Stenning; beyond their heads the street shone glimmering in the rain. We were in Baker Street. I knew that neither of them would dream of turning round and that it was up to me to get on with it, and make the most of my opportunities. It was quite a nice wombat; I wish I could remember its name. And so I talked to it about the play that we had seen—*Lilac Time*. A good dinner, a play like that, and then a nice long drive in the narrow back seat of a warm saloon, in the dark. It should have worked all right.

Stenning was in the game. He took his right-hand corners normally because I was sitting on the right-hand side, but on the left-hand ones he swung her round as if he was road racing on a dry road in the summer. And after the second or third of those I found that she was snuggled in against my shoulder with my arm round her, and there was Schubert in the car. And she said:

"They'll look round." I can remember her little whisper in the darkness as she raised her face to mine.

"Not unless you scream," I said. "And I don't think that would be a very good idea, myself." And true to programme I bent and kissed her, because it's perfectly absurd for a man like me not to be married, with all my money. And true to programme, she whispered: "You did that because you know I daren't scream."

And as I held her in my arms I knew that here was a termination of the matter, and that Joan had failed. I had set a new mainsail on *Runagate* before I came away, and I was worrying whether I had left enough slack in the clew to allow for the shrinkage of the wet weather. I wanted that sail for racing, and it wouldn't do to have the shape all spoilt. I knew that I oughtn't to be thinking about that sail with the wombat in my arms; that I should have been giving my whole attention to the job in hand. And I wasn't.

The lights dipped and swung as we ran out into the suburbs. It was warm and comfortable in the saloon, and the wombat seemed to fit my shoulder pretty well. She was very quiet after a bit, and I was worried about the sail and not sorry not to have to talk. And presently I realised that she was asleep. Asleep with my arm around her and her head on my shoulder. I have never had a girl like that before or since. If I hadn't been a bloody fool I should have married her, I suppose, but I was much more worried about the sail.

And presently I took my arm from her, and stopped the car, and got out by the roadside. It was where the road ran not far from the sea; the rain had all gone and left a dusty road; there was a bright moon on the tumbled water and a sound of surf. And as I crossed the field I had a great desire to get where I could see the surf running up the dim line of the beach; on a night like that it would be silvery beneath the moon, with little flashes of bright fire where it drained. All my life I have lived with no other thought than to satisfy my own desires; at that moment I wanted above all things to see the surf breaking on the beach beyond the field, and so I pressed on across the grass.

And presently it seemed to me that I came to a place where the field petered out in sandhills that ran down to the beach, and the line of the surf perhaps two hundred yards away. There was a vessel there anchored very close inshore and black against the moonlight, not quite opposite me but a little way along. From the set of her one-pole mast she might have been a Thames bawley of about fifty tons, or she might have been like the smacks that I have seen in Rotterdam. I only saw her silhouette. There was a dinghy drawn up on the beach opposite her; the surf was very low. And the surf was as I had known that it would be; it was running up the sand around the boat all silvery in the moonlight, with little flashes of bright fire where it drained.

I moved forward down a valley of the sandhills to where the girl was standing with her back to me. She was dressed in some dark manner, black or blue, and she was staring at the boat and at the running surf, as I had done. And I came quietly through the deep sand till I was very close to her, fingering my apple, and I said: "That would make a dry point. Achaersen could do it, but he couldn't get it into the Academy, could he?"

She swung round on me. "You should have stayed up by the lorry. It's no good your trying to get on board yet. There's half a dozen carpet sweepers to come off." And then she said: "Is Peter coming down?"

I didn't understand what she was saying; I was tired, and I was very lonely. I had nothing but my apple. "You're wrong," I said. "I'm not going to sea tonight. I'm tired. I think I'm going home."

She leaned forward suddenly and stared into my face, and I can remember a look of great anxiety, of terror, as she stared at me.

"Who are you?" she exclaimed. "There's something wrong. You're not the man who was here before. You're English."

I nodded. "I'm a sojourner," I said, "as all my fathers were."

I drew my apple from my pocket, because she looked a friendly sort of girl who would be nice to me, up to a point, and I wanted to show it to her and tell her all about it. But she drew back and stood there staring at me, quite still, and it seemed to me that she thought that something terrible was going to happen in a moment.

And then she said, very quietly: "Oh, don't."

And then it seemed to me that I was down upon my face in a little lapping noise of water and a smell of burning, and somewhere about me there was the beating and tumbling of a sailing vessel in irons in a light wind. And somebody bent over me and said:

"He isn't dead."

And presently they turned me over, and there was a splash of water on my face. I stirred and opened my eyes, half blind with pain. I was lying in a slop of blood and water on the deck. I would have sat up then, but Wallis, leading seaman, pressed me down upon the deck and whispered: "Keep down, sir." And then the snotty came crawling back along the bulwarks with another pannikin of water.

I took it from him and drank. "How many of us are there now?" I asked.

"There's only us," he said.

The vessel was on fire aft and it seemed to me that she was settling by the stern; the whole stern must have been blown out when the magazine went up.

"They stopped the shelling ten minutes ago," he said. "They're practically dead ahead, sir. A little on the port bow."

"Where's the panic party?"

Wallis swore, "The dirty b——rs," he said. The snotty said: "They shelled the boat, sir. I don't think there's anybody left." And then he said: "It wasn't playing the game, sir."

I retched violently. And when that was over I asked: "Is there any armament left?"

"Aye, sir," said Wallis, "there's the port six-pounder and eight rounds. She'll want to be broad on the beam for it, but the gun's all right."

I saw it lying on the deck upon its swinging mounting, behind the bulwarks. It had not been touched. The vessel lay upon the water like a log; she lay heavily and each time she sank into the trough the coming swell sluiced down the bulwarks burying the hull, so that I thought that she was never going to rise. Astern she was awash, so that there was a hissing and crackling, and a great cloud of smoke where fire and water met. I thought of Jardine, dead in the Dardanelles, and of Fordyce.

"This is the end for us," I said. I knew that there would be no relief from the outside; we had sent no wireless for assistance before the action had begun, and that had been the first to go. "It's no good surrendering." I could see the wreckage of the boat astern.

The snotty had wriggled on his stomach to the hawse-hole.

"She's running slow ahead," he whispered. "She's coming round on to the beam."

I wriggled up beside him. The submarine was running slowly across our bows, submerged but for a portion of the conning tower, and the twin periscopes; occasionally, as the waves swept over her, we could see the gun. Then she went down entirely but for the periscopes, and began to travel slowly down the port beam, distant perhaps five hundred yards from us. She was examining her handiwork. Then she got on to the quarter and the smoke hid her from our gaze. We lay motionless upon the deck.

Ten minutes later we saw her again on the starboard quarter, approaching us from the direction of the boat. She came close up to us this time, the periscope passing up the vessel's side not fifty yards away. If we had had a depth-charge thrower left we might have got her then, but all that stuff had gone.

She turned slowly across our bows, and broke surface dead ahead. I couldn't see her from my position; I had to depend on whispers from the snotty. And then I saw her. She was running on the surface very slowly, perhaps two hundred yards away, and turning to pass down our port side again.

"Come up to finish us off, I reckon," whispered Wallis.

"Be ready for it," I replied.

Her speed slowed to a crawl, and a man appeared in the conning tower, and then an officer. And then in a moment there were men on her deck and about the gun; there was nothing now to wait for. And I said:

"Right. Get on with it." Then we were on our feet and racing for the gun. It swung up smoothly; the shell slid into the chamber and the breech clanged home, and I swung her by the rubber at my shoulder and laid her to the water line below their gun. We got our first shot off before they did and that was a pretty good show, but the vessel lurched as I fired and it went over their heads. They hit us with a burster forward while we were loading, and I laid and fired again. And this time it went well, because I holed her on the water line between the gun and the conning tower, and our third shot burst beside the gun, so that when the smoke cleared there was nobody standing up on deck to serve that gun. The fourth shot I laid more slowly and more carefully, and holed her again at the base of the conning tower and a little aft.

She began to blow her tanks, and the water came foaming up around her all white and creamy and mingled with a little oil. She took a list to port, and then the hatches opened both forward and aft. Men began to stream up on deck out of the forward hatch; they held up their hands and one or two of them waved to us.

There were three of us, and thirty odd of them.

I snapped the breech open and the case clanged out, but the next shell was not there. The snotty was holding it and staring at the submarine crimson with excitement. He was yelling:

"Oh, damn good, sir. Bloody good."

"Stop that row," I snarled. "Get on with it."

He stared at me. "Aren't they surrendering?"

I ripped out an oath, and the shell slid into the bore. I clanged the breech to, and swung the gun till it bore upon the fore hatch with the men still coming up. And then I glanced aside, and that damn boy was staring at me in a sort of horror, and I cursed at him again. . . .

And then began my struggle towards consciousness. This was no real scene; it was a dream that I had will and power to prevent. This was no new experience to me; it was my fever dream, the recurring nightmare that has been with me for the last twelve years. But I still had my will; still power to prevent this frightful thing. And with a stern effort I awoke, and opened my eyes to an unfamiliar room, white paint and green distemper.

Nurse Malone was there, bending over me. I could not move in bed, but I was damp with sweat and quivering with fright and with the horror of the thing that I had done. I knew that I was awake and safe, and I burst out to her:

"I don't want to do it again."

She smiled a little, bending over me. "It's quite all right," she said. "I'll see that you don't do it again. But now I want you to lie quite quiet and not try to move about. Just see if you can have a real rest. You know, you've had a motor accident."

# CHAPTER 2

THE NEXT point of significance in my story is a conversation that I had with Dixon in the nursing home after my accident, a few days before I was taken back to my own house.

He came and sat beside my bed one morning when he had examined me and the nurse had gone away; he must have had an easy round that day. "I'm going to move you back into your own house next week, I think," he said. "Would you like that?"

I was as weak as a kitten. I had a continuous headache, and I was pretty miserable at night. I told him this, and said that I didn't think that I was fit to go.

He eyed me seriously. "You don't get over an accident like this in a day, or in two days, you know," he said. "For one thing, you evidently lost a great deal of blood from the wound in your head. Quite apart from the concussion."

Irrelevantly I cut him short and asked what I had wanted to know for some days now. "What's happened to my car?"

"It's been taken down to Walker's garage and they're waiting for your instructions before beginning on it. I saw it the day after the accident, and I was very much interested."

I asked: "Is she very much knocked about?"

"The radiator and the wings were very badly damaged," he replied, "and there was a lot of glass broken. But I found the most interesting part to be the hole in the fabric of the roof over the driver's seat, where your head had hit. Your head must have gone very nearly through the roof—I never saw such a thing. You must consider yourself very fortunate that it was not a coach-built body."

I was quiet for a time. "It's a hundred-and-fifty-pound job, I suppose," I said at last, a little painfully. "She must need re-upholstering with all that blood and muck."

He wrinkled up his brows a little. "I doubt if she does," he said. "There was a little mess on the roof, but the inside of the car was quite clean. I think you must have done your bleeding out of the window. She was lying on her side, you see."

I asked: "How long was I there?"

"A labourer found you on his way to work—one of the men on Halls Farm at Stoke Fleming. He must have found you at about half-past six. When did you leave Plymouth?"

I tried to recollect. "I think it must have been about half-past twelve."

He nodded. "You must have been lying there for about five hours. You know, seriously, you're extremely lucky to have come out of it so well. You might very well have died in that five hours."

I said: "Providence looks after fools and drunken men."

He stared at me, and nodded again. "Yes. You may have been a fool—I don't know about that. But I do know that you were drunk."

"So do I," I said, a little shortly.

There was a little silence then. He sat tapping his pince-nez on the palm of his hand and eyeing me, till at last he said: "You know, you're simply knocking yourself to bits. It's time you pulled up and lived like everybody else."

"Damn it, man," I said. "You talk as if I was a bloody dipsomaniac."

He was patient. "I didn't mean your drinking. I mean just this—that you're knocking yourself to bits. You don't take care of yourself. Do you, now?"

I lay and stared at him, half expecting to see him furtively consult his notes. He was not at all at his ease, and suddenly it seemed to me that he'd set himself a job that he didn't like doing. "You'd better tell me what you mean," I said.

He cleared his throat, and considered for a moment. "I don't know that I've ever had a case quite like you. I've never had a patient of your general physique through my hands so often as you, and with such a variety of ailments. Just look at them. You broke your arm in two places last summer in the races, and very nearly lost it, I may say."

"Gybing in the devil of a sea," I put in. "You can't always rely on a vessel when she's like that—especially if she's over-canvassed for racing. You know that."

He nodded. "That's why every other boat but you made a wheelbarrow tack at the buoy. Then, the winter before, you managed to turn a simple touch of flu into a pleurisy, simply because you wouldn't lie up."

"I had some work to do," I said. "That might have happened to anyone."

"The point is, that it doesn't. Then, before that, you got water on the knee—not very serious, but you neglected it, and it's only the mercy of Providence that you're not lame yet. Frankly, at the time, I thought that it was becoming chronic."

He paused. "Do you know that you've been in my hands six times in the last two years? And it's only for want of a little care."

I hadn't much to say that was worth saying. "I've been a pretty good source of income to you, taking it by and large," I said. "As good as half a dozen old ladies. You don't want me to mend my ways?"

I must have stung him up, somehow. "Well," he said drily, "I want you to go on being a source of income to me, anyway."

There was a little silence.

"I see," I said. "You think I'm a bad life."

He thought about it for a moment. "No, I don't. I didn't like that pleurisy at all. You've not got the resistance that you ought to have, but that's the infection you picked up in the war. But if you take care of yourself, I see no reason at all why you shouldn't live to be seventy or eighty."

"God forbid," I muttered.

He was annoyed. "On the other hand, if you carry on as you're doing now, you'll probably be dead within the next five years. You'll gybe in a squall when there isn't a motor boat to pick you up, or you'll get a pleurisy when I'm not there, or you'll crash your car where labourers don't come. And then you'll die."

"Yes," I said. "That's very likely what will happen."

He was a little disconcerted and lost the thread of his argument. I lay there staring out of the window while he was marshalling his fancies into order again and I heard a steamer's siren from the river, a sharp double blast. "You might have a look and see what vessel that is," I said.

He stood up. "A little collier. About five hundred tons."

I was interested. "The *Black Prince*?"

He shook his head. "I don't know them. She's got one black funnel with a double blue band." And then he turned from the window and stood looking down on me, his back to the light, his hands in his pockets. "You know," he said, "speaking as your medical man, I should advise you to get married."

I was hardly listening. It was the bi-weekly collier from Barry, but she must have had a good passage, because she had saved a tide. Old Penrose, who had had her since the war, had retired a month or so before and the owners had given the command to his nephew, who used to be her mate; a smart young chap who wore a brown bowler hat with his reefer jacket when he came ashore. I wondered if he had taken to forcing her in good weather, and whether she would stand it. Then I came back to earth and Dixon was talking at me still.

He was very earnest. "I don't know that I've ever recommended this before—to anyone. But it's what you need."

I eyed him for a minute, and he didn't like it. "You think so?"

He said: "I do think so. Living alone as you do, you're simply knocking yourself to bits. And you don't care a damn about it—do you?"

"No," I said. "I don't know that I do."

He came and sat down beside my bed again. "Look here, Stevenson," he said. "I want you to realise that you're a case to me, and nothing more. This is a matter of business to me. I'm not trying to ferret round among your private affairs; I don't know anything about them, and I don't want to. I'm not trying to get at you. All I want to tell you is that, as your medical adviser, I should advise you to get married. I think if you did that, you wouldn't find yourself in my hands quite so often."

I nodded. "You mean that I ought to get someone to look after me," I said. "I expect you're right."

He was relieved. "I'm glad you see it like that," he said frankly, "because I don't like giving this sort of advice at all. I was afraid that you might think it a considerable impertinence."

"Not at all," I murmured. "Who do you suggest that I should get?"

He smiled. "Anyone you like. There are any number of nice girls about who'd be only too glad to get married to a man of your position and your means. You won't have any difficulty in that way."

"Yes," I said quietly. "I've got the money. And that's all that really matters, isn't it?"

He hesitated. "It goes a long way," he said.

I agreed. "It does. I can pay for anything I want. You produce the medicine, and I'll pay for it all right."

He laughed. "I'm a doctor—not a matrimonial agency. I can't go chasing round the country finding girls for you to marry. But I can promise you, you won't have any difficulty. Any girl would marry you. You must realise that you're a very eligible man."

There was a little silence then. Dixon was right, of course, in what he said; I had realised it myself five years before. A man who lives entirely without women has only two alternatives as the years go on. He gets self-centred and dirty, or he dies.

I laughed. "All right," I said at last, "I'll have Irene. I suppose she'll do as well as anyone. You might tell her when you go home. You'd better send her up to me this afternoon."

I forgot all that he said to that, nor am I sure that I should write it down if I could remember it; he was very deeply hurt. His wife was dead and he had only the one daughter, and a son who was abroad. I had known the girl for some years by sight; I had watched her grow from a gawky schoolgirl into a plump and homely young woman who kept house admirably for her father, performed indifferently on the tennis courts, rode a bicycle about the town, and read some woman's paper from cover to cover every week. A most estimable young woman and as dull as ditchwater, but he thought the world of her.

He went away, very grieved and hurt. On reflection I thought that he might see a certain element of humour in the situation, but when he came again he was cold and professional, and I didn't stir him up.

I got back into my house in the following week, and as soon as I got back I went to work. Dixon was pretty rude about it— and to do him justice, I don't think it did me a lot of good, myself. I used to go down to my office at about ten o'clock and dictate a few letters that Tillotson would generally have to correct for me, and I would listen to him while he outlined his plans for the freight programme in a series of delicately-worded suggestions for my approval. Then I would send him away and sit in my office for a bit with my head in my hands, nursing a tearing headache; at half-past eleven Miss Soames would bring me a cup of tea and I'd take a handful of aspirins with it, and go for a walk round the yard. By then it would be time for a couple of drinks before lunch, and after lunch there were generally things that needed my attention in the yard. It was during that time that *Thelma* came in with her bitts carried away, warping at Fowey for the clay. That kept me busy for three days and sent me a journey to Newton Abbot to pick the timber that I wanted for the job, but mostly I spent the afternoons setting up new running gear in *Runagate,* and trying not to think about my head.

I might have stayed at home for all the good I was. But down at the yard there were things happening and people to talk to; I've never been one for sticking in the house by myself, much.

My car took about a month to repair; in that month my cousin Joan Stenning became Lady Stenning. Stenning received his knighthood within half an hour of his landing on the Thames, having sweated and cursed his way through his forty-thousand-mile flight alone round the world in the little Rawdon Dabchick flying-boat. He took nine months over the flight, which was more of a business trip than anything else, and he returned with orders for over a hundred Dabchicks, booked upon the way. He took a cinema camera with him and made films which were worth a considerable sum; his machine was literally plastered with the advertisements of the firms who had supplied him with equipment free. His flight showed a profit of six hundred per cent on the capital involved, an achievement only comparable with that of his progenitor, Sir Francis Drake.

His knighthood created a situation in my family which was not without its quiet humour. Joan had married him in 1925, and had gone to live with him in Golders Green, in undistinguished style. The family didn't like it a bit, Stenning was a professional pilot, and for a long time after their marriage, if you flew from London to Paris, the chances were that you would see him sitting patiently in the cockpit of the aeroplane, high above your head, as you embarked. Even now, if you go to the Rawdon Aircraft Company to charter an aeroplane the chances are that you will be chauffeured by a Knight of the British Empire. The material profits of his flight went mostly to the financiers who had backed him, leaving him with little but his knighthood and experience.

My family didn't quite know what to do about it. Sir Philip Stenning could no longer be ignored; it was no longer possible to refer to Lady Stenning as poor Joan. I wrote to congratulate him, and got a letter back from Joan in which she asked if I would like to run her up to Scotland for a week.

I really wasn't fit to drive again, but I wanted that holiday with Joan. It took me two days to get to London because I had to stop in Shaftesbury and go to bed. Stenning had gone to Greece to try to get rid of a few more Dabchicks. I hadn't let anyone know that I'd been ill, but Joan was very decent about it, and after a couple of days we set off up north, Joan driving the Bentley.

We got to the MacEwens' at Carthness in time for dinner on the second day; if I had been fit we should have done it in a day and not been tired. I stayed up there for ten days playing golf with Joan, and sailing their dinghy, and watching the birds. In that ten days my headaches went away, and I never got them back again. I get over these things pretty quickly as a rule.

Joan was up there for a month, but ten days was all that I could spare from the yard, and so I started off for home one morning in the Bentley. I took it easily because Joan had made me promise to spend two nights upon the way, and as she had been decent and not worried me about the crash I was inclined to keep my promise to her.

By six o'clock I was at Boroughbridge and wondering where I should put up for the night. York was not very far away, but I had stayed at York on the way up in a very famous hotel with faded lace curtains in the dining-room, and had not been impressed. And so for a whim, and because I wanted to see people of the sort that I do not usually meet, I went to Leeds and stayed in a very large and rather garish hotel in the middle of the town.

I was very lonely that night. I had left people who liked me in Scotland to come back down south to my empty house and to my own work, and though I knew that I should be content with my life when I got back to Dartmouth, for the moment

I was discontented and upset. I dined alone and rather expensively in the more select of the two restaurants of the hotel, and at the table beside me there was a party of young men and women dining not wisely but too well. In the south they would have been thrown out with the hors d'œuvres, but they were having the devil of a good time and I would have given my eyes to have been with them. There were two or three parties of elderly business men with their unattractive wives drinking champagne in solemn state, and there were two or three fat, elderly foreigners dining alone like me and, like me, trying to pretend that they were enjoying their dinner. I got tired of the pretence half-way through and cut it short, ordered a cup of coffee, and went out.

In the hall one of the waiters found me a cigar. I hung about there for a bit and managed to get into conversation with the hall porter, and was pleased to do so. He told me about the theatres that were on and I didn't like the idea of any of them, and then he started on the cinemas. And finally he said:

"There's a good Palais de Dance if you're fond of dancing, sir. Quite a good class place tonight. This is the two-shilling night, you know."

I don't dance more than once or twice a year, but I am very fond of it. This was something rather new to me, and so I said:

"They have professional partners there?"

He smiled fatly. "Oh, yes, sir. Sixpennies, you know. Sixpence a dance, or sixpence a sit out, which ever you happens to prefer. Nice respectable young ladies they are—mostly."

I nodded. The more I thought about it the more I liked the idea. I could not face the thought of going throught he evening alone, but for a pound or so I could hire a girl to spend the evening with me. For once in a way my money was some good to me, and so I went upstairs and changed my shoes, and went out to the Palais.

I sat at a table by the floor for some time before dancing. It must have been a pretty slack night at the Palais, because there cannot have been more than a dozen couples in the place. The sixpennies sat in a pen in the corner, smoking cigarettes and reading magazines; four or five girls in black silk dresses and the same number of slightly effeminate young men in dinner-jackets. There was one girl there that I liked the look of most, a little older than the rest, perhaps, and one who looked as if she wouldn't be much effort for me to entertain. And so at last I walked up to the barrier and caught her eye, and I said: "Would you care to dance this one with me?"

She glanced quickly up and down the little row of girls; a sort of commercial rectitude that insisted that she must be quite sure that the invitation was to her, and not to her neighbour. And then she looked up at me and smiled, and said: "Me? I'd like to very much."

So we danced, and she asked me if I had been long in Leeds, and I made the usual talk about the band and the floor and my own dancing, and she gave little stilted answers. And suddenly it struck me that she was busy, almost too busy to talk. Then I fell over her feet and she said quickly: "Would you do that again?" I did it again, but her feet weren't there that time. It took her about a minute and a half to learn my tricks. By the end of that quickstep I could do exactly what I liked; she danced magnificently. The dance came to a truncated end and the short encore; I walked her off the floor and put her back into the pen.

Three minutes later I got her out again for a waltz. Again she was busy at first, so that I left her alone and we danced that one in silence. I was taking her back to the pen again when she turned to me and said:

"You know, you don't need to put me back in the pen again after every dance unless you want to. They let us go and sit with gentlemen at the tables, if you like."

I said something suitable, and so we picked a table and sat down. And hardly was my chair drawn in when she remarked:

"Would you like anything from the soda fountain? A cup of coffee or anything? I'll fetch the waitress for you, if you like."

So I ordered a cup of coffee for her; she would not eat anything because eating between meals was bad for the figure. Then I bought her cigarettes. Then we danced again, and coming back to the table I had leisure to examine what I'd got.

She was not very tall, perhaps a little higher than my shoulder. She had long black hair tied up in coils about her ears and drawn straight back from her forehead; she was extravagantly made up with a dead white complexion and deep red lips. She had very large, black eyes and rather a determined chin; when she smiled she was very friendly to me. Her eye-lashes were separated into little groups, very long, each group waxed together like a little moustache. She wore a plain black silk dress and a very small gold watch upon her wrist.

I said what a pretty little watch it was; she was pleased, and took it off to show it to me. "A gentleman friend gave it to me," she said, "when I was working at Leicester. He *was* nice to me—isn't it lovely? It cost six pounds fifteen, and then he got something off because it was through a friend in the business. Another gentleman told me that you couldn't buy a watch like this for under ten pounds. Fancy! But lots of the gentlemen give us quite nice presents." I murmured something or other, and for a moment she paused to appraise my value. "He was married, but his wife used to go away a lot and then he got lonely and used to come and spend the evening with me. Are you married?"

"No," I said, "I'm not. Are you?"

She studied me for a moment through a haze of smoke. "No," she said at last, "nor anywhere near it."

She told me that her name was Miss Gordon, but her friends called her Mollie. "I do think it's soft," she said, "when professionals make up fancy names for themselves, like Edwina or Althea, like some of them do." She laughed. "Fancy me talking like that! I mean, they call me Carmen here on Friday nights, because I do a speciality dance then—tango—I've got a lovely costume for it. I do it with one of the boys here, and he's in costume too." Then we talked about her profession; she told me that she was paid ten shillings a week and half the sixpences she earned. "But then there's the tips," she said, with studied nonchalance. "Some of the gentlemen are very generous. Then other times you'll dance all night with a gentleman and never get a bean beyond the sixpences."

She told me a little about her pay. It was a good week when she took home thirty shillings from the management; living by herself alone in rooms she could hardly have got along without the tips. I was sorry then that I had made her dig so laboriously for her gold, and so I said:

"How do the tips run out? Do people double the sixpences, or something like that?"

She looked across the table at me with something that was very much like friendship. "Not many," she said generously.

34

"You see, that comes to an awful lot if you dance all evening."
She eyed me for a moment. "You've not been to a Palais much,
have you? It must be expensive for the gentlemen, having us
girls for every dance. Would you like me to go back to the
pen and dance again a bit later? Lots of people do that, you
know."

"Rather not," I said. "I've got money to spend tonight, and
I'm just beginning to enjoy myself."

She laughed with me. "I like it when people have a good
time here," she said, "because it makes it much nicer, doesn't
it?" And then she asked me: "What's your job?"

"I work for a shipping firm in the south," I said. "I'm in the
office."

She nodded, and we went and danced again. She was
immensely clever at her job, very cunning in suiting her ways
to mine. And presently she began to educate me a little in the
finer points of her peculiar art. When that happened I knew
that she was beginning to enjoy herself.

She said no more about money, apparently satisfied that it
was going to be all right at the end of the evening. She told
me a little about her life; it seemed that she had been brought
up for the stage in some fifth-rate theatrical school. For a few
years she had scratched a livelihood by occasional engage-
ments in the chorus of provincial companies; then she had
abandoned that for dancing and had wandered in a desultory
manner from Palais to Palais, staying perhaps six months in
each. She told me that her home was in Preston.

"It's not much fun being on the stage," she said, "when
you're out of a job most of the time. I'd rather do this. I've
been in quite a lot of Palais since I started. Bournemouth was
lovely—I was a silly to come away from there. But there was
a gentleman. . . ." She stared absently across the floor, then
roused herself and turned to me. "Sometimes one gets mixed up
in a place," she said quietly, "and then it's time to move on."

I nodded. "How do you like Leeds?"

She shrugged her shoulders. "I don't think I'll be here very
much longer. I want to get down to the south again, with the
summer coming on. Tell me, have you ever been to
Torquay?"

"I know it pretty well," I said. "It's not far from where I
work."

She turned to me: "Is it lovely?" And then, without waiting for my answer, she went on: "I'd love to go to Torquay. I've never been, but everybody says it's lovely there. One of the girls here went there for her holiday last year with a gentleman, and she said it was lovely. It's all on hills, isn't it, looking out over the sea, with a harbour and boats and things?"

"That's it," I said. "The shops are all along by the harbour."

She sighed. "I'd love to get into a Palais there. It must be lovely to live in a place like that. But they don't get many vacancies in those places. The girls down there, they know when they're well off."

We danced again, and came back to the table.

"Been to many shows?" she asked.

I tried to remember when I had last been to the theatre. "Not many lately," I replied. "I expect you go to lots. Or can't you get away from here?"

She blew a long cloud of smoke. "It's not very easy. You see, if you get a boy that wants to take you out he has to book you out for the session, and that costs twenty-five bob on top on what he spends outside. It's only the old ones that can do that, and I don't like going out with them. They get so silly. But I do love a show, better than anything. I expect you don't care for them much?"

I had had a long drive that day, and a good dinner. I was leaving Leeds on the next day, and it was unlikely that I should ever see this girl again. Sometimes it's a luxury to speak the truth. "I like a theatre," I said. "I like to go and have a really good dinner somewhere, and go on to a theatre, and then go and dance for an hour or so before bed. But you want to have somebody to go with; it's not much fun doing that alone."

She nodded. "Haven't you got any girl friends to go with?"

I knocked the ash off my cigarette. "No," I said. "They don't seem to come my way much." I looked at her and grinned. "That's why I have to come and pay sixpence."

She nodded, without laughing. "You're too particular," she said shrewdly. "There's ever so many like you come and dance with us—you'd be surprised. There's some that just don't want to do anything but sit and talk for a bit. It's like as if they don't seem able to fancy the girl friends they can get, and can't get the ones they fancy, and so they come here. It's funny, isn't it? My brother now, he's just the same as you."

I was watching an unpleasant youth dancing with an anæmic girl, an extraordinarily graceful pair. "What does he do?" I asked absently.

Evidently she was very proud of him. "He's in the motor transport business. He's got a lorry of his own. I hadn't seen him for over three years, and I didn't know where he was or anything, but he turned up here on Friday last week, and booked me out all Saturday, and we had a lovely time. They told him at home that I was here. He's doing awfully well, down somewhere in the south. He takes carpet sweepers and things that come from abroad from the boats and drives them to the factory, or something. It's all-night work."

She paused. "He's just the same as you—never seems to fancy the sort of girl that he can pick up." She bent a hostile eye upon the single ladies sitting at their tables all alone. "And there's some that don't take much picking up, either." She paused. "We always used to do things together when he was home, and it was lovely seeing him again."

The evening was drawing to a close. I was tired and ready for my bed and I had the suspicion of a headache which I wasn't anxious to provoke. "I'm going home in a little while," I said. "Would you like something from the soda fountain before I go? An ice, or anything?"

The hard, painted harridan of our first meeting had merged imperceptibly into the girl friend that she had spoken of. "That 'ld be lovely," she said. "What can I have?"

"Anything you like," I said, a little surprised. "What do you want?"

She hesitated. "Some of the things are rather expensive, you know."

I had never had that said to me by any girl before. I smiled at her. "It's nearly the end of my holiday," I said quietly. "I've got a lot of money to blue before I go back home." And she laughed, and said: "If that's the way of it, I'll have a banana split."

So I ordered two of these things, and when the bill came it was half-a-crown. "I told you they were terribly expensive," she said, a little ruefully. We finished them and went and danced again, and after that I sent her to find out my reckoning for me.

She came back. "It's twenty-five dances. "That'll be twelve

and six, won't it?" So I gave her twenty-five shillings, feeling that it was miserably inadequate for the evening that she'd given me, and she said: "Oh, that's an awful lot. You are kind!"

We shook hands. "I've enjoyed this frightfully," I said. "It's been the nicest evening that I've had for years."

"It has been nice," she said simply. "I've loved it. You'll come back when you're in Leeds again, won't you?"

And so my hostess said goodnight to me, and I went back to my hotel alone. Next morning I set out for home.


# CHAPTER 3

STENNING has kept a little black cutter, *Irene*, with me for the last three years. She is about seven tons yacht measurement; she is about thirty years old, I think, but the hull is still quite sound. She is planked with Baltic redwood upon oak frames; the only vessel I have ever seen like that. I don't know why redwood isn't used more; it's cheap enough. They use it on the east coast a bit, and that's rather interesting, because this boat was built at Yarmouth.

He makes her earn her keep by chartering her out among his friends; when she is not away she lies moored up Bowers Creek just across the water from my yard, with *Runagate*. He uses her for his holidays and long weekends. About a fortnight after I came back from Scotland he came down with Joan to cruise in her for a couple of days; they arrived by road one afternoon, and went on board to get squared up for an early start next morning. I put off to them after I had finished at the office, and stayed and had a meal with them on board.

It was the first time I had seen Stenning since his return from the flight which made his name, and he was rather interesting about it. His technicalities were beyond me, but he had lived on shellfish for a week when he got lost on some rotten little atoll near Hawaii, and he had dined with Royalty. By his own account his journey had been uneventful and the flight from the Bermudas to the Azores—two thousand miles of open sea—had bored him stiff, but he had very nearly died of eating onions in the tropics and that gave him a great fright. He didn't like Australia, and his nearest approach to a flying crash came when he was coming in over Lambeth Bridge and nearly got bumped down on to it.

Joan produced a sort of Irish stew for supper and we sat for a long time over it and after it, smoking and talking in a desultory manner. Stenning is a fine practical seaman of the rough-and-ready type. It's in the blood, of course. His father was a commander, RN, and his grandfather; it's a pretty good old naval family. His mother was a Portsmouth chorus girl. That marriage came to an end, and Stenning's father died, and Stenning went with his mother to the north to live with her new husband, who kept a chain of drapers' shops in places like Ilkley and Skipton. He cut away from it when he was fifteen years old and went as odd boy in a garage; then for some years before the war he was a chauffeur. That went on till the war, when he enlisted and was commissioned into the Flying Corps in 1916. He became a Captain, Acting Major, and collected decorations. In 1918 he was sent home as an instructor, and for him that was the end of the war.

He became a civilian pilot after the war and got to be pretty well known in golf and rugger circles; he had plenty of spare time and a natural aptitude for games. He lived a bachelor life and he lived it hot and strong, culminating in a month for being drunk in charge of a motor car. His life at that time was full of episodes, some creditable and more discreditable, till in the middle of one of these he met Joan and married her out of hand, to the disgust and indignation of my family. But Joan knew what she'd got hold of when she picked on Stenning; I don't think she has regretted it. She is now Lady Stenning, which may make up a bit for the things my family said to her when first she got engaged.

Stenning had been abroad since he came back, to Greece and then to Rotterdam—a series of business trips mainly in connection with the marketing and foreign manufacture of the little Dabchick flying boat. By virtue of his job Stenning moves about a good bit, and he spent a long time this evening developing to me his views upon the flow of trade in the world. He has a very clear head and exceptional opportunities for observation; if he had capital—which he hasn't—this

39

combination would make him a wealthy man. I remember that he talked this evening for a long time about the rise of Spanish South America, and what he said was sound and made me think about my stocks.

The evening drew on; in the hatchway the sky turned slowly to deep blue and on to black, and we sat smoking there in the saloon. Presently we stirred and went up through the hatch into the little cockpit; it was ten o'clock and time that I was getting home. In the bright light of the saloon behind us Joan began to tidy up the mess that we had made, and then I saw her pulling down the bunks.

My dinghy was lying out astern, her painter stretched, and sheering gently in the running tide. Down the river the white lights of the town made dappled streaks upon the water; it was very calm. "Time I got along," I said. "That's a rotten reefing gear you've got. Remind me about it next year when you're fitting out. I'll put a crane up at the hounds and fit you Jersey pattern."

He stared up at the one-pole mast and the pencilled tracery of ropes in the dim light of the riding-lamp. "There's room for a crane," he said reflectively. "I suppose the spar would stand it." He had only half his mind on the reefing gear; we were both of us still thinking of the flow of trade, and of the coming general election.

"The safeguarding will go," I said.

Sir Philip Stenning spat into the sea. "I'm not a bloody soothsayer. I can only tell you what I've seen happening to-day. I can't say what's going to happen if the safeguarding comes off. But I tell you this, that there's a darn sight more light manufactured stuff comes into this country than goes out of it. You see it at every dock, safeguarding or no. Motors, electrical household gadgets, carpet sweepers—all sorts of stuff. Seems as if every country in the world can produce cheaper than we can."

I had been considering his reefing gear, straining my eyes into the darkness at the hounds and not paying much attention to what he said. "Damn it," I said absently, "everybody's talking about carpet sweepers these days."

He took me up. "Well, that's a case of the production on the Continent that I was talking about. You'd think that the only country that could produce against the duties would be

America. Well, it's not, and it's time we realised it. The carpet sweepers I'm thinking of are shipped in Rotterdam, and shipped in funny little tubs not much bigger than this. They'll be Jerry stuff. I tell you, the sooner we re-cast our ideas of import and export trade in manufactured goods, the happier we shall be."

I nodded absently. "Maybe." I stood for a moment looking out over the water, then I threw away my cigarette and bent down at the hatchway. "I'm going ashore now," I said to Joan. "Hope it's a decent trip. Did you see the potatoes?"

She came and stuck her head and shoulders up on deck. "Two stone, are they? Tell Adams I'll pay him for them when we come back. We'll be back on Thursday evening, I expect. It's lovely to have seen you." And so I pulled up my dinghy and uncast the painter, and pushed off and left them there together, Sir Philip and Lady Stenning. And as I pulled away they waved at me together across the dappled, inky water, he standing with one arm around her shoulders, till the darkness dropped a curtain round them and I was alone again, and pulling for the slip.

They sailed away next day, and I went on in Dartmouth. After my holiday I had slipped back very readily into my old life, drinking a little more than before my crash, perhaps, and working a little harder. I have my set routine now, after ten years, that fits me like a glove. I get to the office at about ten, leave it at half past twelve for lunch, and leave it again at seven for my dinner. Sometimes in the afternoon I work on *Runagate* or one of the others; I put in most afternoons in the yard. On Tuesdays and Fridays I go up to the RNC for bridge after dinner, and very occasionally I dine there. On Saturdays I go to Plymouth to the club.

I don't entertain much at the Port House because there's not much to do there after dinner, and I can't take any pleasure in being host to more than one or two people at a time. One wants a wife to help one out with that sort of thing. But now and again I get a man in to dinner who doesn't mind just sitting in the library afterwards with a cigar, when I can play him a record of Mozart on the gramophone and talk about my ships. Colonel Fedden comes in for an evening of that sort sometimes, and I remember that he came about a week after Stenning went away.

Fedden is Chief Constable in my part of the world; a quiet, youngish man of fifty, who cruises in a little yawl *Seamew*, ex-*Happy Day*. He was just back from the Bay, or at any rate the Isles de Glenan, and I wanted to hear how he'd got on down there. We sat down to dinner at about eight and talked ships, and rose at about half-past nine, and no sooner had we got settled in the library with the cigars and brandy than the telephone bell rang for him.

I listened while he spoke. They were ringing from the police station at Newton Abbot, and they wanted him to go over there at once; so much I gathered from the one-sided conversation. There was a little backchat then, that I didn't understand; in a few minutes he hung up the receiver and came over to me by the fire. He had to go.

I glanced out of the window. It was a fine, blue evening with the remains of a red sunset lingering in the sky. "I'll run you over in the Bentley," I remarked. "Then we'll come back here for a whisky before bed. You won't be long?"

He hesitated. "I don't quite understand what it is that they've got over there," he said. "Something about a burnt-out motor lorry. In any case, I don't see that we can do much tonight. No, I probably shan't be very long. But I don't want to drag you out."

"I'd like the run," I said. So we went out to the stables and got the Bentley, and drove out on to the cool, brilliant roads with our cigars.

At Newton Abbot I waited in a lobby for the greater part of half an hour. Through a glass partition I could see Fedden in the next room, in business with a superintendent and a sergeant. A constable gave me an evening paper and I sat there reading it, and studying the printed and photographed descriptions of various miscreants on the wall, till at last the door opened behind me, and there was Fedden.

"Sorry to have kept you so long," he said. He did not stir from the door. "I won't be a moment now. But in the meantime, I should be glad if you would come in here for a minute, if you don't mind. For your advice."

I followed him into the room. There was a table, and on the floor behind the table there was a large deal packing case, about the dimensions of a coffin, but not so long. The lid of this packing case was standing up against the table, and looking down into the box I saw the blued glint of steel.

"This must be confidential, Stevenson," said Fedden. "But I want you to have a look at that, and tell me if you've ever seen one like it before."

I laid my gloves down on the table and stooped over the case. The gun lay neatly on chocks on the bottom of the case, surrounded by its accessories in little racks upon the sides. I stood erect again. "I've seen something very similar," I said; "but they never came my way much. May I lift it out?"

He nodded, and I stooped down and lifted the gun from its case. It was a sort of light machine gun designed to be fired from the shoulder. It was heavy; not quite so heavy as the infantry-type Lewis, perhaps, but still much heavier than the service rifle. It was served by a long clip of cartridges which fed in underneath the lock, rather in the manner of an automatic pistol. I examined it pretty thoroughly, but I found no indication of the maker's name, nor any mark or numeral of any sort.

I looked up at Fedden. "Is this a Thompson gun?"

He shook his head. "I know the Thompson. We took a lot of them in Ireland."

I laid it down carefully on its chocks within the case, and stood erect again. "I saw something very like it in Zeebrugge," I said, "just after the Armistice. It was a German gun; a major in the Inniskillings had it as a souvenir. It wasn't quite like this. It had a different lock, and it hadn't all that cooling stuff. I think it was lighter. He said it was an aeroplane Parabellum gun. That's the nearest thing to it I've ever seen."

I stood and eyed it for a moment. "I should say it came from Germany," I said. "I'm afraid that's all I can tell you about it. I'm sorry."

I glanced at the case for any further information, and then at the lid. There was a label pasted on the lid, a large white one, coloured with a crude illustration in red depicting a vacuum cleaner of the Hoover type sweeping a white swathe upon a spotted carpet. Below the picture there was a legend in large block lettering: THE PANPHAGON SWEEPER. That was all.

"No," said Fedden. "It occurred to me that there was just the chance that you might know about these things. How-

43

ever. Now, if you don't mind . . . just for a few minutes?"

I went out into the lobby and sat down again with the paper; in the office that I had left I heard his voice upon the telephone. After a quarter of an hour or so he came out into the lobby with the superintendent, and this time he was ready to go home.

We slid out of the town upon the Dartmouth road. "You're coming back to my place for a drink?" I said.

He was hesitant. "I really don't know that I ought. I've got to go to London over this damn business first thing tomorrow morning, and I ought to see my wife."

"Time for a quick one," I said. "You've got to come back with me, anyway, to get your car." And so we went back into the library and took off our coats, and while I was fiddling with the siphon and the glasses he sat down in one of the chairs before the fire, and he was unusually quiet.

I passed him over a tumbler. "I take it that you don't want me to say anything about that gun," I remarked.

He shook his head. "If you don't mind. I wouldn't have brought you into it if I didn't know that you can keep your mouth shut."

I laughed. "No need to worry about that," I said. "I've got nobody to talk to here. Nor likely to have."

He glanced across at me. "No," he said quietly, "I can't imagine how you stick it here alone. I can't imagine why you don't pick up some girl and marry her."

I was gingerly manipulating a very full siphon as he spoke; it went off suddenly and I squirted half the whisky from my glass. I refilled it carefully. "This gun," I said. "Would it be stretching professional reticence to breaking point if I was to ask where it came from?"

He considered for a moment. "I don't think so. We got it off a burning motor lorry last night, on the Exeter road. There were three of them. The other two were burnt."

I crossed over to the fire. "Oh," I said. "What had the driver got to say about it?"

"There wasn't any driver," he replied. I raised my eyebrows. "The lorry was deserted. It was found at about four o'clock this morning, about a mile this side of Ideford, burning like a furnace. There wasn't a soul with it—just the lorry blazing by the side of the road."

44

"What about the gun, then?" I inquired. "That gun wasn't burnt."

He nodded. "That case was found behind the hedge, about fifty yards up the road from the lorry. It was found about lunchtime by the farmer, who gave it to the police. When the lorry cooled off they found the other two in among the wreckage—all burnt up, of course. And that's literally all about it. No owner—nothing. Nothing but this one packing case behind the hedge."

I smiled. "It looks as if the owner's got a packet coming to him," I remarked. "You'll be able to trace him by the numbers on the lorry, I suppose."

"We could do if they happened to be genuine," said Fedden cynically. "But they're not. That's what worries me most about the whole business. It makes it look so bad."

I frowned. "Is there no way of tracing the lorry?"

"That isn't my department. I should think it's going to be pretty difficult for them. The lorry was an old one, and it's pretty well burnt out."

He got up, and swallowed the remainder of his drink. "I was going up to town this week anyway," he said, "so it's not much loss." He turned to me. "You'll be very careful about this, though?"

"I'll not talk," I said shortly. And so he went away, and when he had gone I filled myself a nightcap and sat down again before the fire for a few minutes before going up to bed.

I don't know how long I sat there, or how much the decanter held when Fedden went away; I know how much it held when I went up to bed. I must have been a little drunk that night, because I was beset with dreams and memories. I lay and tossed in bed and watched the moonlight on the wall, consciously trying to sleep and resolutely preventing myself from thinking. I forced myself to think about the gun. Then, with an active mind running round in circles, I found myself going over and over my memories of the night before my crash in the Bentley; I lay and felt the wombat in my arms again and saw the white, glimmering surf running up upon the shore beneath the moon. I rolled over on to a cool patch of pillow, and I was in Leeds listening to the dancers and the dance music, and talking to rather a pathetic, painted girl that I had hired to entertain me for the night. Her brother ran a motor-lorry. I turned restlessly again and listened for the soft muttering of the sea down by St Petrox to see what sort of a night it was, and I was with Stenning listening to the ripple of the water on *Irene*'s topsides, talking about the safeguarding of industries and carpet sweepers from the Continent.

And suddenly I was most startingly awake. I lay on my back in bed for a minute and looked about me at the dim outlines of the furniture around the room, no longer feverish and sleepy but with a cool forehead, a clean mouth, and a clear and understanding mind.

"My God," I said aloud. "I wonder if there's anything in that?"

I did not know, I think, quite what I meant, except that I had the peculiar feeling which I sometimes get in business, that I was on to something important. I got out of bed and went and had a drink of water at the wash stand, and passed a cold sponge over my face. And then I went and stood beside the open window, and listened to the sea. It was a fine moonlight night; I could see all the rocks and hazards of the entrance, and the chequered buoys. There was a gentle southerly night wind and the tide was running out; the black weed on the rocks showed that it was near low water.

"I must go over and have a look in the morning," I said quietly. "To see if the place is really like I think it is." And with that I went back to bed with an easy mind, and fell asleep at once, and slept quietly till I was called.

I went down next morning as usual to the office, but I finished up about eleven. I went up home and took the Bentley from the stables, and started out upon the Slapton road. I passed the corner where they told me that my car had been discovered in the ditch and went on, puzzled and a little disconcerted at seeing nothing that I knew. At last I reached Slapton and drew up, and thought about it for a little. Then I turned round and drove back along the road that I had come, with eyes half closed and with a lazy mind, and at a considerable speed. Till suddenly I trod on everything and drew the car in beside a gate which led into a grassy pasture on the right. Beyond that lay the sea.

It was about a couple of hundred yards short of the corner where my crash had taken place.

I got out of the car slowly and went through the gate, and

on across the pasture. And presently I came to a place where the field petered out into sandhills that ran down to the beach, and the line of the surf perhaps two hundred yards away. There was a little valley in the sandhills straight ahead of me, and I moved a little way down it in the loose, powdery sand.

"This is the place, if anywhere," I said aloud. "I'd swear to it."

I was certain in my own mind that I had been to that exact spot before on the night of my crash, when I was very drunk, and that I had spoken some nonsense to a girl. I stood there for a long time trying to puzzle it out; more than that I could not recollect. I could not understand how I could possibly have got into the sandhills there. To have crashed at that corner I must have passed the gate into the field at sixty miles an hour. And then I thought that I was wrong; that I was suffering from an illusion, that I was still ill and I must realise it. Till, presently, tired and a little out of sorts, I sat down on a hummock of speargrass and sand for a little before going home. Whatever were the rights or wrongs of this affair, it was pleasant in the sun.

I had shuffled up the loose sand with my feet into a little heap while I had been puzzling about this thing. And as I sat there listening to the martins my eye fell upon this heap, and it seemed to me that the fresh sand that I had uncovered was not like ordinary sand. I turned it over with my toe and frowned at it; and then I got up and went over to the spot and knelt down, and scraped away a little area with my bare hands to see what had been there.

And straight away I was back in the days when I was a boy. Once, coming up barefoot through sandhills on a Cornish beach, I had cut my toe rather badly on a broken bottle buried in the powdery sand, and it had bled so much that it had to have stitches put in it. For weeks the place was one of awe and veneration to us children; it was a hallowed spot—blood. We never cleaned it up. In spite of rain the sand was discoloured till we left.

I must have cleared an area of four square feet before I found the limits of that stain. One thing was quite clear then. Whoever had been there before had bled a bucketful.

And as I rummaged in the sand my fingers struck on something soft and round. I pulled it out and dusted it, and turned

47

it over in my hands; and then I sat there in the sunlight holding it, quite still, while the martins swept and wheeled about my head between the dunes. I was thinking of the little things that please us in a childish mood, that comfort us when we are quite alone.

It was a rotten apple. Now that was a funny thing to find there in the sand.


# CHAPTER 4


ALL THAT afternoon I sat working with Tillotson in my office in the yard. He had got some book on management that had a chapter upon cost accounts, and we were trying to thrash out a means of harnessing the ancient art of ship repairing with the reins of modern business. I remember that particularly because it was a job that would take some doing at the best of times, and I had only half my mind on it that afternoon.

I broke off for a minute in the middle of the afternoon, and rang up Dixon on the telephone. I wasn't certain that he could tell me anything I didn't know, but I made an appointment, finished up early at the office, and went up to see him. after tea. He greeted me by asking how I was.

"Pretty fit physically," I replied. "Mentally—perhaps not quite so good."

He grinned. "You're looking very well."

"Lunatics often do," I said. "You should know that. Now, what I've come about is this. I want you to tell me all about that injury to my head."

He frowned in perplexity. "Tell you about it?"

I nodded. "I want to know exactly what sort of condition I was in when first you saw me, after the crash."

He raised his eyebrows a little and reached for a ledger on his desk. I watched him with some amusement while he adjusted his eyeglasses. He turned a few pages, and then stopped.

He coughed. "I saw you at seven-forty-five am," he said. "Well, you were quite unconscious . . . blanched appearance."

He scanned the page. "A lacerated and contused wound in the occipital region. Slight hæmatoma—that's bleeding under the scalp, you know. No hemiplegia. Reflexes sluggish. Pupils equal, slightly dilated. Smell of alcohol."

He glanced at me. "Is that what you want to know?"

I sat for a little time in thought. "I suppose it is," I said at last. "There's just one thing. You told me that you saw my car before it was repaired. You said it had a hole in the roof. Would you say that that injury is in keeping with the hole?"

"I don't understand."

"Well," I said, "the car's got a fabric roof. From the inside, there's first a soft cloth ceiling, and then a layer of felt, and then a few small laths, and then the outer fabric. There's nothing very hard. You say I rammed my head through the lot. Is that the sort of injury that you'd expect?"

He smiled. "I really couldn't say," he replied. "I've never seen it done before. But it's the sort of injury you got."

There was nothing to be gained by staying on. I got up and picked my hat and stick up from the chair. "Oh, well," I said, "it's interesting to know. Just one thing more. I suppose that injury could have been caused by any sort of blow? Of course, actually it happened in the crash. But you wouldn't have to be in a car to get an injury like that?"

"Oh, no. It could happen in a great variety of accidents."

I laughed. "It would be just like that if some kind friend had slugged me on the head from behind?"

He laughed with me. "I should think so. Just like that."

I nodded. "That's all I wanted to know. Put it down to the concussion if you like, or drink."

But he got to his feet, his brows contracted in a frown. "You weren't speaking seriously?"

I moved towards the door. "It doesn't pay to be serious," I said. "It only means that people laugh behind your back, instead of to your face." And so I went away, and back to my own house to dine.

That evening I wanted above everything to have a talk with Fedden. I rang up his house as soon as I got home, but they didn't know when he was coming back. He was staying at his club in town. I went up and dressed for dinner, as I always do when I'm alone, and went down to the dining-room to eat. I cut it short and had coffee and my cigar in the model room;

I can remember wandering restlessly about the house all evening, unable to settle down to anything.

Finally I put in a call to Fedden at his club. I was lucky in getting on to him there, and I made an appointment to dine with him on the following night.

I drove up to London on the next day. Looking back upon that time I am surprised that I should have gone to London upon such a whim; I think it would take more to stir me now. For many men, I suppose almost any excuse would serve for a few days in town, but not for me. I hate the place. I don't go there more than once in six months, and then only when I can't avoid it. When I have to go, I get into my club and stay there as much as possible; it's a rotten town unless you've got a pack of womenfolk about. The best solution is to go and stay with Joan.

Fedden dined with me that night. I told him that I had come up upon business. He told me that he had spent both days between the Home Office and Scotland Yard; I found him worried in his manner, and a little tired. In my club there is a little smoking-room at the top of the house, that looks out over St James's Park; I took him up there after dinner because I knew that we should have the room to ourselves at that time of night, and we settled down with our cigars before the fire.

I forget what we talked about. I only remember that he was reticent, very reticent about the business that he had been engaged on up in town. I tried once or twice to edge the conversation in the direction of the gun, but he sheered off most adroitly; Fedden is a bit of a diplomat in a quiet way. Till at last I got fed up with it. I took advantage of a pause, dropped the ash of my cigar carefully into an ashtray at my side, and said to him:

"About that gun you showed me the other night."

He turned a very cold, grey eye upon me. "Well?"

I said: "You'll think it's none of my business, and perhaps you're right." I passed my hand absently across my hair—what Dixon had described as the occipital region. "At the same time, I think I've got something to tell you about it which may help, if you want to hear it. In fact, that's what I came up to town about."

He shifted in his chair and turned to me, frowning a little

in perplexity. "You mean that you've come up about the gun?"

"You'll think me a damn fool," I replied, "but that's exactly what I have done."

He lay back into his chair again. "If you've got any evidence which will help us in the matter, we should be very glad to have it," he remarked. It amused me to notice his retirement behind officialdom.

"You mustn't credit all I have to say," I said. "I don't know that I really credit it myself. You must form your own opinion." The darkness fell slowly in the room as I sat there with him, telling him my groundless little tale of disconnected incidents. I told him my memories of the night before my crash, so different from the official story of the accident, when I thought that I had gone across the field till I had met a girl and seen a vessel on the beach. I told him about my apple, and the carpet-sweepers, and the foreigner, and the man called Peter, and I described the boat to him.

A servant came to draw the curtains of the room and take away our coffee cups, and when he had gone we sat on in the light of the fire and the one soft reading lamp behind our heads, and I told him of the girl who had been kind to me in Leeds, whose brother owned a motor lorry and took carpet sweepers by night from the boats to the factory inland, away somewhere in the south. Over the park we heard a bugle blowing the Last Post, and I told him how Stenning had been in Rotterdam and had seen or heard of carpet-sweepers being shipped in little boats for export into England. I reminded him of the label on the packing case that had contained the gun.

And finally, I told him how I had come to find my apple in the sand, and how somebody had had a nasty accident among the dunes.

Then he sat quiet, until at last he said: "It's none of it evidence."

"I'm sorry about that," I said.

"It may give us a line to go upon. I should like you to give it us again at Scotland Yard tomorrow morning, if you will?" He paused for a minute, and then he said: "There are certain features in this thing which make it very difficult."

I didn't know what comment I could make on that, and so

said nothing at all. And after a little time he said: "So much depends on where those guns were going to. Until we know that, our hands are tied . . . most damnably." His tone was strained and worried. "If we could get the lorry driver, he might tell us that. The dancing-girl's brother—if there's anything in what you say."

I smiled. "There may not be," I put in quietly. "I've had concussion recently, you know."

He turned and eyed me for a moment. "Yes, I know." And then he said a damn queer thing. He said: "Do you believe in God?"

I knew Fedden to be a deeply religious man—many soldiers are. I had had this sort of thing from him before, but that didn't prevent it coming as a fresh surprise. "Well," I said, a little awkwardly, "I don't go to church much. But I've been to sea a lot. I'm a master mariner, you know."

He nodded slowly. "Yes, I know." And then he said: "Personally, I believe every word you've said, but I'm not so sure that Carter will. I believe God sent you to help us clean up this affair."

I couldn't keep my end up in a conversation conducted upon theological lines, and so I asked:

"Who is Carter?"

"Sir David Carter," he replied, "the Chief Commissioner."

Better than God, I thought, and to direct his mind into more mundane channels I asked how he had spent the last two days. It seemed that he had been most of the time in consultation with the sleuths at the Yard. Some aspect of the matter that he had learnt there had upset him seriously, but what it was he would not say. Finally, at about midnight, he went back to his own place to sleep, having secured me for the following day.

I went to Scotland Yard with Fedden next morning after breakfast, and for a time I sat in a lobby waiting for him while he went about his business. Presently a sergeant came to fetch me, and I was ushered down long stone passages till we stopped before an office door.

It was a fair-sized, decently furnished room in the government style; very high and rather bare, strewn with heavy mahogany desks and furniture, with mournful leather chairs and a settee belonging to a bygone age. Fedden was waiting for me there with two other men. One of them was a keen-faced, youngish man of about my own age; this was a Major Norman. The other was a serious, white-haired man, not very old. I shouldn't say that he is more than fifty, though he is quite white. That was Sir David Carter.

I told my disconnected little tale again in reply to a sort of questionnaire from Fedden, and this time it seemed thinner, more unlikely than it had ever seemed before. I was ashamed to tell it. It seemed to have lost the quality of realism here; what was clear and definite at home, in sound of the sea and almost within shouting distance of the sandhills, seemed no more than the wildest guesswork and hypothesis in Scotland Yard.

Fedden came to an end at last, when he had extracted from me all that I had to say. The other two had listened to us in perfect, disconcerting silence; it was impossible to tell how they were taking it. At the end the man called Norman glanced at his chief, stirred, and took up the task of questioning me, and for a further quarter of an hour took me backwards and forwards over the story till he was satisfied that I could tell him nothing more. And then there was a silence in the room.

Sir David Carter, sitting behind a very massive desk, tilted back his chair and sat staring up at a cornice of the ceiling, immersed in thought. At last he said:

"This is a very unusual story, Commander Stevenson. I must thank you for coming up to give it to us so readily."

I cleared my throat. "You must understand that I can vouch nothing for its truth. Colonel Fedden will have told you that I've recently been ill." I paused. "Each time I tell this story it seems more likely that I may be wrong about it all—that I'm imagining things."

He tilted his chair forwards till it rested on its legs again, and faced me steadily across the desk. "On the contrary," he said courteously, "we are very much afraid it may be true."

I did not know what to say to that, and presently he went on:

"It fits very closely with information that has come to us from other sources." I wondered what the other sources were, but he did not enlighten me. He was quiet for a little then, but presently he spoke again.

"Commander Stevenson," he said, "I must tell you that it is not our custom here to take witnesses into our confidence. So much you will appreciate. In the normal course of affairs I should now thank you for your courtesy in coming to us, and I should send you home. If I do not follow that procedure now, it is exceptional."

He paused for a minute, and went on: "Sometimes a witness becomes so deeply involved in the investigations which we carry out that it becomes necessary for us to break our rule. In such a case, we demand the most complete discretion. Colonel Fedden has told us that he regards you as a discreet man, not much given to talk."

I stirred in my chair. "I don't go gossiping about the place," I said. "I don't particularly want to be mixed up in anything, but having this evidence, I thought somebody ought to know about it. If I can give you any further help I should be very glad to do so. Otherwise, I'm quite ready to go home."

He nodded slowly. "We appreciate your attitude very much."

He leaned forward, resting his elbows on the table, and began to talk to me in very general terms. I sat there listening to him, puzzled. I couldn't imagine what he was driving at, why he was talking to me in that way. He was giving me a little discourse on gun-running and its objects, couched in the most general terms.

"In this instance," he went on, "the problem cannot be very difficult to solve. If a rising, or revolution, were contemplated in this country today, the source from which it emanated would not be very difficult to trace. So many sources may be discounted that the field becomes narrow. For example, it would be difficult to imagine an armed revolt in this country for the purpose of overthrowing the monarchy—today."

I was beginning to understand. "I see what you mean," I said. "There's only one revolutionary agency in England to-day—or only one obvious one. You mean Russia, I suppose. Communism."

He inclined his head. "I think it very likely that if these arms are really smuggled in we should find such an agency in the background." He paused for a moment, and then he said:

"I should not have indicated this conclusion to you if it

had been merely speculation on our part. Unfortunately, we have had other evidence, apart from this affair, that something of the sort might be in train."

I stared at him. "Do you know where those guns were going?"

The man called Norman stirred by the fireplace. "We know no details," he replied. "We only knew that something of the sort might be on foot."

I nodded. "Stenning may be able to tell you some more about where the guns came from," I observed. "But as for where they were going to, you want the driver of the lorry." I was silent for a minute then, thinking of that painted, kindly girl serving her profession to the beating rhythm and the changing lights.

Sir David Carter nodded: "Exactly so. In fact, our next step should be to secure a little more information than you have been able to give us from the woman in Leeds. The professional dancer, Miss Gordon."

"Well," I said, "that's easy enough."

Fedden coughed. "I'm not so sure about that," he said dryly.

I eyed him in surprise. "Well," I said, "you can have her up and ask her where her brother is?"

The man called Norman spoke up then: "You must understand, Commander Stevenson, that the police have no power to interrogate a witness. They can invite the witness to make a voluntary statement, but the whole conduct of these matters is not so easy as it was."

Sir David Carter leaned forward in his chair. "I see no reason for dissembling," he said. "Frankly, Commander Stevenson, we find ourselves faced with a difficulty in this investigation. I will put it to you as briefly as I can."

He paused for a little time, and then he said: "I would have you understand that in this office our business is to keep the peace. To surprise and to suppress any rising whatsoever that may be attempted against the elected government of the country—no matter what political aspect that rising may assume. Our business is to keep the peace of the country."

He considered for a moment. "In this instance the disturbance which we suspect is identical in character with the Left Wing of the Government. I see no point in mincing matters. We have in this country a moderate Labour Government, and here, in the seclusion of this office, we suspect that these guns are intended to arm a Communist rising of some sort."

I nodded slowly. I was beginning to see something of the difficulty.

Sir David continued: "I trust most sincerely that further investigation will show that our suspicions have no foundation in fact. But if they should have such foundation, then I have confidence that the Government will allow no political complexities to interfere with the proper suppression of any attempt against the peace of the realm, and with the punishment of the offenders. I have that confidence."

He eyed me for a moment. "Supposing, however, a mistake were made in this affair. Suppose that from this office we made public our suspicions of a rising in the Communist interest, which events proved to be groundless. It is not difficult to see the play which would be made with such a mistake by the Left Wing. In this matter, we must have a cast-iron case before publicity occurs."

"I see that," I said.

"I do not think that anyone would describe this as a cast-iron case at the moment," he remarked dryly.

He paused for a minute, and then he went on: "Therefore, we cannot afford to give any publicity to this matter at the moment. And now we come to a further difficulty. You spoke just now of the possibility that we might interrogate this woman in Leeds about the movements of her brother. I wonder if you realise our difficulties, today, in the interrogation of feminine witness?"

I stared at him for a moment, and then I realised what he was driving at. "I see," I said. "You mean Lord Lee's Commission."

He inclined his head. "Exactly. Consider our position in this matter. If we were to interrogate this woman in the manner which occurred to you—and as we might have done a year ago—what should we be doing? We should be taking information from her which might lead, in the end, to the arrest of her brother upon a criminal charge. In all probability we should not have indicated to her the result of any statement she might have been persuaded to make. That would not further our interests, you see—which are, to catch criminals."

He paused. "The British public is very chivalrous, Commander Stevenson—too chivalrous for its own safety. Methods of crime detection which were adequate a year ago, today are hampered and restricted. If we were to interrogate this woman in such a way today, tomorrow the whole matter would be in the hands of her local Member of Parliament. And then . . . publicity."

The window was open at the top; through the opening I could hear the noises of the traffic in Whitehall, and a girl singing, and a piano, in some building near at hand. There was a bee on the window pane, and I wondered where the devil he had come from. I sat on my Victorian leather chair and stared around, at Fedden, at Norman, at Sir David Carter. All of them seemed to be studying me, as if they found in me the solution to their difficulties.

"I see that this case is not an easy one," I said quietly. "What I don't see at the moment is why you have told me about it in this way." And I stared at Carter.

He smiled a little. "Such a question is justifiable. We have told you about it, because in our opinion the matter can most readily be solved with your assistance. I should say that you are at perfect liberty to refuse to assist us, in which case we shall only ask for your discretion when you leave this office."

I stared him in the eyes. "What do you want me to do?"

He bent forward and toyed with a pen upon his desk. "I believe the information that you have given us to be most valuable," he said at last. "We want only one more light upon the case before we take the matter up in earnest. We want to know something more about the woman's brother, the man who runs the motor-lorry. Where he is usually to be found, the name of a friend who knows his whereabouts, the address to which a letter should be sent to reach him—almost anything will serve our purpose. Once we have access to the man we can proceed upon our usual lines without the grave risk of interrogating the woman."

He raised his head. "This woman spoke to you about her brother when you were dancing with her before. We should like you to go to Leeds and dance with her again."

The bee still buzzed upon the window pane, the dull thunder of the traffic still sounded from Whitehall. I was about to speak, but he stopped me.

"One moment. I have said that you are at liberty to refuse

us this service, but I should like you to give it full consideration before you speak. This importation of arms is a serious matter for the country, Commander. It means—it may mean civil war. Imagine it for a moment, if you can, civil war in England, at this time. The country pulling round and becoming prosperous again—industry finding its feet. And then— this thing." The pen-holder snapped in two between his fingers, but he did not seem to notice it. "For myself, I cannot bear to think of it."

He raised his head. "This is a distasteful service that we are asking of you, but a very small one. Even so, I should not have suggested it but for the fact that in you we have a man whose record is—quite out of the ordinary."

I met his eyes and stared him down. "I murdered thirty German sailors in the war," I said harshly. "I suppose that's what you mean. Seems to me that's a damn good credential for a job like this."

Nobody moved when I said that, and for a minute nobody seemed to know quite what to say. I didn't help them; I was busy with my own reflections. I was thinking of the girl in Leeds, and how decent she had been to me that night. I was thinking of how she had been afraid that I was spending more than I could easily afford.

At last I broke the silence myself. "Let me get this right," I said. "You want me to go to Leeds and dance with this girl again, and get her to talk. You want me to find out some information which will set you on to her brother, without letting her know that this is a police matter. That's what you want?"

The man called Norman stirred. "That is what we want. Some means of finding the brother when we want to pull him in."

I stared at him. "I should be glad if you would talk English. Some means of finding the brother when you want—to do what?"

He flushed angrily, and Sir David Carter interposed. "It is very necessary that we should be able to keep the brother under observation," he said smoothly. "You will appreciate that. If this man is simply the driver of the lorry and no more, I doubt if it would be necessary to take any further steps in regard to him."

I sat there for a minute, deep in thought. "What happens if I can't find out anything at all?"

"Then we shall have to deal with the matter with our usual machinery," he said. "It means a grave risk of publicity. And frankly, I do not consider that this case, at present, is strong enough to bear a critical examination."

I nodded. "So that if I don't go to Leeds, you'll have that girl up and interrogate her?"

"In all probability," he said.

I sat there resting my chin upon one hand and staring into the fireplace. I was thinking of the life that I had been living since the war, what I had done and what I had achieved. It wasn't very much—a few old sailing ships gathered into a barely economic trade. It seemed to me that the life I had been leading for the last ten years had done little good to me or anybody else. One must live steadily and do what one can. As for this matter of the girl who had been kind to me—well, that was just my luck.

I raised my head and glanced across at Carter. "All right," I said quietly, "I should be very glad to go."

I got away from there as soon as possible, and went back to my club. Fedden walked back with me, but I had little to say to him, and presently he went away. I lunched and went out to the Academy, and there I put my name down for the little study of seagulls that now hangs in the library above my desk. Then back to the club to spin my dinner out over an hour and a half, and read Surtees till I went to bed.

Next morning I took the Bentley after breakfast and set out up the Great North Road, lunching in Newwark with the best part of the journey done. By teatime I was back in that garish, over-furnished place in Leeds, sitting and smoking in a corner of the lounge, watching the young business men and brokers with their girls, who thronged the place. There was nothing else to do, and I sat there till dinner, wondering what was going to happen to me that night. I dined alone, and went out immediately afterwards to the Palais.

The place was fairly full. I sat for a little while at a table alone, watching the dancers and wondering how to set about the business I had come upon. The girl was there. I could see her sitting in the pen, reading a magazine and now and then passing a desultory glance a round the room. I knew that she had noticed me, and presently I went and fetched her out to dance.

It seemed to me that she was changed in the weeks that I had been away. The set phrases, the fixed smile were all the same, but beneath it she seemed listless and depressed. I took her out for a waltz; she danced beautifully, but there was no life in it; it was as if she had lost all heart and interest in her work. I cursed myself for a fool that I had ever come upon a crazy job like this, took her back to my table, ordered her a cup of coffee, and gave her a cigarette.

She roused a little when the coffee came, and made a definite effort to entertain me. "I'm so glad you've come in again," she said. "I often thought about you, and wondered if you'd come back. I said to Phyllis only the other day, I said I wondered if you were coming back again ever. It's ever so nice when people come back."

I smiled. "Who's Phyllis?" I inquired. I didn't particularly want to know, but I did want to make it easy for her to talk about the things she knew.

"One of the other professionals here—that girl over there." I saw a lithe young girl with very fuzzy hair, dancing with a Jew. "I've been teaching her to swim at the baths in the morning. I do think swimming's lovely. Would you like to dance this one?"

We went and danced to the slow, haunting rhythm of a fox-trot in the changing lights. It seemed to me that that Palais was a place where one should dance exquisitely or not at all; the floor was too large for the mediocre. I said as much, regretting my deficiencies.

"You're not so bad," she said. "Not half so bad as a lot of the gentlemen. I could give you a lesson any morning, if you like," she added hopefully. "It's only five shillings."

I repressed a smile; it was a sign of returning animation that she was looking about for business. "I think I shall be busy all tomorrow," I replied. "I'm only up here for a day or so."

"Have you come up on business?" she inquired. I said I had; so much at least was true. "It must be fun travelling about like that," she said, a little wistfully. "One gets tired of just staying in one place always. . . ."

The dance came to an end, and we went back to our table

and the lukewarm coffee. "You haven't been down south since I saw you?" I asked. "To Torquay or anywhere?"

I was very much alert that night, on the look out for any detail which might help my game. I saw at once that I had touched upon some tender spot; she laughed, but not for merriment. "No," she said. "You don't get away much when you're in a Palais."

I nodded sympathetically. "You must get fed up with it," I said. "Do you like Leeds?"

She shrugged her shoulders. "It's not bad. But I don't like towns at all—not really. Or maybe that it's just the holiday season." She was depressed. Then she roused herself and said brightly: "I say, you must think me mopey tonight. Aren't I awful!"

I eyed her for a moment. "Not a bit," I said. "I think you're very tired. What you want is a good holiday."

"My holiday begins on Sunday," she said simply. "But I'm not going to take it after all. Maybe I'll get it later on."

"Why not?" I asked. "I'd take it if I were you. Do you good."

For a time she wouldn't tell me, but presently it all came out. It came in little disjointed, disillusioned sentences, fragments that I had to extract and piece together one by one. And when I had it all, I found I had a story that had something of a tragedy in its ordinariness.

Her working hours were from three in the afternoon till midnight, six days a week with no half holiday. Unprotected by any union or organisation of that kind, her working year included all Bank Holidays; Easter to her was a Sunday and no more; she worked on Boxing Day. She was paid ten shillings a week, plus her commission and tips; this gave her an average income for the year of about two pounds a week. She was allowed one week's holiday a year, unpaid.

It was pathetic, the importance which she set upon this holiday. She didn't say much, but I gathered that she had been saving all the year for it, garnering her two-shilling pieces and half-crowns week by week. By careful economy she had amassed nearly seven pounds towards it; she was going to Scarborough with a girl who worked in an office in Pudsey, and who hadn't got a boy friend either.

Man proposes, but God disposes. She got influenza and had

a whole week off duty; that knocked her back over three pounds, with her living expenses, doctor's fees, and medicine. Since she had been back her business had been rotten, and she had been forced to draw still further on her little store. Finally, the manager told her that she must get a new pair of shoes because hers were getting so shabby.

I don't think I've ever been really short of money, all my life; all my life I've never had to work harder than I wanted to. It took me a little time to realise the magnitude of the disaster. I said:

"Isn't there anyone who you could borrow from, and pay them back later?"

She eyed me for a moment quite inscrutably. "I expect so. I know lots of gentlemen who come here who would lend me money if I asked them."

There was a subtlety in that that put me in my place; I remember thinking how very wearing it must be to be on the defensive all the time. I said:

"I don't mean strangers. But haven't you got any relations, or anyone like that?"

She smiled, and softened a little. "There's only Billy. He's doing awfully well. He's my brother, you know—I told you about him before."

This was the business I had come to Leeds about. For a moment I wondered absently whether anyone at Scotland Yard really cared a tinker's curse about the peace of the realm, or whether they just sat there and earned their money in the job that they were paid to do, comfortably unimaginative.

"You could go to him, couldn't you?" I asked.

She shook her head. "I don't know where he is. I wouldn't mind borrowing from him."

I wrinkled my brows in perplexity. "Don't you know where he is at all? I mean, you could get in touch with him if there was trouble at home, or anything like that?"

She shook her head again. "He's down in the south somewhere, but I don't know where. If anything happened really, I suppose we'd ask the wireless. Like those SOS messages they always have."

She said: "He never was one for writing much, or reading a book. And they're the same at home."

I took her out upon the floor for a waltz and thought about what I had learned. It was clear that she could tell me nothing of her brother's whereabouts, and, frankly, I was glad. I hadn't fancied the job from the outset, and now it seemed to me that I was free to go back to London and report that I could find out nothing. The police, I thought, could get along and do their own dirty business now.

I knew what they would do. They would assume that I had been clumsy in my methods. They would begin where I left off and have her up and put her through a sort of Third Degree. In the end such an interrogation might quite well prove awkward for the police, but that was their look out; it seemed to me that this girl had trouble coming to her more serious than the loss of her holiday. I wondered absently what they would trick her into saying about brother Billy.

We went back to the table. I offered her a cigarette, and then I sat there silent, staring out across the floor at the dancers and the band, wondering what would come of this affair. Some little movement of her roused me.

"I'm sorry," I said. "I was going to sleep."

She laughed. "What were you thinking about?"

I smiled. "As a matter of fact, I was just thinking there must be some way of getting in touch with your brother, if you wanted to. Do you know the number of his lorry? You could do it that way."

She shook her head. "I only saw it just the once."

"You know what make it was?"

She looked worried. "He did say. Something beginning with D. Not David."

I nodded slowly. "Was it a Dennis? A thirty-hundred-weight Dennis?"

She brightened. "That's what he said—I remember now. Thirty-hundredweight Dennis. Are they good?"

"I think they're very good," I said. "There's an awful lot of them about, though. You wouldn't find him that way." I eyed her for a moment. "I don't suppose you could pick that lorry out from amongst a lot of others like it in the street, could you?"

She laughed and dimpled. "Oh, yes. It's got horseshoes on it."

"Horseshoes?"

"Mmm. They're ever so lucky. Billy said it isn't easy to get horseshoes now." It seemed that he had decorated his lorry with a shoe on the radiator and another on the tailboard at the back. "So I'd just go along the line till I saw a lorry with a horseshoe on the front, and I'd know that was the one, you see."

We went and danced again, but I asked her no more questions. She had told me all she knew, and my work in Leeds was done. She had no means of getting into touch with her brother, though she could identify the lorry; it was very probable that she could identify it even in its present burnt-out state. That was my report to Sir David Carter; I had done what I could for them, and they must get on with their investigation in their own way now.

As the evening went on, things improved. Her depression disappeared and I had little to do but listen while she talked to me about the little matters of life; how she had been teaching her friends to swim, and how they had got tickets for a trade show at the talkies, and they were lovely. She had changed her rooms since I had been there last because her landlady got ill; and she liked the tweed of my suit, it was ever so soft and nice. A quickstep wasn't a slow foxtrot and I mustn't dance it like one. Phyllis had got a boy who was doing awfully well in Bradford and was taking her out quite a lot; wasn't it lovely for her? The band was leaving next week because they had had a row with Mr Banks; it was awful, and the new one was coming from Wimbledon. Two of the men professionals had left and gone roller-skating at Scarborough. The cat in the kitchen of the restaurant had had kittens and the cook said she might have one, but she would have to see her landlady about it first.

I don't know how she did it, but she got me talking to her that night. I don't generally say very much; I sit and hear what other people have to say. But that night I remember doing what I could to make her see my life; I sat there talking to her about the things I like. The way the porpoises come up and play round the vessel on a summer evening, diving underneath her keel all silvery and green, and coming up alongside her to blow. The subtlety of the tides and the pleasure of the dawn at sea after a night on deck, and the smell of bacon from the galley. The great loneliness of a bell buoy, the smell of oilskins and salt water, and the crash and thudding of the cold grey seas when you're beating on a wind in winter. The slow framing of a vessel in the yard, the smell of hot tar, the litter of oak shavings on the slips and the piles of sawdust by the droning band saw in the shop.

And she said: "You do like your work, don't you? I mean, the sea, and ships and all." She was looking at me rather queerly.

I smiled. "I'm frightfully sorry—I must have been boring you stiff. I expect everyone you get in here wants to start talking about his job."

She shook her head. "They don't—not much. Sometimes it might be nicer if they did . . . I've never heard anyone talk like you. I've been to the seaside, but I didn't know it was like that. You've been a sailor, haven't you?"

I nodded. "I was in the Navy in the war." And then, to kill those memories, I took her out and we danced again very merrily, and coming back I said: "You'd like a banana split after that, wouldn't you?"

She dimpled. "It would be lovely. I haven't had one, not for ever so long. Fancy you remembering!" And so we ate these things and counted the cherry stones, and danced, and smoked and danced again.

Till in the end the opening bars of a tune brought us both up to our feet staring at each other in amazement, for it was midnight and the band was playing God Save the King. The table before us was littered with spoilt menus of sundaes and ices, because I had drawn a ship for her, and she had drawn a pig, and from that we had progressed between the dances through the whole field of animal and naval art. I stared across the table and said:

"I had no idea it was so late." Then we went together to the desk and I paid her her dances and her tip. She took the money without glancing at it, but stood looking up at me a little wistfully, and she said:

"You'll come in again some time, won't you?"

My work in Leeds was finished; I had nothing now to do but to get back to London and report. I said: "Of course I will, Miss Gordon. I'll probably come in tomorrow night."

She smiled. "That'd be lovely." And so I walked back to my hotel and up to bed, tired and content.

I had all next day to kill. I took the Bentley after breakfast and went out of the city rather aimlessly in the direction of York. In an hour or two I was well back into the past and wandering all through the lanes and byways of the York and Ainsty country, where I used to stay with my uncle Jim in the holidays, long before the war. They used to mount me on a strawberry roan, a beautiful little mare. They're none of them there now. Arthur Cope was killed at Passchendaele, and Mary married and went out to India, and Uncle Jim died soon after the war, and I went wandering through the lanes that day in my expensive car alone. Things change.

I was slowly making up my mind. My report to the police was that the girl could probably identify the lorry even in its burnt-out state; she had no means of access to her brother. I knew what they would do. Rightly or wrongly, Norman would 'pull her in' and take her down to see the burnt-out wreck; if she identified it she would be submitted to a sort of Third Degree in the hope that she would let slip some admission which would put them on to the track of her brother. The police were right. Their business was to catch criminals, to rout out the whole truth of this affair, and that was undoubtedly the way to set about it.

The most that I could do was to make things a little easier for her.

Eight o'clock found me back in the Palais at the conclusion of a very boring day. The girl was there, waiting for me in the pen. I went to get her, and she came out to meet me on the way.

"It was nice of you to come," she said simply. I don't know why, but something in the way she said that startled me. She said it almost humbly, as if in dancing with her I was doing a great kindness to a lonely girl.

We went and danced, and chose a table by the floor, ordered our coffee and danced again. We were very well together by that time; the band was good and the floor clear. I had never danced so pleasantly in all my life. She was less depressed than she had been the previous evening. She chatted freely to me of her little interests, and presently I asked if she had thought any more about her holiday.

She shook her head. "I saw Ethel today, and she's fixed up to go with another girl in her office. Scarborough it was, you know." She stared absently around the room. "I'll stay on here and maybe get a holiday in the autumn."

I said: "It's rotten luck."

She turned to me and smiled. "No good getting mopey about things, is it? I expect you've found that. It doesn't do any good."

I was silent for a moment. "No," I said at last, "I don't know that I have." She looked puzzled. "But anyway," I said, "I've never had to lose a holiday like this. So I don't count."

She eyed me seriously. "I've not lost my holiday. It's just that I haven't the money to do what I'd like to do. Seems to me it's just a question of being happy with what you can get, and not bothering with the things you can't afford. It's the same for everyone that way." She bent across the table to me, earnestly. "I mean, it is, isn't it? I mean, you're fond of the sea and ships and things. But you don't go worrying because you can't go on an ocean cruise on a liner, like they advertise. To Monte Carlo, and that. Fares from a hundred and fifty guineas."

"No," I said, "I've never worried about that. But then I don't specially want to go."

She said: "You couldn't go if you did want to, and so you just don't want to. It's just like me and Scarborough—only you're more sensible." She smiled, a little bitterly.

"I think it's you who's the sensible one," I said quietly, and we went and danced again. I had no courage to match the courage she had shown, no experience to help her in the disappointment of her holiday. All that I could do would be to give her money and so spoil her confidence.

She began to tell me about the various habitués of the place, pointing them out to me one by one. She had something of a flair for character and a very shrewd knowledge of men— the chief defensive weapon in her armoury. I rallied her on this and provoked her to a laughing defence of her judgment. She said: "You just get to know. I mean, you don't have to dance with a man more than once or twice to know what he's like and what he does."

I laughed with her. "Including me, I suppose."

She dimpled. "You told me all about yourself, so that doesn't count."

"Tell me something that you've found out for yourself,

that I didn't tell you." I paused. "I'll give you an easy one. What's my income?" I asked, a little ironically. "How much money would you say I made a year?"

She blew a long cloud of smoke, and eyed me for a minute. "Not less than six hundred," she said at last. "I don't think very much more."

I smiled. "Why not more?"

"You'd have got married," she said simply. "A man like you."

I laughed; I had no answer to that deductive reasoning. "That wasn't a very good one," I remarked. We sat for a moment in silence looking out upon the floor and at the dancers in the moving, changing light. At last I said:

"As a matter of fact, I make a good bit more than that." About forty times as much, but there was no point in splitting hairs. "I didn't tell you any lies when I said I worked in a shipping office in the south. I do work there, but I'm the owner of the line. The ships are mine." I paused. "And then, of course, there's other things. . . ."

I smiled. "And so you're a bit off the map about me getting married," I said. "I could afford to, but it's never quite come off. You'll have to think again for that one."

"You're too particular," she said. "It's not often that I'm wrong like that."

We went and danced again; it was a quickstep and a merry one at that, so that we were laughing when we came back. I said: "This holiday of yours. Will you be here next week?"

She shrugged her shoulders as she lit another cigarette. "I suppose so. They think I'm going off, but I'll have to see Mr Banks and see if he'll let me stay on now, and have it later. I expect he will."

I laughed. "You'd better come down south with me," I said. "I'm motoring down tomorrow."

She eyed me quietly across the table, but said nothing at all to that. There was a long, tense silence while I waited for her to say something, wondering whether I was going to be chucked out of the place with ignominy. She sat there opposite me, very still, smoking and staring at me across the table, inscrutable. I thought of Norman and his methods, and I said:

"You could do that. I live at Dartmouth in a biggish sort

of house, with only a housekeeper and a couple of servants. If you care to come down there for a week I'd——" I got stuck in that sentence and began again. "It would be a very great pleasure to me," I said quietly.

I had roused her curiosity. She moved a little and looked puzzled. "I don't understand. Do you live all alone like that, in a house? Don't you have anyone to look after you, or anything? Just servants?"

"Just servants," I replied.

"Isn't it sort of lonely?"

"It is at times. That's why it would be so very good of you to come and stay with me."

She stared at me, a little helplessly. "I don't know what to say." And then she said: "Is this place near Torquay."

I know now that Torquay had been a dream city to her for all the years she had spent in the grey business districts of the north. "It's not so far away," I said. "Go over there as often as you like."

She said: "It's lovely, isn't it? All on hills above the water, with shops on the quay, like you told me. Everyone says it's lovely there. . . ."

"You'd better come and see it for yourself," I said casually. "You'd be quite all right. All my bedroom doors have keys on the inside. And all my guests pack up and go away after the first couple of days because they can't stand me any longer. So you needn't let that worry you."

She smiled. "I'd not want to do that."

We went and danced again. That was a foxtrot and a very stately dance; we never spoke at all. At the end we went back to the table and ordered something called a fruit parfait, which she said was lovely. And sitting there I turned to her and said:

"Don't worry if you'd rather not come down with me. You can go to Scarborough just as well; I'd like to stand you that, if you'll let me. I've had a damn good time these nights that I've been here, and I'd like to know that you could get away."

"It's been lovely for me," she murmured. "It's been so different."

I had an envelope all ready for her in my pocket, and now I passed it to her across the table. "I don't suppose I'll be coming here again after tonight," I said quietly. "But there's ten pounds there, if you'll take it, and it'll give you a decent holiday in Scarborough. Or if you'd like to come with me it'll give you something to spend, and if you don't like the way I carry on you'll be able to get away from me. But either way, I'd like you to have a proper holiday this year."

The parfaits came, and proved to be a tinned peach and an ice mixed up together in a cup. "I shouldn't be able to give you all my time," I said. "I've got my work to do. In the mornings you'd have to amuse yourself. But it's by the sea and there's boats and things to play about with, and I expect you'd like it if you came."

She sat there staring at me absently. "You are a funny one," she said after a time. "Let me think."

She sat there staring out across the floor, her chin resting on one hand. She looked very tired, and older than her years. An unpleasant little Jew moved by and spoke a word to her; mechanically she smiled at him. A waitress came and swabbed our table with a dirty cloth. The air was heavy with the acrid smoke of very inexpensive cigarettes; it was hot in the Palais with a moist, unpleasant stuffiness. Above the jazz melody and the shuffling feet I heard the rattle of the machine that issued tickets for the sixpennies.

She turned to me. "All right," she said at last, "I'll come away with you."

They were playing a Blues. The saxophones wept and moaned, the dancers walked upon the floor in long-drawn graceful movements, the lights swung and changed colour to the plaintive rhythm. A draught from some door brought a sudden whiff of clean air into the place and made me raise my head. I heard the wind sighing in the rigging of my boat, I heard the halyards flapping on the mast, and I wondered if the mooring chains were chafing at the bobstay in the running tide.

# CHAPTER 5

SHE HAD a bed-sitting-room in the district rather to the west of Leeds; I found the house next morning with some difficulty. It was in an industrial neighbourhood. It was one of many little streets of drab brick houses, semi-detached and each with a little front garden for the cats; not quite a squalid street, but very nearly so. It was called Acacia Road, and she lived in the house of a man who worked in the goods office at the railway. The road was a playground for the children of the neighbourhood.

It was just after ten o'clock when I drew up before her house; the children swarmed around, staring and fingering the car. She must have been on the look out for me, unseen, because as I got out of the saloon the door of the house opened and she came out to me, suitcase in hand. I went forward to meet her; in the front window a faded blind was pulled aside to disclose a woman's face pressed close against the glass.

I smiled and took the case from her, bulging a little and cracked and gaping at the corners. I think it had in it all that she possessed, or nearly all. She was in grey; grey shoes, grey stockings, grey overcoat, and grey felt hat; she had taken great pains over the adornment of her face. "It's going to be fine," I said. "We'll have a good run down."

She hesitated motionless upon the pavement. "Oh!" she said. "Is this your car?"

I never did like little cars, and my Bentley suits me pretty well. A dead, dull black saloon with a silver radiator and fittings, it loomed immensely in that narrow street; it seemed to shame the cramped style of the little villas. She moved forward on the pavement and peered in through the window at the deep, low seats, the hide upholstery and the gleaming wheel. "Oh!" she said. "Is this your car?"

I nodded. "Do you like her?"

She breathed: "It's awfully grand." And then she said: "Are you going to drive it yourself?"

She thought, I think, that the driving of a car like that was a professional matter and that lurking somewhere round about would be Adams in his livery, who at that moment was mowing the lawns of the Port House, down in Devonshire. I smiled at her. "I am," I said. "That is, unless you'd like to take her for a bit, later in the day."

She shook her head. "I only drove a car once, one day with Billy. He said it was a Morris—Morris something. But I couldn't drive a car like this."

I swung her suitcase into the back of the car beside my own and opened the front door for her. "All right," I said equably. "Then you'll just have to sit and watch for the best part of three hundred miles."

She stared at me wide eyed. "Is it as far as that?"

"Something over two-fifty, anyway," I said. "It may be over three hundred. It'll take us most of the day, taking things easily. But it's a good day for a run."

She hesitated for a moment in the door, examining the car and feeling the upholstery. "I used to go out with a boy who had an Essex coach, in Birmingham," she remarked. "But that wasn't like this. . . ."

I thought of Le Mans. "This isn't quite so handy in a busy street," I said politely. "It's too big." And with that we got into her, and moved away down the road.

We went down through Huddersfield, through a bleak and blackened land of little fields and little mills. Between the towns it was bright and sunny on the road; Sixpence sat quiet by my side. I gave her a map to study, but she couldn't read it, and so we went on more or less by dead reckoning, eked out by signposts and by my memory of the road. Before we had been going for ten minutes I had absently thrown off my hat into the back seats of the car; I generally drive bareheaded in a saloon.

She turned an eager, delicately-painted little face to me. "May I do that too? Take off my hat, I mean?"

I smiled. "Of course. Better make yourself really comfortable; we've got a good way to go." I reached behind and got her a rug; she took off her hat and patted her hair into shape before the mirror of her bag, powdered her nose, and settled down happily beside me as I drove.

"There's cigarettes there, if you like," I said. "You might give me one. . . ." I had to show her how to use the lighter then, and that amused her almost more than anything we saw that day. All morning I was smoking cigarettes; with each cigarette she pressed the button till the unit glowed, lips parted, watching it entranced; then she pulled it out and handed it to me. She couldn't make out how it worked at all.

I gave the Midlands a miss that day and went down the Welsh side. We got up on the high land after Huddersfield and went across the moors, skirting Manchester, to Buxton; then down to Newcastle-under-Lyme. It was there that Sixpence asked in all innocence if my car was a fast one and we got her up to eighty-six before I had to shut her down for a corner, but mostly we were running at about fifty. We turned away from Staffordshire and cut down through Market Drayton to Shrewsbury, and when we had passed through that we began to think about our lunch.

I chose the Chequers at Church Stretton, a place that I had had meals at before. The house dates back to the sixteenth century; a grey stone building, rather rambling, and full of open fireplaces burning wood. They have restored it and built on a dining-room within the last few years, and spoilt it altogether. They run it as a show place now, with prices commensurate, and no good American goes home without having spent a night in the room where Charles II slept and knighted Perrhyn.

We left the car by the grass plot in front and went into the hall, ushered by a porter in brown livery. I knew that I had made a mistake as soon as I got inside; we should have lunched at some little pub by the roadside. The place was all white paint and glass panels inside, like a hospital; the mere travesty of an English country house. The new dining-room was very white and spacious, with tables round the edge of a bleak dancing floor.

I was occupied with Sixpence at the beginning of our meal, and we had finished the fish before I was free to look about the room. Over in an alcove by the window there was a lady lunching with a couple of children, very neat and clean, in charge of a neat, clean nurse in the uniform of some institute or other. Something about the lady seemed familiar to me and drew my attention; I stared at her a little harder, and it was Marion.

Marion, whom I hadn't seen or heard of for the last nine years since we parted in the stables down at Courton, crying her eyes out because she didn't want to marry me. Why she should have cried like that I never understood; if anyone had a right to cry it should have been me, but I can only remember feeling a bit uncomfortable about it all. Nine years is a long time; she had filled out and collected a couple of children, but it was Marion all right. I seemed to remember having heard that she was married; I wondered what her name was now.

Towards the end of lunch the nurse marshalled the children and went out with them, and she was left alone for coffee. I bent across the table to Sixpence.

"I've just seen an old friend of mine at that table over there —the lady. Do you mind if I go over and speak to her for a minute or two?" And so I crossed the room to her table.

"Good morning, Marion," I said quietly. She looked up in surprise; then she recognised me. "Malcolm!" she said. "After all these years. My dear!"

I sat down beside her table and talked with her for a few minutes of the old days and friends that we had known. She had a neat and orderly mind even in the old days; with the years this had grown on her and now she was very social, very rigid in her class. She told me that she was living in the hotel with her two children for the summer 'because the air was so good for them'; I heard no mention of her husband, nor of any home that they had made. I sat there listening, thinking that I could have done better for her than that.

In turn she wanted to know my news. "There's nothing much to tell," I said. "I still live down in Dartmouth, just the same. I have my work down there, you see, and that's all one really wants." I smiled. "That," I said, "and a certain amount to drink."

She said: "Oh, my dear. Do you mean you've never married, all these years?"

I laughed. "Lord, no," I said; "nor likely to. You should know that."

She said: "Oh, Malcolm!"

She leaned across and put her hand on mine. "Malcolm," she said, "we were good friends once, and I've sometimes thought I didn't treat you very well." I said something or other—I don't know what. "But you're still a young man, and it's not too late now for you to marry some nice girl and be happy with her, as you used to want to be. There's ever so many nice girls about, Malcolm. You mustn't go and hurt all your old friends by getting down too low. I know what men are, of course . . . but don't go down too far, Malcolm." And she glanced across the room at Sixpence, sitting all alone.

I knew that Sixpence wasn't happy there. It was not that she was unaccustomed to a good hotel, because she evidently was; she knew the ropes all right, but there was a bleak austerity about the place that might have daunted anyone. She was sitting rather stiffly on her chair, ill at ease and anxious in the menacing presence of the waiters. In the freezing cleanness of that room she looked a little shabby and a little over-dressed; the paint upon her face showed up most cruelly.

I smiled. "Looks a bit high and dry, doesn't she?" I said cynically. I knew that I must get back to her; it was bad luck for her to be made to feel like that upon the first day of her holiday.

"Who is she, Malcolm?"

I glanced at Marion for a moment, thinking what a different life I should have had to lead if we had gone through with it. Some things cannot be explained; I knew that Marion would never understand me if I talked to her all night. I shrugged my shoulders. "One of my little friends," I said. "I picked her up in Leeds."

She withdrew her hand. "You've changed a lot, Malcolm," she said quietly.

I nodded. "I dare say. It's probably as well we never married, Marion."

She had nothing to say to that.

I ground the stub end of my cigarette down upon the tray. "Things change," I said, "and people. And one gets to think about things differently. It's been jolly seeing you again, Marion, but now I think I must get back to her." I smiled. "I paid her ten pounds to come away with me, you see, and I must get my money's worth."

She sighed a little, and I left her to her life of freezing clean hotels, her two hygienic children and their nurse, and all the Best People that she knew, and I went back to Sixpence. "This room simply shatters me," I said, and glanced around me with distaste. "It's like a ruddy ice house."

She rippled softly into laughter. "Oh, you are funny!" she

said. "I mean, I've been feeling like that, too. It's terribly grand, isn't it?"

She had finished lunch while I had been talking to Marion. "Let's get out of it," I said.

She stared at me. "Don't you want any more to eat? You haven't had half enough, driving all that way."

I smiled. "Don't want any more," I said. "The food would choke me. You want to trifle with lark's tongues in aspic and talk about Marcel Proust when you lunch here."

She stared at me. "Who was she?"

"I don't know," I replied. "That's why we're going." And I sent the waiter for the bill.

We settled down again into the Bentley and went wandering south between the hills to Ludlow, running at an easy speed. All afternoon we ran southwards by the border, through Ludlow to Hereford and down to Ross. Then we cut across to Gloucester and down beside the Cotswolds, till finally we ran into Bristol in good time for tea.

I turned to Sixpence as we drove through the suburbs of the town. "I chose that place for lunch," I said, "and it turned out to be a dud. You'd better have a shot this time, and choose where we have tea."

I thought for a moment. "We'll have to have supper on the road, I think. We'll be a bit late getting in, and I haven't told them we should want a meal. Would you like a meat tea and a light supper somewhere?"

She looked up at me doubtfully. "Would you like that? I mean, is that what you have?"

I laughed. "I had my way about lunch. You've got to choose where we have tea."

She laughed with me. "Let's just walk about a bit and see what the places are like. I mean, fancy asking for an egg to your tea in where we had lunch. Wouldn't it be awful?" And so we slid into the centre of the town among the traffic.

We found a place to park the car and walked out into the streets, looking for our tea. In the end we found a place, a sort of teashop, not too pretentious; she paused outside and looked up at me doubtfully, and said: "Do you think this is nice?" So we went inside and ate a meal of tea and poached eggs and iced cakes. Sixpence finished up with a strawberry ice, but I couldn't face that; at the end she sighed happily and said: "It is nice here, isn't it?" I helped her on with her coat, and for that little service she turned to me impulsively and said: "You are kind!"

And then I went and spoilt it all. I don't know now exactly how it came to happen; some tone or inflexion in my voice, I suppose, that brought her little castle tumbling down. She asked if we had time to walk up the street a little way to look at the shops, and so we strolled on slowly, pausing every now and then. First it was a leather shop that caught her eye, and she paused to admire the bags and dressing cases in the window. Next it was a window full of evening frocks; that held us for a long time, and I was told that she looked best in green. All the girls said so.

This shop-inspecting expedition, I could see, was going to cost me money. That put things on a different footing; to me it became a matter of business then, and I began calculating the chances dispassionately. My job was to get her safe to Newton Abbot and hand her over to the police for the identification of the lorry; I had sent a wire to Norman to say that I was bringing her down. While she was in my hands my business was to keep her quiet and amenable; what happened when I had delivered up the goods was no concern of mine. The next move was evidently that I should buy her something and I was quite prepared to play my part. What to buy I neither knew nor cared.

It was in this frame of mind that we came to the jewellers, and we stopped a long time there. First it was a pendant that attracted her, and then a brooch; in my preoccupation I was amused to study her and to notice that her taste was by no means bad. We stayed there so long that I became aware that it was here that I must do my stuff. I don't suppose there was a thing in that window worth much more than twenty pounds.

It was a brooch, a single bar of platinum with an emerald in the middle, that she was admiring at the time. I smiled, thinking it was like giving toys to a child to make it be good. "You can have that, if you like," I said. "Or any of these other things."

As soon as I had spoken I knew that I had done it wrong. She stared up at me, wrinkling her brows. "Do you mean you'd give it me?" she demanded.

I didn't quite know what to say to that. "If you'd like it," I

77

replied. "Either that or anything else in there that you'd like."

She stood there staring up at me. "Do you mean I can have anything I like out of that window? Anything I like to ask you for?"

I nodded. "If you'd like anything there."

There was a silence. She stood looking in at the window without speaking for a minute, and I knew that things had gone most desperately wrong. In an endeavour to retrieve the situation I said awkwardly: "Would you like to go inside and have a look round?"

She shook her head. "I don't think I want anything now. They're not very nice."

I was humbled and amazed. We went on looking at shops in a desultory manner, but all her pleasure in the walk was gone. She seemed listless and depressed, and after a decent interval she suggested that perhaps it was time we got on the road again. So we went back to the car. By that time I knew what was wrong. I had hurt her very deeply by the way in which I had offered her the whole contents of the shop; I could imagine that in her parlance that was not the way a gentleman would give a present to his girl friend. The worst of it was that I could see no way in which to put things right.

We slid out of the town into the suburbs and up the hill upon the Axbridge road. It was a lovely evening on the road, but that didn't do us any good. Before, she had been chattering to me all the way, pointing out things by the roadside and lighting cigarettes for me, but now she sat quiet by my side and even the automatic lighter failed to amuse. From time to time she said something with forced gaiety, but there was a constraint between us that the swift passing of the miles did nothing to remove.

We went down through Axbridge and across Sedgemoor, through Bridgwater to Taunton. With the coming of the evening we ran into Devonshire and down to Exeter. It was about half-past seven when we passed through that; I took the Dartmouth road. I was in my own country by this time. Chudleigh was my destination for this stage, and twenty minutes later we pulled up at the Running Hart for supper.

Try as I may, I cannot remember much about that meal. I suppose we ate in silence punctuated by little forced remarks; I know that nothing happened which would make the situation any easier. Only one thing I remember. They know me at the Running Hart, and they gave me to wait at table a boy that I know something of, whose uncle is a shipwright in my yard. This boy is a pretty good golfer in his leisure time; he got into the semi-final of the South Devon Championship that year. I think he must have told us about that as he served the meal, because I cannot think of any other way in which I should have known.

It was nearly dark when we had finished. We had a cup of coffee in the lounge; several times during that I felt that Sixpence wanted to say something, but it didn't come. At last we went out to the car. I had turned her off the road into the stable yard, and there she was standing on the cobbles by the mounting block, gleaming a little and enormous in the dusk. Sixpence had followed me, a pace or so behind, but as I opened the door for her to get in she stopped motionless beside the car.

"Mr Stevenson," she said, so low that I had to drop my head to catch her words. "Please, I don't think I want to come on any further with you. I'm so dreadfully sorry. . . ."

There was a bat wheeling and darting round the yard against a deep blue sky. I stood there staring absently into the dusk, at the dark shadows in the open stable doors, the tin advertisements of poultry food upon the russet walls, the haystack by the gate. This was the England that I knew; in coming down from Leeds I had come south from a foreign land, and brought with me a foreign girl.

I bent towards her. "It's exactly as you like," I said. "You needn't come with me unless you want to, you know." That wasn't true, of course. Now that I had got her so far she would certainly complete her journey to identify the wreck at Newton Abbot, whether with me or with the police.

She hesitated, at a loss for words. "I think I'd better spend the night here," she said at last, "by myself. And then I'd go up north again by train tomorrow."

I nodded. "I'm so very sorry this has gone wrong," I said quietly. "I mean that. If you could tell me what's the matter— I'd do anything I can to help, you know. Don't worry if you'd rather not."

She looked up at me. "I feel so awfully mean telling you," she muttered, "after all the trouble you've taken, and the things you've done, and everything. It's just that I don't want to go on with it. . . ."

I smiled at her. "That's quite all right," I said. "You don't want to worry about that." I knew that sort of scene by heart; it happens to me every eighteen months.

She raised her eyes and looked me straight in the face. "I'm so dreadfully sorry, and I didn't mean it to end like this when I came away with you—truly I didn't. I suppose it's that I'm not really the sort of girl for this. And you're not the sort of man, either."

I was staring into the dim expanses of the field beyond the gate; the bat was still sweeping and circling about the eaves. "Why do you say that?" I asked, without looking at her. "Why do you say I'm not the sort of man?"

She hesitated, and then said: "The way you were talking to the waiter. . . ."

She came a little closer to me in the dusk. "I'd like you to know," she said simply, "because you've been so kind, and perhaps you won't think so bad of me. Lots of the girls go away for holidays with gentlemen and just don't seem to mind, but I never did that. Only once, and I didn't know about things then; I was seventeen, and I didn't know. And that was ever so long ago—I'm quite old, you know." She smiled up at me tremulously. "And then you came, and it was all so different. I'd never had a gentleman quite like you before, although I've met lots, you know, coming to dance. And then I couldn't have my holiday, and I was sort of silly about that, although it doesn't do to be silly about things, does it? And then you came and asked me to come away with you. And I thought it didn't matter. . . ."

It seemed to me that this young woman was labouring under a considerable misapprehension as to the nature of her holiday. I stood there resting one foot upon the running board of the Bentley and I was silent for a minute, considering the position. At last I said:

"You can go home if you like—you know that—and I'll fix up a room for you here, and go away. But you're quite wrong about me."

She looked up at me. "I don't understand."

I dropped my foot down from the running board and stood erect. "I'm thirty-nine years old," I said, "and I must be a damn fool, because although I've got plenty of money I've never taken a girl away the way you mean. Not even when I've had it chucked at my head. You were right when you said I'm not that sort of man, and I don't take any credit for that, either, because it's how you happen to be made."

I paused. "You think that because I offered to buy you anything you wanted from that shop, that I was trying to buy you. Well, I wasn't, as a matter of fact. I meant you to come down to my place for an ordinary holiday, like I told you."

She stood there looking up at me. "I don't understand," she said again. "I've never met anyone like you a bit. . . ."

I smiled at her. "We aren't going on our honeymoon," I said, "although I know it looks a bit like that. I meant it to be just an ordinary holiday for you—sort of staying with friends. Only there's only me and the servants in the house."

"You mean you just wanted me to come and keep you company, sort of?" She paused. "Not anything more than that?"

I nodded. "Nothing more than that."

There was a little silence then, and then she said, half to herself: "Just because you were lonely, like, living all alone." I hadn't anything to say to that.

She raised her face to mine. "I'd like to come on with you," she said simply, "if you'll let me now. I didn't know it was like that. You must think me awful, though. . . ."

It was very dark and shadowy in the yard. It seemed to me that I had slipped back fifteen years, that I was still a boy with all the glamour of a young man's life in front of me, that I could mould my life to what I chose and make it good.

"My dear," I said, "I think you're simply sweet."

In the dim light her upturned face was like a flower. "You've been so kind to me," she murmured in the dusk. "I don't know what to say."

The bat was still wheeling and flickering above our heads against a deep blue sky, the poultry food advertisements had faded into dim shadows on the russet walls, the night was very still. She stood there very close to me, her face upturned to mine; we were more together then than we had ever been. With a little sigh she came into my arms and rubbed her face against my overcoat.

It was over seven years since I had kissed a girl.

6                    81

After a little time we came unstuck, and got into the car. I swung her out of the stable yard on to the road, and then we sat quiet for a time in the gloom behind the headlights, very close together, talking in low tones. It is twenty miles from Chudleigh to my house. It seemed like two to me, that night.

We passed through Dartmouth and up the shoulder of the hill. At the top I swung the car in through the gates and up the drive, and we came to rest on the gravel sweep before the house, three hundred miles from Leeds. I switched off the engine, and the silence closed down on us, infinite, complete. We sat there for a moment silent in the dark; then I stirred, and we got out of the car.

The front door opened and Rogers was there with one of the maids; he came forward and busied himself with our luggage. I spoke a word or two to him; from the open door a stream of light poured out into the darkness where we stood. Then I turned to where the girl was standing by the car.

She came up to me: "Is this where you live?"

"That's right," I said. "Let's go indoors."

She hung back a little by the car. "It's awfully big," she breathed. "It's like the pictures. . . ." And then she said: "Whatever is that noise?"

I listened for a moment. I could hear nothing beyond the usual small noises of the night, the rustling of branches in the breeze, the low murmur from the beach. I laughed. "That's the sea you hear," I said. "On the rocks, just down below that lawn. You'll see it from your window in the morning when you wake."

For a little time we stood there listening, sniffing the sea air. "That's it," I said. "It's when the wind's in the south-east that it makes that noise. Blows straight in."

"Oh——" she said. "It's going to be lovely here."

We went into the house. Mrs Rogers, my housekeeper, was in the hall; I noticed that she looked at her a little bit askance. I spoke a word or two to Mrs Rogers on the subject of spare rooms and light refreshments, and by the time I'd finished she had clearly understood that her position would be vacant if she gave me any nonsense of that sort. She went away then, and I had no further trouble with her in that way.

Both Sixpence and I were tired from the drive; there was a fire in the library, and we went in there. She was shy and very quiet, very observant of the house. She refused a drink, but jumped at the proposal of a cup of tea and a piece of cake before the fire; I poured myself out a whisky and put on a few records on the gramophone to allow her to keep quiet. Then we were ready for bed.

I took her up and showed her to her room. There was a bright fire burning in the grate and the room looked very comfortable; her things were all laid out. She hadn't very much. I looked round and made sure that she had everything she wanted for the night—soap and towels and all the rest of it. I crossed with her to the window and drew back the curtain; two hundred feet below the moon cast dappled shadows on the water at the harbour mouth. "There's the sea," I said. "You'll see it all when you wake up."

We turned back into the room.

"What's that door?" she asked.

I crossed the room and opened it, smiling a little; the light shone brightly on white tiles and silver pipes. "That's your bathroom," I replied. "Not my bedroom, as you might suppose."

She rippled into laughter. "Oh, you are funny. I mean, I didn't mean that when I asked you what the door was." She sighed. "It's all so lovely here I don't know what to say."

"Better say goodnight," I remarked. "That's a safe one, anyway."

She came up to me. "Goodnight," she said simply. "And thank you so much for the lovely day I've had."

"Goodnight," I said, and went down to the library again. There were one or two letters to be opened, and one or two instructions to be given to Rogers about matters of the house. And then I sat smoking for a long time, irresolute, staring into the fire. At last I reached out for the telephone and rang up Fedden at his house.

"Well," I said, "I've got the girl down here. What do you want done with her?"

There was a moment's pause. "One moment. Where is she? Where are you speaking from?"

"Speaking from my house," I said. "You don't want her tonight, do you? I've sent her up to bed."

"I can't do anything with her tonight," he replied. "We'll examine her in the morning. You know Norman's down here?

He came down this afternoon. About this girl—has she made any statement to you?"

"None at all. I haven't tried for one. I brought her down here because I thought she could identify the lorry."

He paused. "I don't understand. How did you get her to come down here, then?"

"Personal charm," I said laconically.

"Oh. . . ." There was a little silence then, because Fedden is a better sort than I am. "Then she doesn't know anything at all about this matter—why you've brought her down?"

"Nothing whatsoever," I replied. "Still, I've got her here. What do you want me to do with her?"

He considered for a moment. "Bring her to Newton Abbot police station at half-past ten tomorrow morning," he said at last. "I'm meeting Norman there at ten. In all probability he'll show her the lorry there."

"All right. Are you any good at scenes?"

"Did you say scenes?"

"Yes, scenes. You'd better come prepared for one, because we're pretty sure to have it."

"Oh. . . ."

"One thing more," I said. "I take it that my responsibility ends tomorrow, when I hand her over to you. I'll arrange to have her clothes packed up and sent along to you later in the day. The position is that I deliver her to you at Newton Abbot, and you take charge of her from then onwards."

He hesitated. "If you like. I don't see that we can ask you to do anything further in the matter after that."

"That's all I wanted to be sure about," I said. "Goodnight."

I put up the receiver and moved the decanter over to a table by my chair. The fire was dying in the grate; I threw on more coal and beat it savagely into a blaze.

I sat there till the room grew cold and dark. Then I went up to bed.

# CHAPTER 6

I CAN'T have got much sleep that night, because I was awake at dawn. That was about four o'clock, I should suppose; it must have been about the second or third of June. I lay and watched the light growing in the room till I could see from the glow that there was sunlight out of doors, and a clear sky and an easterly wind for settled weather.

It was no good lying in bed; I gave up the attempt to sleep, got up, and had a bath. Then I went downstairs in my dressing gown and pyjamas and wandered absently about the house a bit; my chair and glass were as I had left them in the library an hour or two before. I went through into the model room and drew the blinds. The morning sun streamed through into the room and I stood there idly for a little time, studying the hull shapes on my drawing board. At that time I was working on the design of the small cruising yacht that I laid down last month when I came back to Dartmouth; I think she will turn out a pretty little craft, embodying all that I have ever learnt about the game.[1] I stood there studying the lines till I became absorbed, moved T-square and curves, and stood there working at the hull until I heard the servants moving round the house.

I went upstairs to shave and dress, and when I came down again Sixpence was before me. I came down into the hall treading quietly on the thick carpet of the stairs, and stood there for a moment sorting through my letters. Then I looked up and through the open door of the library I saw her standing at the entrance to the model room. She had not heard me in the hall.

I watched her for a minute. She stood there very quiet, staring about her, taking it all in. She was dressed in the same grey costume that she had worn the previous day and had taken the same pains over her face; her thick black hair was coiled about her ears. I watched her as she moved slowly forward into the model room, treading very softly as though she was uncertain if she ought to be there at all. She passed

---

[1] This vessel was on the stocks at the decease of her designer. She was purchased and completed by Mr L. A. Stone of Salcombe, who christened her *Mazurka III*. [ED.]

into the sunlight by the window; deep colours showed up in the folds of her hair and warm tints on her neck below the powder line; she moved with a quiet grace that was, perhaps, in part an attribute of her profession. She stood there for a time by the window in the sun, looking about her at the models, careful not to touch the cases as she moved. Presently she slipped over to my drawing board and paused for a long time over that, uncomprehending.

I smiled, and went up a few steps of the stairs, and came down upon the resonant woodwork at the side. I turned into the library and found her there. "Morning," I said; "did you sleep well?"

She nodded. "Lovely," she said. And then she said: "It is a lovely house. I think it's just a dream."

I smiled, and moved forward to the door. "This is the model room," I said. "Where I do my work—some of it. What I don't do down at the office I do here." I stared around. "There's not much here but ships."

She said: "The maid told me when she came to wake me up. Oh, and I mean—I've been calling you all wrong. You must think me awful! But you never told me different. I've been calling you Mr Stevenson all the time."

I laughed. "That's what I ought to be called. It's only because I have to do with ships that they call me Commander. I was only in the Navy in the war."

She looked up at me uncertainly. "Oh . . . I didn't know." And then she said: "She said you were up working, ever so early. Didn't you sleep properly? I slept lovely after all that driving."

"You don't sleep so much as you get older," I replied. "I often get up early in the summer."

This was an opening she knew. "Oh, you are funny," she replied. "You aren't old."

I grinned at her. "I've got enough grey hair, anyway," I said.

She looked around, and sighed. "I'd sleep for ever in a lovely house like this," she said.

We went through into the dining-room for breakfast. I saw her glance around as she sat down, a swift circular glance that seemed to take in everything from the silver on the table to the portraits of my family upon the walls. "I've got to go over to Newton Abbot this morning," I remarked as we sat down. "Would you like to come too?" I paused. "I'm running over in the car."

She looked at me doubtfully. "Are you sure I wouldn't be in the way? I mean, it's all so lovely here I don't want you to bother."

I smiled, a little bitterly: "You needn't worry about that. I'd like it if you'd come to keep me company."

She smiled at me. "It would be lovely. I do like driving in your car. It is a nice one, isn't it?"

"It goes all right," I said, and so we got on with the meal. I had grown queerly callous by that time and could listen quite unmoved while she chatted to me about holidays that she had taken with her brother, years before, holidays at Colwyn Bay and Southport. I listened with a detached, critical interest while she spoke of him, trying to make out from her account what sort of man this brother' of hers was. She had a great regard for him. To her he was everything that was fine and manly and courageous; it was the idolism of a child. I wondered what the man was really like.

He was three years older than her. That put him at about twenty-eight years old, I thought.

We left the house soon after breakfast; that was a rotten drive. I was silent and preoccupied, and after a little time Sixpence grew quiet and didn't worry me. I noticed that at the time, and I remembered wondering if she had smelt a rat. In any case, there was nothing she could do about it now; my business was so nearly over.

It was in that frame of mind that we drove into Newton Abbot and drew up before the police station, exactly at the time agreed upon. The town was all spattered with election posters. I remember that because it was the first time I had seen the things that year. It must have been about six weeks before the poll.

As the car came to a standstill, I said: "You'd better come inside with me. I shan't be long." She looked a little startled, but I turned away and she followed me in through the door and into the same room where I had been shown the gun. Norman and Fedden were waiting for us there.

I spoke first: "This is Miss Gordon, who's come down with me," I said. "Major Norman—Colonel Fedden."

They bowed to her, and she murmured something that I couldn't catch. I didn't care to look at her.

"We have the lorry outside, in the yard," said Norman. "I think perhaps we'd better go and see that first." He turned to the girl. "Will you come, too, Miss Gordon?" he said pleasantly.

She smiled at him, and we went through the door and out into the yard. There was a mass of wreckage beneath a tarpaulin in a corner of the wall; two constables were uncovering it as we went out.

Norman turned to the girl, and when he spoke his voice was very grave. "Miss Gordon," he said quietly. "I think you told Commander Stevenson that your brother was the owner of a motor-lorry—a thirty-hundredweight Dennis lorry." He paused. "I am very sorry to say that we have had an accident down here recently—rather a bad accident. Do you think you would know your brother's lorry again?"

She stared at him, wide eyed. "I don't quite understand." And then she said quickly: "Do you mean something's happened to Billy?"

His manner was perfect. "Please, Miss Gordon," he said, "there's nothing to distress yourself about at the moment. I want you just to walk round this lorry with me, and see if you can see anything on it that you can identify. That's all."

The wreckage was completely uncovered by this time. It lay there on the asphalt of the yard, broken and twisted and already red with rust. I was standing with Fedden a little way apart. He looked at me awkwardly, and said in a low tone:

"Norman is very experienced in dealing with these cases. You can safely leave her in his hands, if you'd rather slip away now."

I glanced at him sharply. "I'd rather stay," I said. "I want to see how this is done."

He made no answer, but stood there fidgeting a little—a decent man in an impossible position. Norman had moved closer to the lorry with the girl, and was talking to her in a very gentle tone. She had forgotten we were there, I think.

"It caught on fire in the middle of the night," he was saying, "on the road, not very far from here. There was nobody there at the time, and when help came it was burning so fiercely that no one could get near it to do anything. Everything in it was destroyed—we don't even know what it was loaded with.

88

As you can see, it was completely burnt out...." He hesitated. "And the driver...." He stopped.

She was staring at him, dumb with horror. "Please ..." she whispered in the end. "Please tell me. What happened to the driver?"

He paused for a moment, as if he didn't quite know what to say. "I am afraid, Miss Gordon," he said very gently, "we don't quite know what happened to the driver. It was all so utterly burnt up, you see."

It was a moment before she realised what he meant; then for a minute I thought she was going to break down. But she had guts, that girl, and all that happened was that she began fumbling at the catch of her handbag, mechanically trying to open it. It would not come undone and she stood there fumbling at it desperately, her head bent down. I don't know what it was she wanted out of it, perhaps a handkerchief.

"Come," said Norman, "there's nothing to distress yourself about. We don't know that this is your brother's lorry. Perhaps it may not be."

She swallowed once or twice. "I—I should know Billy's lorry," she said at last. "I think so. She looked up at him pitifully. "It had horseshoes on it."

He spoke to her very gently, immensely kind. "Then let's just have a look at it together," he suggested. "Two heads are better than one, aren't they? And you can tell me if you see anything you recognise."

I stood there looking on at this dumbfounded, amazed at the cleverness of the man. He had said nothing that was not true. It was true that the lorry had been burning fiercely when it was discovered, true that he knew nothing of the driver's fate. I could see that he would get the whole of the evidence he wanted without the slightest difficulty; if she had anything damaging to tell she would commit her brother up to the hilt without ever knowing she had injured him. The whole of her examination was being cast into the form of an inquiry into the supposed death of her brother, and she would tell everything she knew.

A more educated, more sophisticated girl might possibly have broken out of the snare that he had made for her by puzzling over the circumstances that had brought her to that yard; she might have smelt a rat. I could see that Norman had

89

nothing to fear from that. The girl was very nearly in tears, hanging back a little from the wreckage in the corner that he was trying to get her to inspect.

"Come, Miss Gordon," he said, "we must just have a look at it, you know." There was an air of gentle authority in his voice which made her come to him at once. Together they walked slowly up the length of that tangled, rusty mass of iron.

They moved round to the front. I saw her stop, I saw the muscles of her face working. I saw her catch her breath as she pointed to something on the ruins of the radiator. I couldn't see what it was from where I was standing. I saw Norman bend down to her, infinitely solicitous.

"Is that your brother's?" he asked gently.

She nodded once or twice, dumbly. "It was a little one—just like that. He—he said it was a donkey's. . . . There was a big one on the back."

Norman inclined his head. "We found a big one on the road, underneath," he said quietly. "It must have been nailed on to some wooden part."

There was an infinite silence in the yard.

"Come," said Norman, "just one more look, and then we'll go indoors. I want you to tell me if there's anything else that you can recognise. There might still be some mistake, you know."

They walked together slowly down the other side. The steering column was bent and twisted down; the thin bare core of the wheel stood up forlornly. Below the wheel a little clip was mounted carrying a ring, clumsy, amateurish fitting at the best. She laid her hand on this.

"He used to put his pipe in that," she said in a low tone. "He put it on himself, because he told me." She turned to him with a trembling lip. "Please—mayn't we go indoors now?"

"I think we may, Miss Gordon," he said kindly. "There's nothing more that we can do out here." He hesitated for a moment, and then said: "I am so very, very sorry."

She made no reply to that; I don't think she was capable of saying anything. She walked across the yard with him towards the door we had come out of; Fedden and I followed them a few paces behind. It seemed to me that the art of criminal investigation had advanced a step or two since Sherlock Holmes.

At the door Fedden made another effort to get rid of me. "There's nothing more for you to stay for, if you'd like to get away," he said. "We can take care of her now, and send her back up north."

I gave him a grim stare. "I should prefer to stay," I said shortly. "I want to see what fancy games you gentlemen are going to play with her." He winced at that, as I had meant he should.

He said something or other, but I brushed past him and followed Norman into the office. He was already seated at the table there, the girl opposite him. He gave me a sharp glance as I came in, which I ignored; I knew that he could do nothing to eliminate me without arousing her suspicions. I took up a stand on the far side of the room, half turned away from them, looking out of the window. Fedden came in and closed the door, and stood by me. At a corner table there was a sergeant taking notes, armed with a notebook and pencil.

"Now, Miss Gordon," Norman was saying, "just one or two questions that we have to ask, about this accident. I am sure you won't mind."

She looked up at him dumbly.

"First of all, what was your brother's name?"

She answered in a low voice: "William Hartop Gordon."

"And his age?"

"He was thirty last October." So she was older than I thought.

"Where did he live?"

"It was somewhere in Birmingham, but I don't know the address. He used to be in Wolverhampton, up till about a year ago."

"Was he a married man?"

She shook her head without speaking.

"Do you remember where he lived in Wolverhampton?"

"He was in lodgings. Twenty-nine Elmer's Crescent was the address."

Norman smiled at her kindly. "Just one or two more questions, Miss Gordon." He paused. "When did you see your brother last?"

She swallowed. "In Leeds. I think it was about a month ago. You see, he came and booked me out."

"I see," said Norman; "and you went out with him. Did you go in his lorry?"

She tried to speak, and failed. She shook her head, and then she said, a little piteously: "Please, do you think I might have a glass of water?"

The sergeant rose, lumbering from his table, and went out of the room; he returned in a minute with a dripping cup. She took it from him gratefully and drank; Norman sat patiently till she had finished.

"That's better," he said kindly. "Now, Miss Gordon, did your brother work for anybody? or was this lorry his own property?"

She said: "I think it was his own."

"I see." He was silent for a minute, and then: "Did he ever tell you what work he used to do, or who he used to work for? I mean, whose loads he used to carry in the lorry?"

She said: "Oh, yes." I swung round sharply by the window, and she stopped and looked at me.

"That's enough of this damn foolery," I said harshly.

There was a momentary silence. I stood there staring down at Norman at the table, watching the deep colour mounting in his face. He turned and beckoned to the sergeant, who got up and came towards me. "I'll see you about that afterwards, Commander Stevenson," he said easily. "In the meantime, perhaps you wouldn't mind waiting outside?"

The sergeant opened the door for me.

I laughed shortly. "If you like," I said. "In that case I shall go straight up to town. I can get a question asked about this matter in the House tonight."

Fedden stirred uneasily beside me, and I swung round viciously on him. "Yes, by Christ," I said, "and you'll be in it, too. Chief Constable of the County!" And I laughed again.

"Don't be a fool, Stevenson," he retorted, not unkindly. "You must go home and leave this thing to us."

"I'm damned if I do," I said.

The girl sat staring at us, red eyed and uncomprehending, gripping a little wad of handkerchief in her lap. Norman got up from the table. "I think it would be better for us to talk this over outside," he said smoothly. "In consideration for Miss Gordon."

"I don't," I said curtly.

I crossed the room to where the girl was sitting by the table. "You'd better come along with me," I said. "We're going home."

"Sit down!" said Norman sharply. She collapsed into her chair again, and I saw a tear fall down her cheek. He turned on me, red with anger. "As for you, sir, you must get out of this room. Go to town or go to hell for all I care. Get out!"

I put one foot up on to a chair and stared at him; there was an awkward silence after that outburst. "I'm a friend of Miss Gordon's," I said at last. "I want this inquiry adjourned till she has had an opportunity to consult her solicitor."

Fedden broke in. "Don't talk such nonsense," he said irritably. "The girl hasn't got a solicitor."

I raised my eyebrows. "Louden, Jenkinson and Priestley are acting for her," I replied. "Either Jenkinson or his junior will be here tonight."

Norman broke in: "That's a London firm."

"Don't be a damn fool," I said sourly. "Do you think I put my business with a hedge solicitor?"

There was a momentary silence, and I followed up: "I would have you understand that I am making formal application for an adjournment of this inquiry, in order that Miss Gordon may take legal advice. You clearly understand that, Major Norman?—and Colonel Fedden?" I swung round on the sergeant. "You too. You may have to give evidence on this in Court. You understand what I want?"

"That's enough," said Norman sharply. "He understands well enough."

The girl stirred beside me as if she wanted to say something, but I silenced her with a motion. "Look here," I said to Norman, "you want to get to the bottom of this thing; so do I. I want to know who cracked me on the head that night. But I'll be no party to a trick like this."

Fedden stirred. "Have you any alternative procedure to suggest?" he asked coldly.

I eyed him for a moment. "None at all. My solicitor deals with legal—and illegal—matters of this sort for me. I think you will find that he is able to suggest some alternative procedure to this sort of thing." I paused. "I imagine that he will advise Miss Gordon to make a statement to you, under his guidance."

Norman interposed: "She can make a statement now. This matter is urgent." He swung round on me. "You're playing the fool with matters you don't understand. How do you know what this delay may mean?"

I shrugged my shoulders. "You'll have to take your chance of that. You've waited four days for me to bring her here, and you can wait a fifth for her solicitor." I considered for a moment. "I'll say this for her: Miss Gordon will give you a statement of some sort tomorrow afternoon."

"Tomorrow morning," he said.

I shook my head. "It can't be done. Jenkinson can't get here till late, and Miss Gordon won't be fit to work with him tonight. Tomorrow afternoon."

He turned on his heel and swung over to the door. "You'd better see your friend off the premises," he said bitterly to Fedden, and then he was gone. Fedden said something or other, but I ignored him and turned to where the girl was sitting by the table. She turned a tear-streaked face to me.

"Please, Mr Stevenson," she said—"oh, I mean, Commander Stevenson—I'm sorry, I didn't mean——" She abandoned that sentence and started again. "I don't quite understand what's been happening," she said, a little pitifully.

I smiled. "I know you don't," I said. "I'll tell you about it when we get home. We'll get along now and"—I searched my brain for words of feminine comfort—"you can have a cup of tea and a bit of cake, and lie down for a bit if you want to. Come on." I stared around. "Got all your things?"

She got up and picked her bag up from the table. "There's one thing you may as well know right away," I said. "Your brother's all right. He wasn't in that lorry when it got burnt up."

She stared at me. "Did he go to Hammersmith?" Fedden was there, all ears, and I said hurriedly: "That's enough about that."

I spoke sharply, I suppose, because she started crying in real earnest then. I was too much occupied in getting her out of the building before she put her foot in it again to pay much heed to that. I got her out and into the Bentley in double quick time, and she sat there crying by my side as we slid out of the town. A policeman on point duty looked curiously at us as we swept past, and I wondered if he thought I was abducting her. If I were, I reflected, it was from the police.

She dried up after a mile or two, but all that drive we never spoke a word. I thought it best to leave her to herself, and so we went along in silence all the way. We got back to the house at about half-past twelve. I left the car standing on the drive and took her through into the library, sat her down in a chair, reached out for the telephone and put in a trunk call to Jenkinson. Then I turned to her.

"Now," I said, "what are you going to have? Cup of tea? Lunch will be ready in about three-quarters of an hour."

She shook her head miserably. "Please, I don't want anything."

I stood there looking down at her, and thought that I had never seen a girl less likely to enjoy her lunch than this one. I rang the bell, and told Rogers to get her a cup of Bovril and some toast. It was the best thing I could think of. "You needn't have it if you don't want it when it comes," I said. "You can just sniff at it then go upstairs and lie down if you want to."

She smiled up at me weakly. "You're ever so kind to me." And then she said: "I don't understand a bit what happened over there."

"No," I said, "I don't suppose you do." I paused for a minute, and lit a cigarette. "It's a very long story and I'm not going to tell you now—not all of it. I'll tell you after dinner tonight, when you've had a rest. But the bit you want to know now is this."

I paused, and looked at her reflectively. "Those men over there were police officers," I said. "Did you know that?"

She shook her head. "I didn't know who they were."

"Well," I said, "you know now. They were playing a trick on you. They wanted to find out something about your brother."

She stared at me, her brows wrinkled in perplexity. "They said he'd had an accident."

I shook my head. "Not him. He wasn't in that lorry when it got burnt up—he's very much alive somewhere. They just told you that for a trick, so that you would tell them everything you knew about him. You would have done, wouldn't you?"

She stared at me, wide eyed. "Of course I would." And then she said: "What did they want to know about him for? Has he done anything wrong?"

I shook my head. "I'll tell you this evening," I replied. "It's nothing very bad. He's got himself mixed up in a much bigger business. But you don't want to worry about that. It's going to be all right."

Her Bovril came then, and my trunk call. I picked up the telephone and spoke to Jenkinson in London.

"Look here," I said, "I've got myself into a bit of a mess down here, I'm afraid, with the police. Yes; no, not a motoring offence—something rather more serious than that. I've got a CID man from Scotland Yard down here sitting on my doorstep waiting for a statement. Yes. Do you think you could slip down tonight? One of your juniors would do if you can't, but I'd very much rather you came if you can, old boy. If it's not terribly inconvenient. That's really very decent of you. Well, you can catch the 5.30—gets to Exeter at 8.45. That's the easiest way. Tonight, that is. Yes I'll have the car there, at Exeter, at 8.45. Right you are. See you then. Goodbye."

I hung up the receiver. "That's your solicitor," I said. "He's coming down tonight."

She wrinkled her brows. "Is that what you were speaking about over there?" she asked. "From London?"

"That's right," I said.

"Oh——" And then she said: "Please, I don't think you quite understand——" She came to an end there, and I was puzzled; I couldn't make out what she was driving at.

"Couldn't I have somebody from here?"

I stared at her. "But this is one of the best men in the country—much better than anyone in a little town like this. He'll have these policemen absolutely taped. He handles all my work."

"I know——" She hesitated. "But coming all down from London like that. You see, I haven't got very much money." She looked up at me appealingly. "You do understand, don't you?"

I was silent for a minute. When I spoke, I said: "My dear, he's coming down for me. I didn't mean it to cost you anything at all."

She was troubled. "I don't know what to say. It's bound to cost a terrible lot, coming all that way."

I smiled, a little ironically. "Not more than I can afford," I said. She had finished her toast and Bovril. "Now look here, you'd better go upstairs and tidy yourself. You'd like some lunch, wouldn't you?"

She shook her head.

"All right," I said. "Go and lie down for a bit, or have a bath, or anything you like." She smiled. "I've got to go down to my office after lunch, but I'll be back about half-past four and we'll have tea in here. In the meantime, you can explore the place. You can go anywhere you like, you know," and I told her roughly the boundaries of my land. "Only don't go bathing till I show you where to go. The tide runs out a bit fast round this point."

She nodded obediently, and went upstairs. I went in and ate my lunch alone, and then took the car and went down to the yard. I spent the afternoon with Tillotson in the office, getting the hang of what had happened in my absence in the north. I had a ketch docking for a refit that day on the evening flood, the *Sweet Anna*, and I should have stayed to see her in. I usually do. But that afternoon I broke my rule and left the ship to Tillotson, and I went back to Sixpence in my house.

I found her in the model room when I got back. I saw her as I passed into the hall. She was sitting quietly on the window-seat gazing out through the open window over the sunlit garden to the deep blue sea. I don't know what I had expected to find her doing, but I was surprised. She seemed to be doing nothing at all but sit there looking out over the harbour mouth. In an idle moment I might have sat like that myself.

She got up when I came in. "I've been looking at the little ships," she told me. "They are lovely, aren't they?"

I turned with her and looked at them. This room is a hobby for me, a room of reminiscences. One or two of the models are historical, the caravel and the fifteenth-century pinnace, but most of them are little vessels of my own, ships that I have owned or sailed in in my time, that I keep for remembrance and as pointers of experience. At the moment there are fourteen in the little fleet; all sail except the trawler, *Martin Dodd*.

Rogers brought tea to us in there and I moved about the

room with Mollie, bread and butter in hand, talking to her about my little ships. She was interested and asked a lot of questions, and so we went round the room till finally we brought up at the *Jane Ellen*.

Sometimes I have thought that it would be better if I didn't keep that model, and I have considered sending it to some museum. But there it is still, and she paused beside it. "What are those things on the deck?" she asked. "Are they guns?"

I nodded. "Those three are guns, and those two there are depth-charge throwers. That's a vessel I was in in the war."

She looked up at me, puzzled. I noticed that she had done something to her eyelashes. They were no longer waxed together in little groups, but lay long and soft upon her cheek. I wondered if that was because she had been crying, that they had come unstuck. "But it's a sailing ship," she said.

"Yes," I said, "we used them in the war a bit." I paused. "I wasn't in her very long."

I turned away and went back to the tea, and asked how she had spent the afternoon. She said, a little diffidently, that she hadn't been outside—"it was all so lovely." I took her out on to the terrace and showed her the lie of the hills and of the sea, and then we went down into the garden in the sun.

We spent all evening strolling round the place. Counting the Melcrose land I have about three hundred acres now, but most of that is waste stuff—cliff and bracken. In the made gardens I found that she knew quite a lot about flowers and shrubs—rather more than I do, in fact. She had had a little garden of her own in Preston when she was living at home as a child. I took her through the hot houses, but I don't think she cared much for those; she peered uncomprehendingly into the empty stalls of the stables. She was delighted with the fuzzy.

We call it the fuzzy, but I don't know if that's the proper name for it. It's the coppice that fills the little ravine that runs down to my bathing beach. A stream runs down the middle of it in little waterfalls and it's a great place for wild flowers —bluebells and primroses, and all that sort of thing. The path goes winding down the middle of it, and now and then as you go down to the beach you get a good view of the sea at the entrance. There is a beach at one of the corners, and we paused by that.

In the Range *Sweet Anna* lay at anchor, waiting for the ebb to slacken before going in. The wind was light, and she lay at anchor with both main and mizzen set, and swaying gently in the roll. As we watched the main came slowly down in great folds upon the deck; I stood and watched the hands gathering it up.

Mollie stirred beside me. "What's that ship?" she asked. "Doesn't she look lovely there?"

They were lashing the gaff down on the boom. "All ships are lovely," I said, without taking my eyes from her. "That's one of mine."

"Oh——" she said. And then she said: "What's she doing out there?"

I glanced down at her. "Waiting for the tug," I said. "It should be here any minute now. We'll wait and see."

We sat down on the beach in the sun. "She's a cargo ship, isn't she?" she asked. "Goods, and that?"

I nodded. "She hasn't got anything in her now. She's just come up from Falmouth in ballast. She's come in to refit."

The *Trojan* came bustling into sight down the harbour, shoving a bow wave away from her broad bows. I saw her with pleasure as I always do; that tug is one of my extravagances. I bought her two years ago after a quarrel with the harbour tug-master and, buying a tug, I saw that I got a good one. Twin screw, driven by a couple of heavy oil engines, each of about three hundred horsepower, she's a good seaworthy rough-weather boat; I'd rather go to sea in her than in our motor lifeboat any day. For my work, of course, she is too good. Too powerful, and more expensive than she need have been. That's probably why I'm fond of her.

She ranged up alongside *Sweet Anna* in the calm sea, and they began to manhandle a hawser to her. Mollie turned to me. "What's that they're doing now?" she asked.

"Passing the tow rope." I saw them man the windlass, and across the harbour mouth I heard the clanking of the pawls and the groaning of the chain. "They're getting up anchor now."

They broke it out and we watched the *Trojan* forge ahead, watched the foam gathering at her stern as she put on power, watched *Sweet Anna* stir and move ahead. They catted her anchor as she went, and we sat there watching tug and vessel till they passed from sight behind the point.

"Oh . . ." said Mollie. "Was she really yours?"

I smiled. "She was. We'll go and have a look at her tomorrow, if you like."

In the evening everything was very gold and blue. "Oh," she said, "it must be lovely to have ships like that."

We went on down to the beach; there was a great calm over everything that night, and a faint easterly wind. I showed her the little hut that she could bathe from when she liked, and showed her the current running past the Checkstone buoy. "We'll come down and bathe tomorrow, if it's fine," I said. "I don't know if we'll get Jenkinson to come in."

We walked slowly back up through the wood towards the house. In the fuzzy there were thrushes calling in the evening, and high above our heads the seagulls swept along the cliff against a deep blue sky. We went up through the garden to the house, and stopped on the terrace to pick a few roses for her room.

It was getting on for dinnertime when we went in. She paused for a moment at the window leading into the library and turned to me. "It has been lovely going round like this, just sort of quietly," she said. She stood looking out over the harbour mouth. "I do think it's beautiful here."

I turned into the house. "Let's get a vase to put these roses in."

She went and fetched one from her room, and I stood by the window and watched her while she pottered about arranging the flowers, clipping the stalks and talking about little trivial things. I could have given her nothing that pleased her more at the moment than those flowers for her bedroom, flowers that she had picked herself. I stood there listening to her talk and wondering, a little grimly, if I should ever learn to please a girl except by accident. It was time to dress for dinner, then, and she carried them carefully upstairs with her, and made me come into her room to see how nice they looked.

I didn't stay there long. She had filled that bedroom with her personality; in some subtle way it had become peculiarly her own. I left her there and went on to my own room to dress. I must have taken rather longer than usual that night because she was down first; I found her in the hall examining the player-piano there.

I spoke a word or two to her, and she looked up at me. "Do you think I might play on it sometimes?" She looked doubtful. "I mean, when you're at the office, or like that."

I smiled. "Play on it any time you like," I said. "I'll show you where the rolls are kept."

She followed me to the cupboard. "I didn't mean that way," she murmured. "I meant really play it. It does play properly as well, doesn't it?"

I turned to her in surprise. "Oh, yes. Do you play much?"

She shook her head. "I never had more than a few lessons. But I do love a piano."

She dropped her hands on to the keys and touched a chord. "Carry on," I said.

She moved away hurriedly. "Oh, I couldn't now. I don't know very many pieces."

She was always giving me little surprises of that sort. We went into dinner. She was wearing a dark blue dancing dress with a silver bodice; she had made herself look very pretty in it and I told her so. That set her smiling, and we dined merrily that night. I offered her Pommard, Barsac, or Château Yquem to drink, and found to my surprise that she knew something about wines. She said: "Could I have Barsac? I do like that. It's a sort of sweet, like lemonade, isn't it?" And so we had the Barsac that night.

Later we retired to sit in opposite corners of the chesterfield in the library, full of Barsac and roast duck and caramel pudding, and when Rogers had served our coffee and departed I told her everything I knew about her business. I told her how I had blundered into the affair when I had been as drunk as a lord, and how I had got what I deserved. And then I went on and told her the whole thing, how she had given me a cross bearing on the matter on that first night in the Palais by speaking of her brother and his lorry; I told her about Stenning and his tale of Rotterdam. Then I told her about the gun that Fedden had showed me, and how I had been with him to Scotland Yard. I didn't hide anything from her; I told her how I had been sent to Leeds to get more information out of her, and how I had brought her down with me under false pretences to confront her with the lorry.

She listened to me for the most part in silence, now and again asking trivial little questions. I am not sure that she ever really understood the inwardness of the affair. Finally I came to the incidents of the morning, and explained to her how she had been tricked into giving evidence about her brother.

I came to an end, and we sat for a little time in silence; she didn't seem to have anything much to say about it all. "I'm not very proud of my part in this affair," I said at last.

She stared at me helplessly. "I don't know what to say. You didn't do anything wrong. Lots of gentlemen could have been terribly nasty, but you weren't."

I smiled; her mind, I thought, was running in a groove. "In any case," I said, "you needn't worry much about this thing. Jenkinson's a good man. I think you'll find that Billy will come out of it all right."

She didn't seem to be much interested in him. Perhaps she had confidence in his ability to get himself out of any scrape he got himself into. "I don't understand," she said at last. "If you were on their side, why did you upset everything this morning like you did? They were terribly angry with you, weren't they?"

I smiled, a little grimly. "I don't know. Yes, I suppose they were."

She wrinkled her brows. "I don't see why you went against them like that."

I was silent for a minute. "You can't stand by and see a trick like that go on," I said at last. "You might with a stranger, but not with somebody you know."

She stared across at me with wonder in her eyes. "Oh," she said softly. "You mean you did all that for me. . . ."

There was a long silence after she said that. Presently she leaned across to me. "Please," she said simply, "I think I'd like to go to bed now, if I may. I'm so tired. You said it would be all right if I saw the lawyer in the morning, didn't you?"

And so she went, and I was left to wait for Jenkinson alone.

# CHAPTER 7

I HAD A long talk with Jenkinson that night in the library and put him in possession of the facts of this affair, so far as they were known to me. He sat listening to me in silence for the most part, detached, critical, alert. Now and again he interpolated a searching little question, but not frequently. At the end of it he removed his pince-nez and sat polishing them upon his handkerchief.

"There should not be any great difficulty," he said at last. "We must try and persuade the young lady to give a statement to the police tomorrow. They are entitled to that assistance in their investigations. Under certain safeguards, both for herself and for her brother. . . ."

He replaced his glasses. "Safeguards. I must think out the safeguards which we can impose."

I gave him a whisky and we went to bed.

We had a conference in the library next morning after breakfast. Mollie was there, a little awed by the presence of the lawyer. Perhaps in deference to him she had made herself a bit less ornamental for the occasion; her eyelashes remained unwaxed, and in some subtle manner she had made herself look quieter than before. It may have been that she had less makeup on, it may have been that she was simply blending into the surrounding of my house. I don't know. I only know that I had expected Jenkinson to have something of a shock when he saw what I'd picked up, but it was I who got the shock.

He began by explaining to her again the position that she was in. In his precise, rather meticulous way he outlined to her the inquiry which the Criminal Investigation Department had in hand, acting on behalf of the Civil Power. He showed her that so far the whole of the evidence available tended to the implication that her brother must be involved in business directed towards the provocation of a breach of the peace, if nothing more serious. He said that he had to point out to her the gravity of the situation in that respect, but would emphasise that there should be no necessity for undue alarm about her brother. Similar cases had occurred during the Irish troubles, and he cited one or two cases in which the clemency of the Crown had been directed in favour of persons who were in a similar position in being subordinate to the main issue. He made a point there, that such clemency was only exerted in those cases where a genuine desire to assist the processes of the Law was assured. At the outset of this matter, his advice was to the effect that she should give him authority to express to the police her utmost willingness to assist them in their investigation.

"I am sure that we shall find that this matter will go quite smoothly if we can give them that assurance, Miss Gordon," he said, and paused for her reply.

She was troubled. "I don't quite understand," she said at last. "I'm for Billy. Is that what you wanted me to say?"

I laughed. "No, it's not," I said. "We want you to tell the police all you know about Billy."

She stared at me in perplexity. "But then they'd catch him," she objected.

We moistened the lips and started again, and for a quarter of an hour I explained to her in as simple language as I could the position that her brother must be in, and what we wanted to do about it. She came to understand it in the end, I think.

"You mean that's really the best thing for me to do for Billy?" she inquired. "Just tell them all about him?"

Jenkinson interposed: "Perhaps not quite everything. They may ask questions that they have no right to ask, and I would not let you answer those. We shall both be there to help you answer every question, so there will be nothing to be afraid of. Just tell the whole truth when they ask you anything. I'll stop you saying anything that you ought not to say."

She turned to me: "You don't think he'll be sent to prison? You see, he wouldn't be doing anything bad."

I said: "We don't know what he is doing. But I'll promise you this. If any proceedings are taken against him, he shall have the best legal defence in the country. We'll brief Sir Dennis Scott-Neil for him, or somebody like that."

She eyed me searchingly. "You wouldn't let me down?"

I met her eyes. "I won't let you down," I said. "This really is the best thing to do."

She nodded gravely, and turned to Jenkinson. "Please," she said, "you'll have to tell me when to speak and when not to. You see, I don't know about these things."

I glanced at Jenkinson, and he glanced back at me, and after a moment we went on with her examination. Together we asked her what questions we could think of, to prepare ourselves for what she might be going to tell the police, but we found very little that I didn't know. She knew that her brother had been working on an all-night job, she thought intermittently, for about a couple of months. She could give no further indication as to how to get in touch with him. She thought he was well paid, but who paid him she did not know. She was quite sure he wouldn't do anything wrong.

We came to an end of all she knew quite soon. After a short talk with Jenkinson I crossed the room and rang up Fedden at his house.

"Good-morning," I said. "Stevenson speaking. About this statement that you want to get from Miss Gordon. I've got Jenkinson down here, and we've just been through it all with her. Miss Gordon is quite ready to tell you all she knows, under the guidance of her solicitor of course."

He said: "I'm very glad to hear that. Norman will be back by lunchtime; we'll take her statement this afternoon. I see no point in taking it at Newton Abbott. Will you bring her down to the police station here, at three o'clock?"

I pressed the transmitter to my chest and shot a rapid question at Jenkinson. "Certainly," he said, "that would be quite in order."

I lifted the transmitter. "I'll do nothing of the sort," I said curtly. "Miss Gordon will see you here, in the library of my house, at two o'clock precisely, if you please."

He said: "That's most unusual, you know."

"Miss Gordon had a bad time in your police station yesterday," I replied, "and I'm damned if she's going there again. I should like to think that that was most unusual. This is a purely voluntary statement on her part, and if you want it she is willing to give it to you at two o'clock this afternoon. Her solicitor will be present, and you can bring this Major Norman." I smiled. "I'm willing to sink my prejudices so far as to admit him to my house, on this occasion only. I should like to make that point quite clear."

He said stiffly: "I understand that perfectly. Very well. You can expect us at two o'clock this afternoon."

He rang off, and I turned to Jenkinson. "Glad I'm not a Chief Constable," I said.

There was nothing more that we could do until they came. We went out into the garden; Jenkinson lives at Chislehurst and goes to his office every day in an electric train, and grows begonias and things like that, and takes prizes for them at the local flower show. He is a member of the Royal Horticultural Society, I think; I only know he got me properly tied up, so that I had to get old Robertson out of his hot houses to answer some of the questions that he asked. Together we went round the rose garden, a little absently on my part. I was thinking about what would be necessary for *Sweet Anna*; we had given her a new mainsail in the previous autumn, but topsails and mizzen were getting very thin. I had a long talk with Tillotson next day, and we decided that she ought to have them. We gave her a new second jib, as well.

In the garden Mollie got on well with Jenkinson; he found in her an eager audience for his rather arid little discourses upon begonias. I had one or two things that I wanted to do in the town that day—I forget what they were at the moment. Those two were getting on quite well together and so I left them to it and went down to the town, wondering as I went what questions she would ask him about me. She wouldn't get much out of Jenkinson, I thought. He's too cautious.

I got back home a little late for lunch. They had waited for me, and that made the whole programme late, so that before we had finished lunch Fedden and Norman had arrived. It amused me to send out Rogers to show them into the library and to keep them waiting while we sat and drank our coffee in the dining-room. I had a score to settle with those gentlefolk.

That wasn't the only thing they had to put up with that afternoon. We went into the library and settled down at the big centre table there, and Jenkinson led off with a sour, legal little speech. In his dry way he informed them that he was acting on behalf of both Miss Gordon and her brother, and would continue to do so. He understood that an examination of Miss Gordon had already been attempted in circumstances which appeared to him to have been most irregular. He trusted that he would have no occasion to complain of any further irregularity of that sort. He quite understood that their business was the detection of crime. His own business was the preservation of the integrity of the Law. It would be unfortunate if in the pursuance of their business they again ran contrary to his own.

He let them ask some questions then. They had brought a police sergeant with them who took notes, and we sat for some time while they questioned the girl, and this chap took his notes in longhand. She gave her answers pretty well, prompted and assisted every now and then by Jenkinson.

I forget how it all went, and what they asked. I only know that none of it was new. They asked nothing that was not obvious, and they discovered nothing that we had not known before. The girl was quite incapable of assisting them to find her brother; she had not the remotest notion where he was. She could only suggest that her people up in Preston might know something of his movements, but she didn't think it likely that they would. We sat there for most of the afternoon, and so far as I could see it was an utter waste of time.

It finished up at last; the sergeant closed his notebook and they got up to go. Jenkinson gave them a final word of warning. He told them that he was definitely employed on behalf of Mr William Gordon, and that no statements should be taken from that gentleman, or evidence of any sort, until he had been informed that a solicitor had been engaged on his behalf, and had consulted him.

They went away at last, and we went out to tea upon the terrace looking out over the harbour. I would have asked Fedden to stay, but Norman and the sergeant were with him and I felt I'd had my fill of the CID for the time being.

Jenkinson wanted to catch an evening train back to town. When Rogers brought the tea I sent him to look up trains; it was a warm, sunny afternoon and we sat for a long time over tea, looking out over the rose garden below. We were all a little relieved, I think, that nothing untoward had come out during the afternoon, and glad that it was over. Mollie and Jenkinson were gossiping away together like old friends, and I remember that he was very decent to her in telling her that she was to come to him in case of any further difficulty, whether she was staying with me or not.

His train went from Newton Abbot. I drove him there in the Bentley, leaving Mollie sitting on the terrace; she said that she was tired. I think that may have been tact upon her part. It gave me the opportunity of a word or two with Jenkinson, and I explained to him a little more fully the circumstances in which I had got her down from Leeds, as we drove.

He nodded. "A girl of a good type," he said.

I was silent for a minute. "I've lived very much among my own sort all my life," I said at last. "It's not a very common type, is it?"

He shrugged his shoulders. "I think you get that quiet, refined sort of girl in every class. I used to see quite a lot of them in police work when I was a young man. Shop assistants, typists—girls of every class. You meet a good few barmaids of that sort. Do you see much of them?"

I shook my head. "I don't go into bars much. A man like me has to guard against that sort of thing."

He smiled. "I don't know what's happening to the classes in this country," he said. "One comes on girls like this so frequently—and a good few men, too. The only difference between them and us is that they don't know quite so many facts. . . . Behaviour's just the same. And that's a mighty small difference. . . ."

I put him into his train at Newton Abbot, thanked him for coming down, and saw him off. Then I went back to Dartmouth to my house. I found Mollie in the library; rather to my surprise I saw her sitting curled up upon the chesterfield reading a large book. She laid it down carefully as I came in, and got up to meet me.

"We got that train all right," I said, and glanced down to see what it was that she had been reading. It was Mortimer's *Naval History*, open at the page which describes the action of the *Jane Ellen*. I glanced at the bookshelves, and there was a gap where she had got the volume from.

"So you've got hold of that," I said.

She looked up at me, and nodded; and then she said: "Tell me, was this really you?" She stooped and picked up the book. "I mean, in here."

I took the book from her and glanced down the account a little absently; she came closer and looked over my elbow at the page. "Yes," I said at last, "that was me. Doesn't seem much like it now, does it?"

"I think it's wonderful," she breathed. And then she looked up at me and said: "Mr Jenkinson showed it me. You don't mind, do you?"

I smiled at her. "Lord, no," I said. "Not after all these years. It's all so long ago."

She stood there staring up at me, puzzled. "Don't you like people to know about it? I mean, it says here it was all so splendid, and you got a medal."

"There wasn't anything splendid about it, really," I said quietly. "Only in the history books. It was just bloody murder."

She stared up at me dumbly.

"I shelled them while they were surrendering," I said. "The engagement was over by that time." I stared out of the window at the brilliant, sunlit sea. "I don't know why I did it—I never did know. There was a boy there with me, a midshipman. He wouldn't speak to me when we got back to land —just cut me dead whenever we met. The funny thing is, I don't think he told anyone."

I paused. "When you go and do a thing like that it makes a difference," I said. A herring gull came sweeping down the lawn and banked steeply past the window in the sunshine with a little cry. I stood there thinking of the long, similar years that I had lived in Dartmouth since the war, living alone with my ships and with my work. "Things haven't been much fun since I did that," I said quietly. "Not like they were before."

I glanced down at her. "Not so very splendid, was it?"

She looked up at me, and then down at the book. "I think it was wonderful," she said at last. "Fighting on all alone like that. Nobody could have said anything if you'd given in, could they? I mean, when there was only three of you left."

I laughed. "It wouldn't have done us much good to give in. They shelled the panic party in the boats. We wouldn't have stood much chance in a surrender, and so we just stuck where we were."

She wrinkled up her brows. "You mean that they'd have killed you if you'd given in?"

I shrugged my shoulders. "I dare say. They'd probably have left us out on deck when they submerged."

She came a little closer to me. "Malcolm," she said, and it was the first time she had called me that, "you oughtn't to think so much about the bad things of the war. I mean, everyone who fought had to do bad things, and it was the same on each side. And you only did to them what they'd have done to you if you'd surrendered."

I stood for a moment looking down at her. "That may be," I said. "But it was I who did it."

I was touched by the insight that she had shown; I had never been able to speak to anyone about that business as I had to her. She didn't say any more, and I took her by the arm and we wandered out into the garden for a quarter of an hour before going in to dress. Passing the strawberry bed we stopped and ate a few, and together we picked a few more flowers for her room, although she said the ones she had would last for 'ever so long'. She told me how she used to make flowers last in the Palais when she wore them in her dress with their stalks wrapped up in cotton wool and silver paper, and they kept ever so fresh for days.

Then we went up to dress.

And coming down, I found she was before me in the hall. She had changed into the same blue dancing frock with the silver bodice that she had worn before, that suited her dark loveliness so well. She came up to me as I walked down the stairs, and:

"Please, Commander Stevenson," she said, and hesitated.

I smiled at her. "Spit it out," I said.

She didn't laugh, but looked up at me. "Please," she said, "I've just been thinking. Now that Mr Jenkinson's gone and the police and everything, I'd better go back to Leeds. I thought I'd go by train tomorrow morning, if that would be all right. I mean, you won't be wanting me for anything else now, will you?"

For a moment I was nonplussed. "No," I said mechanically, "I don't know that there's anything else, really."

She stood there looking up at me, dumbly. I moved closer to her and took one of her hands in mine; we stood there together, looking down at it. "You can go if you like, of course," I said. "But won't you stay and have your holiday with me? I'd like it awfully if you would."

She didn't look at me. "Are you sure you really want me

110

here?" she said. "Don't you think I'd be in the way, with all your friends, and that?"

I shook my head. "I meant it when I asked you to come down here for your holiday, that night in Leeds. It was useful for the police, but that was only half. I meant it for you as well."

She raised her head; she had got a colour, and her eyes were very bright. "You mean you really want me to stay the whole time?" she said. "Six more days?"

"Of course I do," I said. "If it's not too dull for you."

She sighed happily. "It's all so perfect here. It's going to be the loveliest holiday I've ever had." She rippled into laughter. "Won't Ethel be jealous when I tell her!" Ethel was her friend who had gone to Scarborough. "And she'll never believe me when I tell her I've been good."

I laughed and took her arm. "I don't suppose she will," I said. And so we went and dined.

I forget what we talked about at dinner that night; I only remember that the telephone bell rang in the middle of it. I left the table and went to it in the library, and it was Joan speaking from her house in Golders Green.

"Is that Malcolm?"

"Speaking," I said.

"Oh, Malcolm—this is Joan this end." I said something polite. "What I rang you up about was this: can we come down and spend the night with you tomorrow—me and Philip? We've got a couple of days for the *Irene*, and Philip wants to have a talk with you. Oh, just one minute, he's here."

Stenning came to the telephone. "Evening, Stevenson; I say, is it you who's been putting the CID on my track again? I had a fellow called Norman call to see me two or three days ago—wanted to know all sorts of things. He said I'd told you, or something. Yes, I met him once before—not a bad cove, is he?" I sometimes think that Stenning must know everybody in the world. "Well, what I thought was this: Joan and I might come down in time for dinner tomorrow night, and we'd have a chat about it before going off in the *Irene*. How's that?"

"Quite all right," I replied. "You won't be able to have your usual room, though. You'll have to put up with single ones."

He asked: "Why's that?"

Some things can hardly be explained over the telephone. I said: "It's occupied."

I heard him laugh. "I remember when I was a young man I used to live in sin a bit myself," he said genially. There was a scuffling noise at the other end; I could imagine Joan throwing a cushion at him. "That's all right, old boy—we quite understand." I smiled; he had an uncanny flair for hitting near the mark. "All right, we'll be down in time for dinner. Can I land in Thompson's field?"

"I expect so. I'll get him to clear that shed. It's a Moth, isn't it?"

"That's right," he said. "All right, I'll see you then."

I hung up the receiver and went back to Mollie in the dining-room. "That was my cousin and her husband," I told her. "Speaking from London. They're coming down here to spend the night tomorrow."

She stared at me in alarm. "Coming here?"

I nodded. "I think you'll like them."

She waited till Rogers was out of the room, then bent towards me. "Please, Commander Stevenson," she said, "don't you think I'd better not be here when your cousins come?" She paused for a moment. "I mean, it looks so funny for you."

I laughed. "Not half so funny as it does for you."

She smiled. "I don't mind a bit about me. But, I mean, it looks so awful for you with your, friends, having a strange girl in the house, and everything."

I buttered a bit of toast. "If my friends don't like the way I carry on they needn't come," I said phlegmatically. "I'd rather have the strange girl, myself," I paused. "As a matter of fact, you don't need to worry about these people—really. They'll only be here for the one night, and you'll like Joan."

She asked me: "What's their name?"

"Stenning," I said, "Sir Philip and Lady Stenning. I expect you've heard about him, haven't you? The flying man."

She stared at me, wide-eyed. "I saw him on the pictures once. Is he your cousin?"

"His wife is. Lady Stenning is my cousin Joan."

"Oh——" She thought about it for a minute, and then she said: "Don't you think I'd better just go away while they're here? I mean, I'm sure Lady Stenning will think it awfully funny, won't she?" She said: "I could just go down and stay in the town till they've gone."

"If you talk like that," I said, "I'll ring up and say they can't come."

She laughed and said I mustn't do that, and we went on with dinner, but I could see that she was not at ease. She talked carefully, and a little absent mindedly, about unimportant things, but said no more about it till the table was cleared and we rose to go into the other room. In the hall she hesitated.

"Please," she said, "I've only got this evening frock, you know, and it's two years old." She looked down at it critically. "It's terribly grubby. Do you think it will be all right for Lady Stenning?"

I smiled. I think she thought that Joan would look at her through a lorgnette, and that Stenning would wear a morning-coat and talk about the League. "I wouldn't worry about that," I said. "They're flying down, so they won't bring much stuff. I don't suppose Joan will want to change at all. And anyway, she hasn't got a dinner frock that's a patch on that one."

She beamed. "I'm glad you like me in it," she said. "It was awfully pretty, but it's an old thing now."

We went into the library and had our coffee sitting on the chesterfield, and over it she told me how she had had that dress in the first instance for a speciality dance she used to do when she was in a Palais in Manchester, and she told me how she had altered it to make it into a dinner frock. And from that we went on talking about dancing and music, till at last I said: "Wouldn't you like to play the piano a bit tonight? I'd like it awfully if you would."

She looked very doubtful. "I don't play very well, and I haven't got any of my pieces here. I don't think I could play anything except dance tunes out of my head. You wouldn't care so much about those, would you?"

"Rather," I said. "Play *Body and Soul*."

She laughed, and slipped over to the piano. I sat over on the other side of the room with my cigar while she crashed into the jazz melody; she played well, with a spirit and energy which made up in that sort of music for her occasional slips.

8                                113

I moved to a chair nearer the piano and presently, warming to her work, she began to sing the words.

She had a trained voice, and for a time I wondered where she had got it from, until I remembered her early training for the chorus. That night she sang those dance songs with a naïve feeling that robbed them of all crudity and gave them a new interpretation to me. She showed them to me as the folk songs of the people that I know so little of, the working England and America that I scarcely knew. I sat there thinking how much I had lived apart since the war, that I knew so little of her side of life.

The night closed down about us and I lit a reading lamp above her piano. She sat there fingering the keys and talking to me about the songs and dances that she knew, showing me the snap and rhythm of the airs, telling me the steps for each. That subject was peculiarly her own. From the semi-darkness of the hall I sat and watched her at the piano, the slim lines of her neck and shoulders merging gently into the silver bodice of her dress. She had gained a colour from her pleasure in the music; in the soft light I saw that she was very beautiful.

And presently she said: "Oh, and I know another one. I do think this is pretty; it comes out of a play called *Bitter Sweet*. It's sort of different to the rest of them." She played the fox trot air for a few minutes, and then sang quietly:

"I believe in doing what I can,
   In crying when I must,
   In laughing when I choose.
      Heigh-ho, if love were all
      I should be lonely!
I believe the more you love a man,
   The more you give your trust,
   The more you're bound to lose—
Although, when shadows fall
   I think if only
Somebody splendid really needed me,
   Someone affectionate and dear—
Cares would be ended if I knew that he
   Wanted to have me near. . . ."

I sat there very quiet, listening to her; she had grown

absorbed in her song. It seemed to me that I was listening to something more than a scene out of a revue, that I was listening to a confession of the philosophy which guided her among the various hazards of the life she had to live. I felt that she was paying me a singular honour in singing that to me, perhaps unconsciously.

Her voice died away into the lonely silence of my house. She dropped her fingers from the keys and sat there motionless. "That was very beautiful," I said.

She turned to me, her eyes shining in the dim light. "You mean you really thought that?—that it was nice?"

I stirred a little in my chair. "It suited you," I said.

She sat there gazing down at me, not quite understanding what I meant. "It's my favourite," she said at last. "It is pretty, isn't it?"

She got up and closed the piano; with that song she had finished singing for the night. I crossed to the side table where they leave my nightcap. "You'd like a drink after all that singing," I suggested. "What would you like?" I eyed the table. "There's whisky here—and lemonade. Would you like a gin and tonic?"

She hesitated. "Do you know what I'd like—if it wouldn't be a dreadful trouble?"

I paused. "What's that?"

"A cup of tea."

I rang the bell and ordered tea, and we went through into the model room. By the *Jane Ellen* model case she stopped. "Was this the ship?" she asked.

I nodded. "That was the ship."

She stood there looking at the model for a long time, very still, one hand resting on the case. And then: "It was a splendid thing," she said.

I couldn't argue it, and so I let her have her way. I moved over to the window. "Tomorrow we'll go down to the yard," I said. "I want to show you all my ships and things. And we've not bathed yet, either."

She beamed. "I've got ever such a lovely bathing dress that I got last autumn in the sales. I haven't worn it yet—only in my bedroom before the glass. I was keeping it for my holiday." She paused. "It's a lovely colour—sort of apple green."

She looked best in green; all the girls said so. So she had told me. "It sounds all right," I said.

She dimpled. "You may not like me in it."

"I expect I shall," I said comfortably. And so we sat there in the half-light looking out over the harbour, and gossiped, and drank our tea till it was time to go to bed. That night, for the first time since my accident, I slept soundly and dreamlessly till I was called at eight o'clock.

I saw Mollie in the garden that morning while I was shaving, coming up from the fuzzy. She had been down to have another look at the bathing place; so she told me while we were breakfasting. She was itching to go in.

I'd have taken her down to bathe at once, since she seemed to be so keen, but I had to go down to the yard that morning for an hour or so. I made her a promise that we'd bathe before lunch; she was content, and as we breakfasted she told me about everything that she had seen on her morning's walk —the birds and the flowers and the trees. She had been up at six. Spreading my toast and marmalade, it struck me that she wasn't missing much.

We went down together to the yard; *Sweet Anna* was still lying out in the stream at anchor. I am a little short of quayside for the vessels undergoing a refit; I should like to build on, but it would cost a lot. That day there was a smack lying at the shore end of my quay and *Pearl Maid* at the outer end; we had been setting up her mizzen with new standing gear, so that there was a great smell of Stockholm tar all round the place. Entering the gates one can always tell what work is going on from the smell: paint, the bark we use for tanning sails, wood smoke, tar—all these in turn provide aroma for my yard.

Mollie came with me into the office, and sat quiet in a corner while I did my letters; I think it was a new experience to her. It was certainly a new one to the staff, and must have given them cause for gossip for a week or so. Miss Soames came in and took my letters and never raised an eyelid from her pad; Tillotson came in to talk about his cost accounts, but took no account of Sixpence sitting in her corner trying to read the *Marine Transporter's Journal and Monthly Advertiser*. He went away, and I sent for Penhill to tell him that *Irene* was to be ready for Stenning by the evening and, as an afterthought,

I told him that I should be wanting *Runagate* next day. Then a short talk with old Captain Sammy Gore, of *Sweet Anna*. He wanted new rudder pintles, or thought he did, but I think it was only because some rumour had reached him far away up on the north-east coast that we had given them to *Mary Thompson* at her last refit. I told him that *Sweet Anna* was a better built vessel than *Mary Thompson*, which was nearly true and matched his own belief, and that we'd have a look when she dried out.

Then the watchman came, as watchmen always do, to say that it wasn't that he wasn't willing, but he couldn't work miracles, and he was doing three men's work and not complaining, and he ought to have some help.

Then I was free to go and bathe.

I took Mollie out of the office and showed her something of my yard and ships. We didn't stay very long because I knew she wanted to get back; that green bathing dress was pulling very strongly. However, I found that she was still worrying a little about Joan and Stenning, because she said, quite suddenly:

"Please, Commander Stevenson, about this evening. When Lady Stenning comes, do you play cards—bridge, or anything? Because I'm afraid I couldn't. I don't know any card games hardly, except Sevens."

I thought for a moment that I'd telephone to put them off, to tell them that they'd better sleep in the *Irene* for the night. And then I thought I wouldn't. For some obscure reason I wanted Joan to meet her, and there was really nothing for her to be frightened of in meeting Joan. That wasn't to say that I could prevent her being frightened. It was the title that did it, of course. If Joan had been Mrs Stenning it would all have been plain sailing.

I smiled. "They don't play bridge," I said. "Not unless they're made to. Stenning's game is poker—he's a tiger at that. But they won't want to play cards, and if they did they wouldn't get the chance. They'll just sit and talk. Stenning talks about yachts and flying, and Joan talks about watercolours and Cairn terriers."

She looked up at me despondently. "I don't know about either. I mean, not to talk to anyone who does. But I do love dogs."

"That's good enough," I said. "Just say that, and Joan'll talk for hours."

We got into the car and went back through the town. Mollie wanted to stop and buy a bathing cap, and wanted me to come into the ladies' outfitters and help her choose it. Dartmouth is a small place and I am quite well known; for many years, of course, my life has been something of a scandal and a byeword in the little town, but always in connection with wine, not women. It took us nearly half an hour to buy that cap and the rest of the things she wanted; by the time we came out and got into the car, Mollie clutching her purchases and laughing with me before all the virtuous housewives of the town, I knew that I had added fresh laurels to my wreath.

We drove up through the town back to my house, left the car on the drive, and went to get our bathing things. Then we went down together through the fuzzy; it was sunny and warm, with the wind somewhere in the south-west so that my beach was in the lee of the cliff. The tide was about half flood; I couldn't have picked a better day to introduce her to the place.

I gave her the hut to change in, and went and undressed among the trees myself. I was ready long before she was, and I can remember sitting on the rocks in the sun down there waiting for her and wondering how this was going to end. I didn't get much further with that speculation because I had little experience to guide me; in all my life I had never lived in such intimacy with any girl before. There's a lot to be said for co-educational schools, I suppose.

She came at last, looking like a coloured picture from a summer magazine. I sat and watched her as she came towards me from the hut, admiring her slim grace. I can see her now.

"That's an awfully pretty dress," I said.

She smiled. "I'm glad you like me in it." Now that wasn't what I said at all, although I might have done.

She could dive a little, and chose to go in that way, near the beach. I dived in with her on the seaward side; she was a weak swimmer and made straight for the shore. I followed her, and in the shallows we told each other how cold it was. One more dive, and she was ready to go and sit in the sun; I think to her that was the best part of the game. I fetched her towel and we sat on the warm rocks for an hour or more, sunbathing and watching the small traffic of the harbour mouth, the sparkling sea in the Range, and the white surf around the chequered buoy.

There was a small cloud on the horizon still. She asked: "Malcolm, when Lady Stenning comes, what ought I to wear? Will the coat and skirt I've been wearing be all right?"

I rolled over and looked at her, and grinned. "I'd wear what you've got on now, if I were you," I said. "That suits you best of all."

She rippled into laughter. "You are awful! I mean, really, what ought I to wear?"

I knew that it would be all right when Joan arrived. "I'd wear something rough and countrified, if you've got anything like that," I said.

She nodded. "I've got a terribly old tweed skirt and a jumper, that I had for walking in. Would that be the right thing?" She was very doubtful. "I'll show it you when we go up."

I smiled at her. "Just anything you like, so long as it's not too smart." She was utterly puzzled. "Don't make her feel too dirty by comparison. You see, she's coming down by air— about two and a half hours' flight in an open machine. She'll arrive with her face covered in oil, or if it's not she'll feel as if it was. She always wants a bath directly she arrives, when they fly down." I paused. "And anyway, Joan always goes about in the most awful things herself."

"You don't think she'll be dreadfully smart?"

"I don't think so," I said.


## CHAPTER 8

THAT EVENING we went up to Thompson's field and sat and waited for the aeroplane. Mollie had gone up to her room directly after lunch, and had come down in half an hour to find me working in the model room. She had changed into a jumper and an old brown skirt, and she had come to ask me if she would do. "I haven't put hardly any powder on, or anything," she informed me. "Do you think I'll be all right like this for Lady Stenning?"

Her mind was still running on Joan. I laid my set-square down and grinned at her. "You're quite all right," I replied. "Looking very nice. You don't want a lot of powder and stuff in those sort of clothes. It doesn't go, does it?"

She smiled, and looked up at me. "You don't like a lot of that, do you?" she inquired. "It's funny how people are about that. Lots of the gentlemen just don't care about taking you out unless you've got a lot on."

She glanced down at her shoes; they were black, high heeled, and ornamental. "I didn't bring my other pair of walking shoes down with me," she said ruefully. "I thought they'd be too old for me to bring here. Does it matter?"

I laughed. "Not a hoot. But would you like to get a pair of country shoes? We'll slip down in the car, if you like."

She said: "I'd love it, ever so. But not now—when you've finished working." And she indicated the drawing board.

"Playing," I said, "up here. I do my work down at the office."

"What is it?" she inquired.

I moved aside the T-square for her to examine the drawing. "It's a ship," I said. "The hull layout of a little yacht I want to build."

She stared at it, uncomprehending. "You do love ships," she said at last. "I wish I knew about them more."

And so we left the house and went down to the town at gossip time, and drew the Bentley up before the local shoe emporium to provide fresh matter for discussion at the local tea tables. I knew all that before we went, of course, but Mollie came back in new brown brogues with tasselled laces and was happy for the afternoon.

They say that a man has licence to take off whatever clothes he puts on to a girl. I thought that I might take that risk, with shoes.

We sat on the gate to Thompson's field for half an hour and waited for the aeroplane. We heard it first, and then we saw it in the sky, a speck above Kingswear. We watched it closer till the engine was shut off above the harbour, and the Moth came in on a wide gliding turn, side-slipped down across the hedge, and ran gently to rest in the middle of the field. Stenning swung her round and taxied in towards us; Mollie turned to me: "Wasn't it pretty the way it did that?"

"He's not got much to learn about an aeroplane," I said.

Joan waved a hand from the front cockpit as they drew abreast of us; I got on to the wing tip and guided the machine towards the barn. Stenning taxied up to it and throttled back; then he reached out and switched off the engine. The propeller kicked and came to rest, and the silence of the evening closed on us again.

Stenning heaved himself up out of the rear cockpit and jumped down; he was in plus fours and a flying helmet. Joan came climbing down the plane from the front seat.

"Had a good trip?" I asked.

"Thick as far as Salisbury," said Stenning. He pulled his helmet off and smoothed his hair. "You've got it nice down here."

Joan dropped down on to the ground. She had taken off her helmet, and she shook her shingled hair into some sort of order. "Cheer-oh, Malcolm," she remarked. "You're looking very fit."

"So I am," I said. "A bat or two still flying round the belfry, perhaps, but nothing to make a song about." I turned to Sixpence: "Joan, I want you to meet Miss Gordon. She's staying here with me for a few days."

Lady Stenning stopped scratching her hair and composed her features into a smile. "Afternoon," she said. "I hope he's been remembering his duties as a host. He doesn't often, I may say."

Sixpence smiled diffidently, and said: "Good afternoon."

I turned to Stenning. He was staring at Mollie in perplexity, slowly passing one hand over his disordered hair. "But we've met before," he said. "Of course we have." He looked inquiringly at her. "Now where the devil was that?"

I asked in some surprise: "Do you two know each other, then?"

"I'm damn sure we do," said Sir Philip. "We've met some place or other." He smiled at her. "I'm so sorry, but I can't just pin it down."

I glanced at Mollie. She caught my eye despairingly, sending an appeal for help. Something was evidently wrong; I didn't know what, but I did all I could to help her out. "Perhaps you met him at some party," I remarked. "I've often met people like that, and couldn't think of where we'd met before."

She forced a smile. "We did meet once before. But I didn't know you were Sir Philip Stenning, then."

"Don't suppose I was," said Stenning equably. "But where was it that we met?"

There was nothing for it, then. "In the Salford Road Palais de Danse," said Mollie bravely. "In Manchester—about two years ago. You came in one night with a party, rather late, and booked me for the evening."

There was a momentary silence after that—the very slightest pause. I moved to her and slipped my arm through hers. "Miss Gordon teaches dancing in the North," I said easily. "She's spending her summer holiday down here with me."

Stenning had recovered by that time. "By God, yes," he replied. "I remember now. I was with Dick Annesley and Holt. I say, it's splendid meeting you again down here."

And Joan said practically: "Now's the time to get my quickstep right. Philip's always going on at me because I can't do enough tricks." She turned to Mollie: "I'd love it if you'd show me, some time."

I sent a little message of my thanks to Joan. "Of course, I'd love to, Lady Stenning," Mollie said. "I know some lovely new ones that Pagani did last season, ever so pretty."

"That's a bet," said Joan. We turned to pushing the machine towards the barn. Before the opening Stenning folded back the wings; we pushed the Moth in under cover and collected their belongings from the locker. Then we made off towards the house, the girls walking ahead of Stenning and myself.

We went inside and Mollie went upstairs with Joan; Stenning and I turned into the library for a drink. He raised it with a meaning twinkle in his eye. "Luck!" he said. "Boys will be boys."

I met his glance. "I brought her down from Leeds three days ago," I said simply. "She's in this business that you want to know about. Norman had a good go at her yesterday, but he didn't get much out of her."

He raised his eyebrows, swallowed down his drink, and set the glass down on the table by his side. "You've got to keeping some damn funny company, these days," he said. "Not but what the girl's all right. Nice, quiet little bit—or was when I met her. But I'd never have thought to find you with the CID."

I nodded. "You're right there. I've had my fill of your friend Norman in the last two days."

I told him that we'd have a talk about it after dinner, and took him up and showed him to his room. Mollie was in her room with Joan; I heard them talking as we passed the door. It seemed that they were getting on all right; I might have known I could rely on Joan. I passed along and saw that Stenning had everything he wanted in his place; then I went to my own room to wash.

I forget what we talked about that night at dinner, but it went all right. The party had settled down, and Mollie was no longer shy of Joan. I sat on with Stenning after dinner in the dining-room, after the ladies had gone through into the south room, and over the port I told him everything I knew about the business.

He was intensely interested. He told me that Norman had been on to him in London to find out what he had heard in Rotterdam; he had had some dealings with Norman previously in his chequered career, and knew Sir David Carter. I found that he had told Norman a great deal more about the episode in Rotterdam than he had mentioned on the yacht. It seemed to hinge about a conversation in a café on the quays, and it went somehow like this:

Stenning had gone to this café for a drink. He was with another man, some engineer or pilot from the aerodrome, and they sat down in the sunshine at a table on the pavement outside. The window of the place was open above their heads and the door was open at their side; in this position they could not be seen from inside the café premises.

They sat there for the most part in silence, not having much to say to each other, sipping their drinks and looking out over the harbour. Inside the room some conversation was in progress about a shipping contract, the majority of which they overheard through door and window. Stenning sat there on the pavement in the sun, listening idly, not taking very much in. In fact, he never really thought of it again until he spoke of carpet sweepers to me that evening on the yacht.

The conversation was in English. One of the talkers was

apparently the captain of a vessel, a young man by the voice, educated, and English. The other one was probably a Dutchman or a German, speaking English with a strong accent. Stenning never saw either of the speakers.

The contract was for shipping carpet sweepers and relays—electrical relays, perhaps, but Stenning did not know. Fifteen sweepers and thirty-eight relays were involved; the smallness of these quantities mildly attracted his attention. Delivery was to be made to Berth No. 16A; an advice note had been sent to the Professor. Stenning heard nothing to explain who the Professor was.

That was all he could remember of the conversation, which indeed had hardly attracted his attention at the time. Later on the same afternoon, however, he had occasion to go down to the docks to see to the unloading of an engine in connection with his work. Walking along the quays he recollected berth No. 16A, and had the curiosity to look and see what sort of vessel was involved. He found a small, single-masted sailing vessel of some forty or fifty tons, a sloop or bawley—he would not be certain which. She was an English rig. He only gave her a casual glance, for he was in a hurry. His impression was of a vessel that was little more than a smack; he retained the memory, however, of a cargo hatch. A crabber, or some vessel of that sort.

That was the sum of Stenning's evidence. It had not provided Norman with a lot to go upon, because Stenning had seen neither of the talkers and was by no means sure that he would be able to identify the boat again. He had only looked down on her, quite casually, from the top of the quay.

Norman had made a search through the police archives at the Yard for the Professor, and had found at least fifteen. He said that every gang in his experience possessed some member, generally of a higher standard of intelligence than the others, who was described like that.

I sat on for some time in the dining-room discussing it with Stenning, but we didn't get much forrader. Finally the clock struck ten, and roused me to the time. It was over an hour since the ladies had gone out and left us talking with the port. I got a little worried then that Sixpence might have fallen down and hurt herself with Joan, and so I rose, and we went through to the south room.

As it turned out, I need not have been alarmed. We found them playing the gramophone and talking about knitted cross-stitch jumpers, or something of that sort, and eating a box of chocolates that Joan must have brought down with her. I could see that they were getting on all right, and I heaved a sigh of relief. I had had visions of finding them silent in opposite corners of the room; one never knows with girls. Or I don't, anyway.

It was a warm, still, summer night. We walked out on to the terrace in the dusk and stood there looking out over the Range, talking idly about the chance of the weather and the sea in the next few days. Stenning was going west next day in the *Irene*; I had other plans, myself, and thought of taking Sixpence east.

In the dim light she came to me, and said: "Please, Commander Stevenson, I think I'm going up to bed, if you don't mind. I do feel ever so sleepy."

"Right-o," I said; "I'm going soon myself." I paused. "I thought if it's a fine day tomorrow we'd have an early breakfast and take *Runagate*."

She looked up at me, puzzled. "Please—I didn't understand."

I smiled. "It's the name of my yacht," I said. "*Runagate*. I thought we might go sailing all day if it's fine. Would you like that?"

She beamed at me. "It would be ever so lovely to do that. I've only been in a sailing boat once, and it was quite rough, and ever such fun." She paused reminiscently. "The gentleman that took me, he was sick."

Stenning laughed. "Red hot!" he said.

She laughed with him. "He *was* cross—what with being with me, and the others laughing at him. . . ." Her voice drifted away to silence in the dusk; a veil dropped upon the story of that pleasure party. "Goodnight," she said, and moved quietly away into the house.

I turned to Stenning and Joan. "We'd better get off early." I said, thinking of the tides. "Breakfast at eight—not later, or we'll find ourselves sweating out over the flood."

"I thought of that," said Stenning. "We'll sail together." I took a turn or two with them upon the terrace before going up. At the corner of the house, in Mollie's room, I saw the light come on and shine out in the night. I saw her shadow move and pass upon the curtains of the room. I knew that Joan was watching, too; I stirred and glanced at her, and our eyes met.

"Malcolm," said Joan, "who is she?" Her curiosity, I suppose was irresistible. "I mean," she said, "it's so unlike you to have anyone."

I eyed her grimly. I knew I had to face this questioning, this prying into my affairs. "She's just a girl that I picked up in Leeds and brought down here," I said defensively. "I gave her ten pounds to come."

Joan laughed softly. "You are a funny old stick," she said, quite quietly. "You needn't think you're going to kid me she's that sort of girl, or you're that sort of man." She paused. "As a matter of fact, she told me all about her work, and how you came to meet. But then there was a lot more that I didn't quite get the hang of; I don't know that she really understood it all herself. All about her brother, and a fire in a motor-lorry, and the police, and staying on to have a holiday with you."

She stopped, and there was a little silence on the terrace; Stenning had walked a little way away. "Well," I said, "she seems to have told you all there is to tell. I haven't anything to add to it."

She stood and eyed me for a moment. And then, quite unexpectedly, she said: "I think you must have been rather a dear."

I stood by the parapet looking out over the harbour mouth; the moon was coming up in a calm night, and there were wreaths of fog or mist down by the sea. "Stenning will tell you all I know," I said at last. "I got involved in this when I was drunk, and played a dirty trick on her. And then I didn't like it when I'd done it. That was all."

I didn't feel inclined to tell her any more, and she didn't worry me to do so. So we took a turn or two upon the terrace, till Stenning said: "I vote we go to bed."

"We'd better have a whisky first," I said. Joan said good-night to us, and moved towards the house. I went with her to the window; on the threshold of the room she turned to me, and said:

"You're very lucky, Malcolm. I think she's simply sweet."

Then she was gone before I could reply, before I could ask her to explain herself.

I went with Stenning to the model room, and we had our whisky there. He wanted the *Irene* got up on the slip as soon as he came back; he said she wanted caulking at the stern post. She didn't, as it happened; what she wanted was new stuffing at the stern tube gland. I fixed up this with him, and then we too went up to bed.

I was up early the next day, but Sixpence was before us. I heard her go downstairs as I was shaving, and saw her in the garden with the Rogers' dog. It was a misty sort of morning with blue sky above; not a breath of wind. I knew what that would mean for the day's sailing—getting up sails that flapped about and didn't draw, and trundling along under power most of the day. Still, it should be calm enough, and it seemed to me that there might be a little wind from the east to bring us home in the late afternoon.

I found her in the garden when I got down, and walked with her for a little time among the rose beds on the dewy paving. Then we went back into the house; Stenning was there in sea clothes, dirty flannel trousers and a fisherman's jersey. Then Joan came down in much the same sort of get-up. I saw Sixpence looking at them furtively, and smiled. "You're not dirty enough for this game," I said.

"I didn't know," she murmured. "I thought you always did yachting in white clothes."

"Not this sort," said Stenning. "That's only when you don't know how to sail a boat and have to have a crew." I think that was unjust, but Stenning hates a crew. So do I for that matter; paid hands are nothing but a nuisance on a boat.

She said again: "I didn't know. I thought yachts always had a crew, like on the pictures."

Joan laughed, and helped herself to sausages. "They don't do any washing up upon the pictures," she observed. "Or perhaps that's what the crew's for. My experience is that a woman's place upon a yacht is at the tub."

We finished breakfast and collected all their gear together with a hamper of our own containing lunch, packed everything into the Bentley, and set off for the yard. Down by the harbour everything was wreathed in mist, thin, with a visibility of half a mile or so. I knew that this would clear off as the day went on; we often have it that way in the summer time.

At the yard we separated. Joan and Stenning started to unload their stuff into their dinghy, and I went into my office for a few minutes to go through the post. There wasn't very much to do; I came out presently and saw them pulling out to the *Irene*. My pram was at the steps; I took Sixpence down and put her in the stern sheets with the hamper, took the sculls, and set out towards *Runagate* in the next berth.

Sixpence sat trailing her fingers idly in the water as we went. "It's lovely here," she said, quite quietly. The mist curled round the hills in slow, thin wreaths; the day was very still. I glanced over my shoulder. "That's the vessel," I remarked to her. "The white cutter."

I brought the dinghy alongside, stood up, and held her off from the topsides. "Hop on board," I said; she slipped nimbly from the little pram on to the deck and stooped to take the hamper that I handed up to her. I let the dinghy drop astern, and followed her on deck. "What do you think of her?" I asked.

She stood there for a moment very still upon the deck before replying, looking round about. "It's all so . . . clean," she said at last. She looked along the sweet sheer to the bows. "It's beautiful," she said. "The way that she goes up like that in front."

I stared at her in surprise; she had picked on one of the outstanding features of the vessel. "You've never seen a boat like this before?" I asked. "Nor been to sea?"

She shook her head. "Only in the speedboats at Bridlington, and that time we went sailing that I told you about."

I pursued the point of curiosity. "How did you know that it was right for her to be like that? That sheer up to the bows?"

She stared at me in perplexity. "The sea wouldn't come over so much, would it?"

I stood and looked at her. "You must have had to do with ships to know that much," I said. "Think, now."

She shook her head. "Only my grandpa. He used to work in some place where ships were built, in Scotland. But he died when I was small."

I nodded slowly, and we went below. She followed me, wondering, as I showed her through the ship. The forecastle, she thought, was terribly small to do the cooking in. She fell in love with the saloon, with the satinwood panels, with the little racks and cupboards, with the recording aneroid in springs. She didn't quite know what to say about the sleeping cabin, with the engine casing down between the bunks.

She turned to me at last: "It would be fun to really live upon a boat like this—for weeks, like."

I smiled. "You'd like it?" I inquired. "It's very rough sometimes, you know."

She nodded. "Fancy sleeping in these little beds. . . ."

I took her up on deck again, and we began preparing to cast off. She was intelligent and quick about the deck; I was continually reminded that she was a dancer as she moved nimbly on the cluttered, narrow deck. Together we got the dinghy alongside, shackled the burton to her bows, and lifted her on board. It was simple getting under way in that dead calm; as soon as the engine was running smoothly beneath our feet I went forward and cast off the mooring chain. The buoy and light line followed with a splash, and we drifted slowly clear.

Stenning cast off almost simultaneously with us. I put the clutch in and the vessel forged ahead in the thin mist, with Stenning following in our wake. He hailed us presently and I slowed down for him to come up on us a bit; he ranged *Irene* alongside, a ship's length away as we went down the river.

"Malcolm," said Joan, "got any salt to spare? We've only got a little in this pot, and I'm putting on a stew."

I turned to Mollie. "Come and take her for a minute while I go below," I said. She came and took the little wheel, protesting that she didn't know about it; in the *Irene* Joan and Stenning stood and watched us, grinning. I stood with her for a minute showing her how it went, then handed it to her. "Now, keep her bowsprit on that point of land." She took it all in, grimly serious. "Give us a decent berth," I said to Stenning, and went down below to look for salt.

There was silence up on deck, so far as there is ever silence in a vessel under way. Once, as I rummaged in the cupboards, I heard Stenning say quietly: "Other way; put it the other way. That's right, now steady her at that." In the stern the motor chugged on easily; at the bows I heard the tinkling ripple from the cutwater. I made a little paper screw of salt for them and took it up on deck; we were cruising steadily beside *Irene* and heading directly for the point. "Let her come up a little now," I said. "About a hand's span from the point." The vessel swung and steadied on her course.

"Like that?" asked Mollie.

I nodded. "That'll do."

The water of the harbour mouth was glassy calm, boiling a little here and there with eddies from the tide. Stenning ranged his vessel alongside and Joan reached out and took the salt from me, then they sheered off again. Mollie made as if to give the helm to me.

"Keep it a bit," I said; "you're doing fine." I glanced ahead. "Keep on as she is; you don't want to go too near the point." I got out of the cockpit and went forward on the deck, and began trimming her for sea.

We passed the Battery and motored out into the Range. At sea the mist was still hanging about in wreaths, the visibility perhaps a mile. I finished my jobs forward and came aft again, and went down into the saloon to fetch a cushion for Sixpence at the wheel.

She beamed at me: "I do think this is lovely."

I nodded: "A good game."

In the Range we parted company with the *Irene*; Stenning was going on down west to Salcombe and the Yealm. At the Mewstone I put her round and headed up along the coast for Berry Head. It was still thick. I put her on a compass course and taught Sixpence to read the card; she was still steering the vessel, keen and engrossed. And then I rested for a little in the cockpit, leaning on the hatch and staring out ahead. I would never have believed that any girl would pick it up so soon. It was in her blood, of course; that shipwright grandfather of hers was probably the last of a long line of merchant seamen. Seafaring is hereditary, I think; I find it so with my own shipwrights in the yard.

The mist grew thinner as we drew near Berry Head; it wreathed apart to show the great, familiar bluff and I felt a faint puff of air upon my cheek. We drew abreast the Head and I put her on another compass course; the wind was steadying down into the east, a light air to the heated land. I went forward and broke out the jib; it flapped and drew lazily in the sun. I gave her the balloon foresail as well, and went back aft; I stopped the motor and we went slipping slowly on under headsails alone. I was in no mood to hurry that day.

"It's lovely, going on like this without the motor," Mollie said. "Quiet, like."

For an hour we drifted on like that, enshrouded in the mist, basking in the sun upon the hot teak of the cockpit and the hatch. Once a Brixham vessel loomed up through the haze and crossed our bows, a great tanned ketch moving slowly under full sail, majestic and imposing on the water's face. On our beam the land showed faintly, Paignton way; occasionally we heard faint sounds of motor horns and barking dogs. For anyone who prided himself on seamanship it was a shocking way to drift across the bay, under headsails only on a day like that. Still, it was pleasant in the sun.

Then Sixpence roused me. "Oh," she said, "what's that?" And pointed dead ahead.

The sun and the light wind were banishing the mist. In front of us the confines of the bay were visible, the flat land rising up into tall cliffs at the north end. There were hills there, and a wonderful town upon the hills that followed the slopes down to the tideway; a magic town, built of white harbour walls and gleaming palaces beside the sea. All this was still half shrouded in the mist; in the bright sun it was all shot with colours, gold and blue.

> Like a flight of rose leaves, fluttering in a mist
> Of opal, and ruby, and pearl, and amethyst. . . .

"Oh," she said again, and turned to me, entranced. "What place is that?"

I glanced ahead, and turned to knock my pipe out on the rail. "That?" I said. "Oh, that's Torquay."

I heard her breathe: "Torquay . . ." and fell to filling up my pipe again. And so we stood like that for a little time until she took her eyes from it, and came to me, and said:

"You're ever so good to me, Commander Stevenson. I don't know what to say. . . ."

I muttered: "That's all right." And then quite quickly, before I knew what she was going to do, she reached right up and kissed me on the cheek.

I put an arm round her, the hand that hadn't got my pipe and pouch in it, and held her for a minute there upon tiptoe; then I let her down again upon her feet. "That was very nice," I said, and grinned at her. I stood there holding her like that with one arm round her shoulders while I pointed out to her the harbour and the pier; I'm not so sure that she was paying much attention. And presently I left her and went forward to uncast the stoppers on the anchor and its chain, and she went back to con the vessel in. And so that moment passed.

I dropped anchor in four fathoms about two cables from the westward harbour pier; it was about half tide. Sixpence came forward from the idle wheel and watched me veer the chain; then for a quarter of an hour we leaned on the main-boom and watched the crowds upon the shore through field-glasses. Then we went below to change for her bathe; first on deck, I got the dinghy alongside to make it easy for her to get out.

She came on deck at last in her green bathing dress; on the harbour wall I saw the telescopes come up at us. We dived in together; she turned and swam to the bows and hung on to the bob stay and the chain, laughing at me, then to the dinghy and so out on deck. I went in again alone; Sixpence was for the sun and the warm woodwork of the deck.

"I do think Lady Stenning's awfully nice," she said as we sat there.

I blew a cloud of smoke. "That's what I told you, but you wouldn't have it."

She wrinkled up her brows. "I know. But she didn't seem like a Lady, not to talk to."

"Well," I said, "she wasn't one last year."

She pondered over this for a bit. "She was ever so nice to me," she said at last.

Presently we went down to the saloon and dressed. Rogers had put us up a sort of picnic lunch: a dressed crab and Chablis, and some sweet or other. We took it up and ate it in the cockpit in the sun. I had put on the Primus and we had a cup of coffee after it and sat there smoking for a time, lazily studying the shore and town.

Then we went on shore. I sculled the dinghy in through the entrance to the harbour and in among the yachts moored there in rows; *Tern IV* was there, and *Coral*, I remember. We went on and left the dinghy in the inner harbour; up the steps to the quay, and there we were before the shops.

We wandered round that town all afternoon. Sixpence had reached the Mecca of her dreams, the Torquay that had meant so much to her throughout her life, and she was missing none of it. We went from the harbour to the pier and then into the gardens where the band was playing; we looked at the sunshine register and saw the veritable Station Road itself. Then we went back and found the Palais and had a look at the outside of that, and then we had to locate Bay View Hotel, where a friend of hers had spent a holiday one summer with a gentleman, and had a lovely time. And then we went to look at shops.

And then that damnable affair cropped up again. It was in the main street that it happened; I wish to God we'd gone back to the boat. We'd got about half way along a line of shops, with Sixpence studying entranced a great variety of articles from furniture to shoes, when we came to a window that displayed a considerable amount of ladies' underwear. I stood there while she glued her nose against the pane, hoping that nobody I knew would pass that way. And suddenly she plucked my arm.

"Oh, look," she said. "That's where Edna works."

She pointed to a ladies' dummy elegantly attired in nothing but a corset, and inadequate at that. "Slimline corsetry," she said. "That's where she works. I wonder if she made that one?"

I didn't understand. "Who's Edna?" I inquired.

She turned to me. "Didn't I tell you about her in the Leeds Palais? She's Billy's girl." She paused. "Only she doesn't seem to care about him, not like he does her."

There seemed to be a sort of silence then; in the busy street the traffic moved about us, but before the window we were very still. This was the first that I had heard of this young woman, but I knew just what it meant. If anyone could tell where Billy was, it would be this girl Edna in her corset factory.

I think she saw that it was something serious. "I hadn't heard of her," I said at last. "Where is it that she works?"

She said: "It's Hammersmith. But I did tell you, back in the police station that day. I *asked* if Billy'd gone to Hammersmith."

She had, and I had shut her up, and then I had forgotten it. By some chance it had not come out in Norman's questioning that this girl might know where he was; this was the first that we had heard of her.

"Do you think she'd know where Billy is?" I asked.

Something of the hard and anxious look that she had had in the dance hall came back to her as she looked up at me. A shadow had come to dull the brightness of our day—God knows, it isn't often that one gets a day like that. It might have happened at some other time.

"I think she would," she said.

We turned and went back to the dinghy at the harbour steps.

## CHAPTER 9

WE WENT on board at once. Outside the harbour a light breeze had sprung up from the north-east; I set to work and got the anchor short, and got the main on her alone. Then with the engine ticking over and with Mollie at the helm I broke her out and set the jib and foresail, and stood out into the Bay.

I kept her off the wind and sailing free until I had the anchor catted and all square forward; then I came aft and luffed her for the open sea. Mollie was by me in the cockpit as we crossed the Bay; I taught her how to steer the vessel on a wind and how to mark the trembling of the luff. But all the glamour of that day was gone. It was still bright and sunny, a calm sea and a steady sailing breeze: the fault was in ourselves.

Once she turned to me and said: "Please, Commander Stevenson. Shall I have to go and tell the police about Edna and Billy now?"

I did not answer for a moment, but stood staring at the land down Brixham way, still wreathed about with summer haze. And then I looked at her, and smiled. "I hadn't thought about it much," I said. "One thing at a time. In any case, we can't do anything till we get home. Let's forget it all till then."

And I stooped down and got a mackerel line from the locker, and showed her how to reel it out, but she was listless and depressed. We caught a couple close off Berry Head, but she was still distrait; I silenced the flutter of the fish and cursed myself that we had gone ashore at all. Better, I thought, if we had been content to look at Torquay from the sea, and so we rounded Berry Head and bore away for home.

It was seven o'clock by the time we were back at moorings off my yard. We came to them under power; to save time I had got the main down as we passed the Battery. I made all square and got the dinghy up, and sculled ashore with Mollie to the steps. In silence we drove up together through the town; I sent her up to change when we got in, and went and had a bath myself before we dined.

It was a little difficult at dinner with the servants there. I forget what we talked about; I only remember that Mollie was restless and uncomfortable. I fancy that I must have sat there talking at her easily, a steady, even flow of meaningless conversation about ships and harbours while I thought of other things. I could not make up my mind whether to let Fedden know at once about this new development, as I should have done. I was sick of the police and their ways. Moreover, I had no idea how far her brother might be implicated in this thing. It would certainly be better if he had a talk with Jenkinson before the police got hold of him.

It was a cloudless summer evening. We finished our dessert and went out on to the terrace, looking out over the Range. Rogers brought out our coffee there, and then we were alone, and I could come straight to the point that we wanted to discuss. "This girl Edna," I remarked, and she looked up quickly at me. "Do you know where she lives? Could you take me to her, for example?"

She nodded. "It's in Hammersmith, not far from the Palais, the one they call Dreamland. She lives with her mother, that keeps a sweet shop in Auburn Road. Just where the Fulham Palace Road goes off, like."

"Do you think she'd know where Billy is?"

"Oh, yes. You see, he's always writing to her, because he told me." She frowned a little. "I think she's ever so silly," she said impatiently.

I stood there, silent for a little, smoking my cigar and staring out over the harbour mouth. If I went to Fedden with this information it was probable that the police would get to Billy first, before I could. I owed it to the girl to see that her brother got the best chance that he could have with the law, and after the affair at Newton Abbot I had no confidence whatever in the integrity of Fedden and the CID. It seemed likely to me that if they got to Billy first he would be allowed to commit himself to God knows what, in ignorance that there were solicitors and barristers engaged for his defence and guidance. That could not be allowed.

The other course would be to go and find him for myself, take him to Jenkinson, and then present him to the police with Jenkinson to hold his hand. That might be the better way, but it would mean the father and mother of a row with Fedden. . . .

I turned to her at last. "My dear," I said, "I think we ought to go to town and have a talk with this girl."

"You mean we ought to try and find Billy?" she inquired. "I'm sure she'd know, because he writes to her, you see." She paused. "Would that be the best thing for him?"

"I think so," I replied. "I think we can probably help him.

She said, a little hesitantly: "I was thinking we might just forget, and pretend I hadn't told you about Edna." She raised her eyes to mine. "Wouldn't that do as well?"

I considered for a moment. There was a great deal to be said for that line of action, but I couldn't see that it would come out right. "The police are sure to find him in the end," I said. "It can be only a matter of a few days now before he's caught. I think we'd better find him ourselves first, and get him into touch with Jenkinson."

She sighed. "I know he wouldn't be doing anything wrong, not really." And then she said: "Will we be going up to London, then?"

"I think so," I replied. "I think we'd better go tomorrow."

There was a little pause. "Just you and me?" she asked. "Staying together in a hotel, or something of that?"

I met her eye, and laughed shortly. "That's right," I said. "In two separate rooms. Two hotels, if you like."

To my astonishment, she blushed at what I said. I stood and watched the slow colour creep from her face down her neck towards her shoulders, and she looked down and made a little pattern in the dust upon the terrace parapet. "I wouldn't want that," she said quietly. "Two rooms is good enough."

I sheered off what seemed to be an unexpectedly difficult subject for her, and we went walking down the garden in the evening light. She had come to know each flower in my garden intimately, as from the bud; I think my garden was the greatest pleasure that she had during the time she stayed with me. We strolled round in the dusk and picked a few roses for her room, till she was tired and ready for her bed. "I do get sleepy ever so quick here," she said. She stood and looked around the hills and sea, dim and already cradled in the night. "It's quiet here, and nice. . . ."

I went with her to the open windows of the library, and paused upon the threshold as she went inside. "Goodnight, Mollie," I said quietly.

She paused inside the window, half a yard from me. "Goodnight, Malcolm dear," she said. "It's been ever such a lovely day. I think it's been the loveliest I've ever had." And so she passed into the shadows of the room, and I was left alone to smoke a cigarette before I, too, went up to bed. I slept quite well, those days.

We went to town next day by train from Exeter. I knew very little of hotels in London, it must have been some fifteen years since I stayed in one. I have my club, and that is all that I have ever needed there. I took her to one of those enormous, modernistic palaces, all glass and stainless steel, that are springing up all over the West End; we had a couple of adjoining rooms there on the third floor, and paid a pretty penny for them. I hated the place right from the very first, but everything was new to her.

"It's awfully nice," she breathed. "It's like the Regal Palace in Manchester, only much grander."

We got there in the middle of the afternoon. She told me that Edna did not leave work till six o'clock; if we called at the sweetshop at about half past six we stood a good chance of finding her. We had our tea uncomfortably in the painted lounge, while the band played somewhere out of sight and one or two couples danced languidly in the hot air on an enormous floor. I sipped the unpleasant beverage they served as tea, and wished very much that I was in my club.

And presently we went to Hammersmith. We got there on top of a bus from Piccadilly; at Hammersmith Broadway we got off, and Sixpence took me walking for some way down the hot pavements till she stopped in front of a little sweetshop and tobacconist.

"This is it," she said, and we went in.

There was no one in the shop. It was small, and not very well stocked, with a tobacco counter on one side and a sweet counter on the other. In the back wall there was a door with a glass window in the upper half of it; through the lace curtain one could see a sitting-room, and people at the table. One of them got up and opened the door, and a fat untidy woman came out into the shop and looked at us inquiringly.

"Good evening, Mrs Tinsey," said Mollie. "I came to see if Edna was here."

The fat woman peered at her for a moment, and then raised her hands. "Well," she said, "if it isn't Mary Gordon!" She raised her voice. "Edna," she cried. "Edna . . . here's Mary Gordon come."

From the back room there came a girl with fair, wavy hair, bobbed, dressed in a white blouse and a dark skirt; a girl with rather a determined look about her—Billy's girl. "Oh, my dear!" she said to Mollie, and ran at her and kissed her. "After all this time! Just fancy!"

Mollie disengaged herself and turned to me. "Edna," she said. "This is my friend." I murmured something that I thought was suitable, and Edna said: "Pleased, I'm sure."

We went through with them into the back room. It was chock full of rather old and inexpensive furniture, and the table was laid for a meal. In the grate I saw the teapot stewing down before the fire; the kipper bones and cherry cake were still upon the table. We put aside their hospitality with some difficulty by assuring them that we had had our tea; I remember in particular that Mother was urgent to 'run out and get another kipper—it wouldn't take but a moment'. We compounded with them in the end by drinking cups of the stewed tea with cigarettes—'stock, my dear'—and I sat and made conversation with Mother about the state of trade, particularly the sweetshop trade, while the girls talked. I gathered from the things I overheard that they had been together in a Palais somewhere in the south. I think that probably Edna had been an amateur and a habitué of some Palais where my girl had worked.

The door bell rang, and Mother rose and went out into the shop to serve a customer. As soon as she had gone, Mollie got straight to the business we had come upon. "Say, Edna," she inquired. "Have you heard anything from Billy in the last few weeks?" She paused. "I mean, that you'd be able to tell me his address?"

Edna nodded. "I got a letter from him somewhere." She rose, and went hunting in a littered sort of escritoire in a corner of the room. Finally she produced a little sheaf of letters from a drawer and opened one. I saw Mollie looking at her keenly—so she kept his letters, anyway.

"Gloucester," she said. "That's the last. Maybe it'd be three weeks back." She looked at the others. "The one before that was there, and the one before that. The one before that was Birmingham, but that was Christmas, that one."

She glanced at Sixpence. "I'd say he was still at Gloucester with the lorry, because he said he was working from there, like." She turned over the letter—"16 Smallpiece Lane was where he wrote from."

I made a note of the address. "You didn't see him lately?" asked Mollie.

The other girl considered for a moment. "He come here one evening last month, maybe six weeks back. It was the night after the fire at Pinsons, because I remember."

Mollie persisted. "You haven't seen him since, not to speak to?"

The other shook her head. "It ain't no good him coming here," she said quietly. "I told him that."

There was a silence after that. In the shop the bell was ringing intermittently; a string of customers was passing in and out. "It didn't ought to be like that," said Mollie slowly. She glanced up at the other girl. "Wouldn't it be any good—not ever? I mean, there never was any other person for Billy, not like some."

I moved a little way away, so far as one could do so in that narrow room, and peered out through the curtain of the door that led in to the shop. Behind me I heard Edna say: "It ain't no good. Seems like he's not the man for me, Mollie. It isn't that I want a Valentino, or anything of that. Billy's all right.

But it'd have to be just right for me to marry anyone, and it wouldn't be just right with Billy—see? I'd rather go on working at Slimlines. Maybe you think I'm silly over it."

Mollie said: "Oh . . . I don't know."

Edna pursued her point. "You wouldn't ever take a chap unless it was just right, yourself."

No reply came to that one, I remember; instead, there came a little awkward pause. I turned back to the room. "It looks as if we'll have to go on down to Gloucester," I said easily. "We can go down there tomorrow and hunt him up."

"That's right," said Edna, "16 Smallpiece Lane. That was where he wrote from last time. I reckon he's still there, maybe."

There was nothing left for us to stay for, then. We made our farewells and got out into the street after some time. When we were out of sight I hailed a taxi, and we went driving round the Park till dinnertime, talking of Billy and the people that we saw in the street. I must say Mollie seemed to be more interested in the latter. This was a holiday to her, and she was out to get the last ounce out of it.

We dined that night in the hotel, and danced a little afterwards to a good band. Then we went to bed, both tired with the day.

Next morning we went down to Gloucester. We lunched there, in the best hotel that I could find, and after lunch went on to look for Smallpiece Lane. It proved to be a shabby little row of urban houses on the outskirts of the town, that ran out and ended in a field, a pasture with worn earth patches where the children of the neighbourhood had played. We found the house and knocked; the door was opened by a thin, gaunt woman in an apron.

"Is Mr Gordon in?" I asked.

"In the garidge," she replied. "You'll find him in the garidge."

"Where is that?" I asked.

It was about two streets away; we went on there at once. It proved to be a sort of yard behind a pair of open double gates, a place with an oily, earthen floor and a tumble-down shed at one end of it. The doors of this shed were open, and I saw the stern end of a lorry sticking out, and an old Morris car.

We passed in at the gates, and crossed the yard towards

the shed. There was a man working on the engine of the lorry; at the sound of our footsteps he straightened up and looked at us.

"Billy," cried Molly. "Bill-ee. . . ."

He was a stocky, pleasant-looking chap, not very tall. A shock of reddish hair hung over his blue eyes; he was very dirty from his work. He wore a soiled blue suit, torn at the back and greasy on the knees with oil and mud. He came towards us, smiling and wiping his hands upon a bit of rag.

" 'Ullo!" he said. "And what brought *you* down here, girl? This isn't half a surprise!"

I glanced at Sixpence, and she was glowing with pleasure. This brother meant a lot to her. "Oh, Billy, this *is* nice," she said.

"Well, well, well, well, well," he replied succinctly. "Not half, it isn't. But what brings you to Gloucester?"

She said: "We wanted to find you, Billy." And then she added: "Oh, Billy, this is my friend, Commander Stevenson."

I put out a hand; he rubbed his own with his rag, and shook it genially. "Pleased to meet you, sir," he said. "Any friend of Mollie's. . . ."

The words died down upon his lips; I saw the laughter go out of his eyes as he stood looking into my face. He let go my hand and stood there staring at me, open mouthed; I stood and watched the colour drain out of his face, and watched the apprehension creep into his eyes. In fifteen seconds he had changed into a different man. "Strewth . . ." he said quietly, so quietly that I hardly heard what he had said.

Mollie said: "Billy . . . whatever is the matter?"

He pulled himself together. "Matter?" he said sharply. "Nothing's the matter. What d'you think?"

She stared at him. "You look as if you'd seen a ghost. Honest, you do."

He forced a smile. "I did get a bit of a turn. Your friend, he's just the image of a man I met one time." He laughed uneasily. "Funny, them turns one gets. . . ."

I had been thinking quickly, studying the weatherbeaten face, the shock of red, untidy hair, the friendly blue eyes. I had never seen this man before, but that might not be necessary. I smiled, and stood staring straight at him. "Maybe you've seen me somewhere before," I said amicably. "Down Dartmouth way, perhaps." I was watching closely, and I saw him blink. "I drive a Bentley Six saloon."

The colour had all gone from his face. "No," he said at last. "I never seen you before." A child could have told that he was lying. He turned suddenly on Mollie. "Here, girl," he cried; "who is this bloke, and where does he come from? What is he to you, eh?"

She pressed my arm. "Billy," she said, a little hurt, "you didn't ought to speak like that. This is my friend."

I stood there smiling at him grimly, still staring him in the face. "I was able to help your sister when she got into a bit of trouble," I explained, "with the police. They found a burning motor lorry, and they thought she might know who the driver was."

There was a long, awkward silence after I said that. In the distance I heard the children playing in the street outside, and the long clanking of an engine shunting in some siding near at hand. He stood there like a naughty schoolboy, looking down and scraping the earth with the toe of his boot. "You're to do with the police?" he inquired.

I shook my head. "Not me."

"Billy," said Mollie, "he isn't with the police. He was ever so good when I was in the station, and stopped them, and got a lawyer all the way from London, and everything. Honest, he did."

I wondered if that sentence was comprehensible to him. I doubt it, for he raised his head sullenly, with an ugly flush. "Then if he's not from the police, what the hell does he want here? I do my business, and don't worry nobody."

"What is your business, anyway?" I asked.

"Lorrying," he said defiantly. "Now you clear out o' this. I've had enough of you. I've got my work to do."

Sixpence said: "But, Billy. . . . You can't just push us out like that."

"Cheese it, girl," he retorted, not unkindly. "You buzz off now, and I'll write to you."

I moved to the Morris Cowley and sat down upon the running board, my elbow resting on my knees. "The police have got your lorry," I remarked, "—the one that was burnt out. They know the number plates were false. They found the

142

three carpet sweepers that you left behind, two burnt up in the lorry, and one behind the hedge. They're looking for you all over the country. They'll have got your description by this time." I paused reflectively. "It was a good game, but it's finished now."

There was another long, uneasy silence. He stood there shuffling a little with his feet, and shooting furtive glances at me as I sat there on the running board. "I don't see who you are," he said at last.

I tried a long shot. "I'm the fellow who was in the car," I said.

"Oh, chuck fooling," he said irritably. "I know that." He was silent for a minute, and then he said: "What I want to know is—what's the game?"

Mollie was standing silent a little way away from us, and leaving the whole thing to me. I sat there for a minute staring out across the littered, oily yard, watching the smoke from a bonfire in a rubbish pit curling lazily up into a light blue, summer sky. My long shot had gone home all right. "There's no game," I replied. "No game at all."

I glanced up at him, standing over me. "When you left that lorry burning on the road, the police were after you like a knife. They couldn't find you, but they got to know that Miss Gordon was your sister, and they took her down to Dartmouth to question her about you. I came in then, and got a lawyer to look after her."

"That's right, Billy," put in Sixpence eagerly. "And all the way from London, too. It was ever so good of the Commander.

I smiled a little, wondering idly where she had picked that up. Only the servants call me the Commander and the men down at the yard. She must have picked it up from Rogers or one of the maids. . . . Then I came back to earth.

I met his eyes. "I'm here to tell you that the police are looking for you now," I said. "You haven't got a chance. You can't even get out of the country, now. If you stay here they'll get you in a day or two. And if you run, they'll get you in a week."

He burst out: "But I ain't *done* nothing!" He stared at me. "Nothing, save lorrying for them, and leaving me lorry on the

143

road. Them things aren't crimes—they can't do nothing to you for that. What do they want with me?"

I motioned him to the step of the lorry opposite me. "Sit down," I said. "There's no sense standing up all day." And Mollie came and sat beside me on the Cowley running board, and I said:

"They want you because they want the other lot. They can't find out anything about them—yet—but they'll get you all right."

He repeated sullenly: "I ain't done nothing wrong. . . ."

Sixpence stirred irritably beside me. "Don't act so soft," she said. "The Commander's all for us, not for the police or anyone. Why don't you tell him what's been going on?"

He looked a little foolish, laughed, and pushed back his cap to scratch his head with an oily hand. "Reckon he knows most of it," he said, embarrassed.

"I'd like to hear what happened when we met before," I remarked.

And cutting short his tale, it came to this. He had picked up two foreigners near Newton Abbot by an assignation, and had driven on down to Dartmouth with them in the empty lorry. They arrived on the shore road at about one o'clock in the morning and stopped a few hundred yards up the road from the corner where my car was subsequently found, towards the town. From there his companions made their signal to the sea and got the reply. His two companions then went down to the shore, and Gordon stayed by his lorry. He had no part in handling the cargo.

About half an hour later the two foreigners came back, carrying the first case; behind them came two men from the ship, carrying another one. One of these men was a young Englishman that he had seen before on these occasions; he thought that he had to do with the vessel that they used.

It was at that point that the car appeared.

They saw the headlights on the road two or three miles away; it was clear to them that the car was being driven very fast. As a precautionary measure they covered up the cases in the lorry, two of them got inside, and Gordon lifted the bonnet as if with engine trouble. But the car stopped short of them. They heard it come along at a great pace, and in the still night they heard the squeal of brakes as it drew up a quarter of a mile away. Then the headlights stopped motionless upon the road, and they stood staring at each other in consternation.

Presently two of the men detached themselves, got over into the fields, and made a wide circuit in the darkness towards the strange car to investigate. Gordon stood waiting by his lorry; after a time the Englishman slipped off and went direct down to the beach.

That was all he saw, but he told me what had happened. "When they got close they seen a man walking from the car down to the beach," he said. "Walking quiet like, over the grass, he was." They went close enough to the car to see that there was nobody else there, and then they followed on the stranger's heels down to the beach. "They took him for a coastguard of some sort. They come up behind him down there somewhere, and slugged him proper," he explained. "With a pistol, with the handle, like."

I felt Mollie stir beside me, and I smiled. "That's right," I said. I paused a minute, and inquired: "What happened then?"

He laughed. "They weren't half in a stew." The next thing he knew was that they came up from the beach to the lorry, all three of them, together with a girl. He had not seen the girl before; he thought that she must have come upon the boat. They were carrying what seemed to be a corpse, and in the party there were bitter words passing. At the lorry they laid the body down and the girl at once began attending to it, removing and renewing a rough, bloodstained bandage on the head. The man was quite unconscious.

They stood there for some time wrangling over what was to be done, and then they went off to view the car up the road, still arguing as they went. And by the time they got there it had begun to dawn on them that there was no significance at all in what had happened at the beach; the man was quite alone, and he was very drunk. Actually, there had been no necessity to strike him down at all; if they had humoured him he would have gone away and would have forgotten the whole thing next day. But there he was, drunk and unconscious, and with a serious head injury. A well-dressed fellow, too—possibly somebody of importance.

They'd got themselves into a pretty mess.

It was the young Englishman who suggested that they should stage a motor crash. He argued, rather forcibly, that the fellow was so drunk that he'd probably have piled his car up anyway before he reached his home, and that it was just as likely to have happened here as anywhere. Nobody had any better solution to their difficulty to suggest, and so they set about it.

Gordon drove the car a hundred yards along the road to the corner and transversely into the ditch in skidding attitude. With the assistance of a crowbar they contrived to turn it over on its side into the hedge—a big job, for it was a heavy car. They went round it with the crowbar then, breaking the glass and damaging the wings, but it was the young English-man who thought of kicking through the roof above the driver's seat. They did the best they could. Taking it all round, I think they must have made a rotten job of it; if any serious inquiry had been made it must have been obvious at once that that was no real crash. But no inquiry of that sort was necessary, I suppose. The fellow's habits were well known.

And finally they brought along the body and laid it in the car. The man was still breathing heavily, and the bleeding from the scalp had stopped. The girl insisted that the position should be such that the head was raised a little, and they had some difficulty over this.

So they finished the unloading of the boat and came away. The man was still in a deep coma when they left, and it was close on dawn. They found out two days later that he had been found a couple of hours afterwards; he was in a nursing home and likely to get over it. It seemed a very satisfactory solution to what might have been a nasty incident.

Gordon laughed, a little ruefully. "They wasn't half pleased when they heard that," he said. "Well out of it, they thought they was. . . ."

I nodded slowly. "Would you recognise the man again?"

There was a little silence in the yard. He hesitated, and then said: "I would, sir. It was you."

"Yes," I said absently, "I suppose it was." I was thinking of the further links I wanted to get out of him and for the moment I was silent, till I said:

"How did that lorry come to go on fire?"

He was annoyed. "Silliest thing you ever saw," he said. "I never seen such!" He glanced at me, irrepressible. "But coo! she didn't half flare up! Filling up, it was. I'd got the filler off the tank and pouring in from the can, and another can unstoppered beside me. An' then one of them went to light a fag." He laughed. "She went off with such a puff I fell backwards off the running board into the road, an' dropped the can and petrol over everything. You never seen such a mess! They fellows was out of the back like a knife and there she was. We just couldn't do anything with her."

I wrinkled my brows. "You had a load on board?" I asked. "I suppose it happened after you'd left the boat?"

"Oh, aye," he said. "We got the most of it off her before it got too bad—all the cartridges and that, but some of the stuff we had to leave. I had the little Morris with me that trip" —he indicated the car beside us—"and we piled it all into her till she was down on her springs. Then she was full, an' still a case or two left, an' we put them down behind the hedge and went on in the Morris. But I reckon they must have been found, because they was gone next day. Still, I don't see what else we could have done. . . ."

I asked him where the stuff was going to, and to my surprise he told me readily. He took it to Trepwll in Breconshire, about thirty miles north of Cardiff. That was a run of about a hundred and sixty miles, which usually took ten hours or so. His garage in Gloucester was handy for this run, and he eked out the business of these journeys with a certain amount of local work of various descriptions.

He told me that in all he had made five trips. I had blundered into the second landing, and his lorry had been burnt upon the last. The lorry that he had now was another one, which he had purchased second-hand as a replacement. He was overhauling it for the next journey.

"When is that?" I asked.

He did not know. It would be in about a week's time; he only got two days' notice of each trip. They paid him forty pounds a trip—not bad, he said, for twenty-four hours' work. For this he promised secrecy.

He deposited his loads at a farm about two miles from Trepwll. Sometimes he had passengers upon these journeys

147

and these were mostly foreigners; once he had gone alone. He did not know the names of any of the men that he had met, and he had resolutely kept his eyes shut upon the nature of the business. He was content to obey orders while things went well; in the event of any trouble he would look after himself, and get out of it as best he could. He got his orders from a man that he knew as Mr Palmer, who came to him personally before each trip.

That was the substance of the tale he had to tell. I liked the man, I must say; if he was a rogue he was a cheerful one. To him the whole affair had been a matter of business and no more; he had made good money, and he wasn't one to worry about ethics. He seemed to have no knowledge of the purpose of the guns, or interest. In fact, he told me that he had not known the nature of his cargoes till the lorry was burnt out, but it made no difference when he did discover it. His business was lorrying.

"Your next trip's in about a week's time, then?" I asked.

"That's right, sir," he replied. He sat there musing for a minute. "I don't know as I'll go on that one now. I don't want to get mixed up with no police. . . ."

Mollie said: "Oh, Billy, you might have thought of that before!"

He looked up at her, and grinned, a little sheepishly. "Strewth," he said, "I never thought of it like that."

It seemed to me that there was information here that Fedden and his policemen ought to have, and that I could not allow this thing to be suppressed. I was equally certain that Jenkinson should be with this man when he made his statement to the police. As far as I could see it, the extent of his wrongdoing would be well covered by a ten-bob fine; they might not take that view of things at Scotland Yard. Jenkinson must be there. I sat and thought about it for a minute, till at last I said:

"The police will be here any day now—you'll have to be prepared for that. You'll have to tell them all that you've told me."

He shifted uneasily. "That's no way to go on. I got good money to keep my mouth shut." And then he burst out again: "I ain't *done* nothing!"

It was Mollie who replied to that. "Oh, don't keep on like

that," she said impatiently. "You been smuggling guns into the country, that's what you been doing, like the Commander says. It's no good you kidding yourself that way."

He scratched his head unhappily. "I dunno what to do," he said.

It took about an hour's hard talking to persuade him that our course was best. But we left that night for London, all the three of us, and by ten o'clock next morning I had him closeted with Jenkinson.

## CHAPTER 10

I DON'T think I need go through in detail the examination which was made of Billy in London. I got him in to Jenkinson, and when we had satisfied ourselves that he could tell us no more than he had told me at Gloucester, we sent for Norman. I had the pleasure of ringing up that gentleman myself, from Jenkinson's office.

I got on to him at Scotland Yard. "This is Commander Stevenson this end," I said. "Is that Major Norman?"

"Speaking," he replied.

"Good morning," I said courteously. "I'm speaking from Mr Jenkinson's office—you've met Mr Jenkinson, haven't you? Oh, yes, I was forgetting. We've got a young chap here that you might like to have a word or two with—I should say, that Mr Jenkinson sees no objection. The driver of the lorry. What? Yes, the driver of the lorry that was burnt out. Miss Gordon's brother."

He burst out: "You say you've got him in your office? How long have you had him there?"

"Oh . . . let's see, now," I replied. "I saw him first in Gloucester yesterday, and brought him up last night. We've examined what he has to say, and there really seems to be no reason why he shouldn't make a statement to you, if it would help you in your work in any way. Mr Jenkinson will be present all the time, of course, to guard his interests."

He said angrily: "See here, Mr Stevenson, if that man gets away I shall hold you responsible for his escape."

"Certainly," I said. "Do I understand that you would like to see him? If so, I'll ask him to wait here for a few minutes."

"I'll be round right now," he said.

"Oh, that's excellent," I said pleasantly. "In about a quarter of an hour's time? I think that will be quite convenient for him."

I didn't get an answer to that one. The line was suddenly cut off; I think he must have been in something of a hurry.

He came in a remarkably short time, and with him was a shorthand man. He was inclined to be a little curt with me, so far as I remember—I can't imagine why. We went through into a sort of Board Room next door to Jenkinson's office, and sat down round a table while Norman asked his questions.

There was nothing new. He didn't know any more than he had told me. Norman pressed him particularly upon the source of his instructions, but he knew nothing other than that the man he knew as Palmer turned up at Gloucester at his garage or his lodgings from time to time and left messages for him. It was from this man that he got his money after each trip, forty pounds in treasury notes. He had no means of finding him at other times. On the morning of each trip the man turned up at the garage and travelled down with him upon the lorry.

He gave a pretty full description of this man, but there was precious little in it to take hold of. He described a man of forty-five or fifty years of age, with grey hair and rather refined speech.

For the destination of his loads, however, he was able to supply clear evidence. He took the stuff to a farmhouse in Breconshire, not far from Trepwll; at this place it was unloaded and carried into a barn. He could identify this farm clearly, though he did not know its name; he gave such positive directions as to how you reached it from Trepwll as would identify it beyond all doubt.

The statement came to an end at last. Norman sent away his stenographer to get it typed, and it was arranged that Jenkinson should take Gordon down that afternoon to Scotland Yard to go over it and sign his deposition. Norman departed then, and I took Mollie and her brother out to lunch, at Mr Lyons' Corner House.

We took him back to Jenkinson at about three o'clock; together they went off to Scotland Yard. Mollie and I took a taxi back to the hotel. She was tired, and a little bewildered by the events of the day.

"I do think it's awful to get mixed up with the police," she said. She had a wholesome dread of the constabulary.

I got a telephone message late that afternoon, summoning me to Sir David Carter at 10.30 the next morning. I wondered who was going to be there. I didn't see what they wanted me for; if ever I was resolved upon one thing it was that I was taking no more part in police affairs. I'd had my fill of that; from this time onwards I was going to devote myself merely to the protection of Mollie and her brother against their irregularities.

Gordon turned up soon after tea; little of any consequence had happened at the Yard. I gave him over to Mollie for the evening, saw that they had plenty of money, and left them to their own devices; I judged that they would talk more freely if I were away. I dined that evening at the club, and took a hand of bridge. By the time that I got back to the hotel they had gone up to bed.

Mollie opened the door as I went into my room; her room was next to mine. She was wearing a kimono and her hair was down her back; in the dim light of the passage she seemed to me to be most beautiful. "I'm glad you're back," she said, a little oddly. "Billy and I, we had a lovely time. We went to the pictures. But it's dreadfully expensive here."

I smiled. "I had a bit of an expensive evening, too," I said. "I was playing cards."

"You wouldn't like a cup of tea, or a whisky or anything like that, would you?" she asked. "I mean, I'll put on my frock, and we'll get a waiter if you like."

"Don't worry about the frock," I said. "You're much nicer like that."

She coloured a little, and told me not to be so awful.

"No, I don't want anything," I said. "Just bed."

There was a little pause.

"Goodnight, Commander Stevenson," she said.

"Goodnight, Mollie," I replied, and went into my room.

Next day I went down to the Yard and saw Sir David Carter. Norman was with him in his room, and Fedden; they must have got him up from Dartmouth in a hurry. They offered me a chair at a long table; Sir David left his desk, and he settled to a sort of conference.

He started off: "I should like to begin by offering my thanks, Commander Stevenson, for the services which you have rendered in this business. Colonel Fedden and Major Norman tell me that we owe a great deal to you, in securing the evidence of the young woman Gordon, and of her brother. I should like you to feel that we appreciate your help."

I had come prepared to hold my own in any bickering, but this old man had rather spiked my guns. "I'm interested in those two," I said at last. "They're a good type, and I'd like to see them clear of any trouble."

He inclined his head. "Exactly so. I hope sincerely that it will not be necessary for us to make any trouble for them. At the moment we do not anticipate that sort of difficulty."

"I'm glad to hear it," I replied. "After what I've seen I should defend them with all the resources in my power," and I glanced from the old man to Norman on his other side.

Sir David Carter coughed. "Leaving that aspect of the matter for the moment," he said, "I thought it would perhaps be best to send for you, Commander Stevenson, before we communicate our proposals to the man, William Gordon. Major Norman informs me that you have considerable influence with both of them; as the procedure which we have decided on is of some delicacy, I think it right that we should put it to you first."

I thrust my chair back from the table. "See here," I said; "I'm out of this. I'm sorry, but I can't do any more for you."

There was a little pause. "Nevertheless," remarked Sir David, "I should like you to hear what we propose."

I relaxed my attitude. "I should be very glad to," I replied. "But I can take no part in any of your plans."

He nodded. "We should not wish you to."

He picked up a pen holder from the tray before him and began playing with it absently, a favourite trick of his. "You will have gathered the position for yourself," he said. "We now know the destination of the guns, and a great deal more about the manner in which they are introduced into the country. We do not know the organisers of the enterprise. We do not know the nature of the ship that brings them, though the evidence of Sir Philip Stenning throws a little light on that. We do know that the guns are taken to Trepwll, and from that we can deduce, without a great deal of investigation, who they are intended for."

He raised his head and looked at me. "There is trouble in that district, as you know."

I did know. It was not far from the Glanferis mines, and the Conservative papers had been full of the Glanferis troubles for the last three months. The coal trouble had virtually closed the pits, and there was much labour unrest. There had been riots and isolated policemen had been beaten up; the papers put this down to Communist incitement. On the eve of the election, with the poll not five weeks off, Glanferis had assumed a disproportionate importance; its news value had been sedulously worked up. Glanferis was a front-page story at that time.

The old man was staring straight at me, still playing with his pen. "I want you to visualise the whole situation, to see it from the broadest point of view. If we go straight now to Trepwll we shall find arms. In that event, we might be forced to the incredible conclusion that the Welsh miners in that district are preparing for an armed revolt against the Crown."

I met his eyes. "You find that quite incredible?" I asked
"Absolutely," he said quietly.

Norman broke in. "We have the most complete reports upon the situation in Glanferis," he remarked. "This comes as a complete surprise. We cannot imagine what section of the disputants could find it to their interest to arm their men. The use of force against the Crown cuts clean across the policy of every party in that district. It would mean political disaster for the party that attempted it. It's inconceivable."

"Still," I said, "there the guns are. You can't get away from that."

Sir David sighed. "Yes, there they are." I was a little sorry for him in his great responsibility.

He pursued his discourse. "I am taking it upon myself to delay the seizure of those guns," he said quietly. "I would not have you think that we are shirking from our duty on account

153

of the election, for fear of the effect that may be produced upon the electorate if guns should be discovered in Glanferis. We are rather concerned to ensure that when the matter is made public for the first time, the whole story shall be quite complete. I would not bring it out in bits and pieces. I want the directing intelligence behind those guns. I want evidence which will show for what reason they are there—in comparison with that evidence the guns are nothing." He turned to me. "This country stands on the eve of a poll, Commander Stevenson. We seem to be in the unfortunate position of having to produce a bombshell for the public, another Zinovieff letter which may change the whole course of the election. If we have to do that we must have solid facts behind us—not merely guns and theories as to what they were intended for. The public must be told the truth of this affair if it be told anything at all."

"I'm with you there," I said. "Give the country the whole truth of whatever may be going on, and let it do what it thinks best. It won't go wrong."

He inclined his head. "Exactly so."

Fedden stirred. "That leads us to the man Gordon," he said. It was the first time he had spoken.

I raised my eyebrows. "How does he come into it?"

Sir David Carter said: "We propose to use him for the next few days for information purposes."

I was about to speak, but he stopped me. "I will tell you first what we propose. We shall send him back to his work at Gloucester, keeping him quietly under observation there. We shall give him to understand that no proceedings will be taken for the slight irregularities of which he may be guilty, on the condition that he supplies us with the information that we want. We want the man Palmer, primarily. Next, we want information about the next landing of arms to enable us to make a capture of the boat. Given those two, I think we shall secure sufficient evidence for us to put the matter to the public for its judgment."

He paused. "I would not have you think that we enjoy these methods that we have to use," he said a little sternly, looking straight at me. "Our business is to catch criminals, and to find out the truth."

I nodded. "I appreciate that point."

I sat and thought about it for a minute, and there was a silence in the room. Their attitude was reasonable; it was the only way to get the information quickly that would settle this affair. Billy must go back to Gloucester and deliver the man Palmer over to the police.

I saw now why they wanted me. They were no fools, and they knew that I had influence with Mollie. They could not make the man go back to Gloucester if he did not want to; they could not make him betray his associates. They were relying on Mollie and myself to influence him that that would be the right thing to do; they must have seen that threats would be of no avail. There was good stuff in that chap.

I could not deny that they were right, nor could I deny them help. The matter was too serious for that. Against my will they'd got me into it again.

I raised my head. "And you want me to do . . . what?"

It was exactly as I had thought. They had not seen Gordon or put this thing to him; they wanted me to do that. They wanted me to represent to him that the police were his friends, only anxious to help him in his difficulties and to guide him out of the mess that he had got into. I was to have a quiet talk with him with Mollie, and then to take him along and introduce him to one or two plain-clothes men the next day. Then he was to go back to Gloucester, and wait for developments.

"There isn't any danger in it," Norman said. "I can assure you that it's a procedure which is often used."

I stared at him. "I am quite ready to believe it," I remarked, a little grimly.

I turned to Carter. "I will see what I can do," I said. "You understand that I can promise nothing—nothing whatsoever. I'll put it to them, and I'll telephone to you this afternoon."

I left the Yard and went back to the hotel. Mollie was out somewhere with her brother—shopping, I suppose. I waited in the lounge for them. They came in presently and we had lunch, and after lunch I took them up into my bedroom for our talk.

I put it to them as fairly as I could. I told them all that I had heard at Scotland Yard, and I told them what the police wanted to find out. I explained as clearly as I could the political reasons underlying the whole thing; I think that Billy understood that more than Mollie did. He was accus-

tomed to reading newspapers. I told them, frankly, that I
thought they ought to help; that what the police were asking
was a reasonable thing. In his small way Billy had helped to
get the country into some sort of a mess, and it was up to him
to help to get it out again.

"I dunno what to say," he said. "It don't seem right to
me. . . ."

But Mollie broke in there. "Don't act so soft," she said. "The
Commander knows what's best. . . ."

Eventually we all went round to Jenkinson, and put the
thing to him. He could not help us very much, beyond the
general advice that where the police demands were reasonable
they should be met so far as possible. He was inclined to think
that their demands were reasonable now, and that our best
course was to fall in with their plans.

So we agreed, and Billy was content to go. I rang up
Norman and arranged for Billy to visit Scotland Yard that
afternoon, and to go down to Gloucester that same evening;
it was obviously desirable that he should get back there as
soon as possible. Mollie and I escorted him to Scotland Yard
and said goodbye to him; he was diffident and uneasy in his
new rôle. I was uneasy, too, but I could see no other way of
handling the situation.

I arranged with him that I would take his sister back to
Dartmouth and we would wait there till this affair was over.
As soon as he was free he would come down to us there.

And so we left him, and went back to the hotel.

Mollie was absent minded and uneasy all that night. We
dressed and dined, and I took her out to a revue; she enjoyed
it, but her mind was never very far away from Billy. She kept
on asking little, difficult questions of the work that we had
sent him on—was it often done that way, and was it ever
dangerous? I answered these to the best of my ability and reassured her, I suppose; I wish I could have reassured myself.
Not one of our better evenings, taking all in all, and I was
glad to go to bed.

We took a morning train to Exeter next day, and Adams
met us with the car. I drove and Adams sat behind; it was a
warm and sunny afternoon. As we got on the road our spirits
rose: the Yard seemed very far away from Devonshire that
day. We went down through Newton Abbot and Totnes, with

Mollie lighting cigarettes for me, and marvelling at the automatic lighter as it glowed.

We got to Dartmouth just in time for tea; it was good to be back home again. I don't like London, and though one goes up there from time to time on business or for boredom, I am always best pleased with my own place, with the sea and with my work. This afternoon as we sat having tea together in the library, with Mollie prattling away of the things that she had done and things that she would like to do in London, I remember thinking what a very good place home was.

And I remember thinking what a dreary place my home had been before the girl had come to stay with me. I remember wondering what I should do when this was over and she went away.

We went down into the garden after tea and picked some roses for her room; she loved her flowers. And then we went a little way down the fuzzy, till we stopped where I had had a seat put up, and we sat there in the evening sun while I smoked a pipe, looking out over the Range and the wide sea. And as we sat there a vessel came into sight from the west, a little cutter under all plain sail, making for the Range and Dartmouth on the evening flood.

"Hullo," I said, and pointed with my pipe. "There's Stenning."

It was only four days since we sailed together, but it seemed much more to us. Stenning had been on a short pleasure cruise while we had been in town, and here he was again, slipping in quietly to his moorings off my quay. "They'll probably stay for the night with us," I said. "They won't fly back tonight."

She glanced up at me. "Couldn't we go down and meet them?" she inquired. "I mean, it might be nice for them if we did that?"

And so we walked back up the fuzzy to the stable, took the Bentley, and went down to my yard. We got there before the *Irene*; I took the yard punt and we went out to the moorings on the calm evening water to wait until they came. Near the mooring buoy I pulled in oars, and we sat and drifted, smoking and talking till they came.

The vessel came slowly into sight, more or less becalmed among the hills, drifting slowly into moorings on the flood with the light airs. Stenning is like me, he never motors, if he can avoid it, in a yacht. Joan was at the helm, anxiously striving with the erratic airs; the vessel came slowly to us, with Stenning busy forward with the gear. He dropped the foresail and set up his topping lift, then with the boat hook in his hand he turned and hailed us as they drifted slowly close.

"Been far?" I asked.

"Only to Salcombe and the Yealm," he said. "This is a holiday, this is."

He caught his mooring deftly and pulled the chain on board; the vessel turned slowly and swung to the tide. I pulled the punt alongside and we went on board.

I went forward to help Stenning with the main; Mollie went below with Joan. "You're not going back tonight, are you?" I asked. "I've got a lot I want to talk to you about."

He cocked an eye at me. "About this other business?"

I nodded.

"Right," he said; "we'll stay and drink your port for you." Stenning has a practical mind.

We gathered up their belongings and transferred them to the punt, and squared up the vessel for the night. One of the advantages of a shipyard is that you can bring your yacht in and leave her more or less as she arrives, secure in the knowledge that she will be properly attended to. We got the sail covers on and locked the cabin up, and then we were ready to depart.

Dinner that evening was a pretty cheerful meal. Joan and Stenning were fit and sunburned with their little cruise, and in good spirits. I was surprised and pleased, too, to see how well Mollie was going down with them. She had lost her shyness and was chatting to them freely about her life up in the North, with little anecdotes about the people she had met and places she had seen. But she didn't like the North, she said. The South was ever so much nicer, with the sea and everything.

She talked a lot about the sea. She was always wanting to know things about it—why the tide went up and down the coast instead of coming in and out, and whether seagulls went south for the winter, and how far out to sea they went. Funny questions of that sort that seemed inspired by nothing but sheer interest—and she never forgot anything I told her in that way. I found her very quick.

I sat with Stenning that evening when the ladies had gone out, and over the port I told him all that had happened in the last four days. Rather to my surprise, I found him seriously concerned about Gordon. He has had more experience of the rough-and-tumble side of life than I have had, and he was by no means certain that the police had power to protect informers from the remainder of the gang. He pointed out what would happen to Gordon if this thing had happened in America; he would have been 'taken for a ride', and nobody would be able to do much about it. Certainly this was not America, but the ways of gunmen were becoming universal in the world. He thought that we were taking a considerable risk.

He was intensely interested in the whole affair. "I must go back tomorrow," he said. "I'm tied up with an appointment that I've got to keep. But if it's any help to you, I'll come down for a day or two after that—when this next landing's due to be made." He paused. "I don't think I'd impress it upon Joan," he said. "I'd like to see *Irene* on the slip, and I'd put it that way."

I told him that that would help a lot. It would be good to have Stenning by my side if there was any trouble coming, and it was good of him to make the offer.

It was still light when we went through into the next room. I had some matters that I wanted to discuss with Joan, and so I cut her out from Stenning and Mollie, and we went walking down the garden in the dusk, talking of little, casual things, until we reached the rose garden and sat a little on the stone balustrade looking away up river to the town. I came to the end of my trivialities down there, and blurted out:

"I came down here because I wanted to talk to you about marrying."

There was a little silence after I said that; she did not reply at once. In the dim light her cigarette glowed softly as she drew. She blew the smoke out and inquired:

"You're not married now, are you, Malcolm?"

I shook my head. "Not yet. I hope I'm going to be soon." I stood and eyed her in the dusk. "You're the only one of my relations that I give a damn about, and I'd somehow rather that you knew about it first."

"It's this girl here, is it?" she asked.

"I shall be asking her if she will marry me, quite soon," I said.

Joan didn't say anything to that, and her silence seemed like a rebuke to me. I wanted to explain to her, and so I said: "Even with all the money that I've got to give them, the sort of girl I want never falls for me. That's idealism, I suppose. Seems to me that the present-day girl has a higher set of ideals than ever before—and I should know. I've tried no less than six times since the war, and failed, with all my money." I laughed. "I must say, it's been an interesting experience. Most instructive."

Joan leaned forward suddenly, and touched my arm as I laughed. "Poor old Malcolm," she said quietly.

I said, a little uncertainly: "I've got a chance of getting married now. I can't go on like this, living alone. Dixon was right. I've tumbled on somebody who really cares for me at last—and not for my money, either. And I'm going to ask her to marry me." I glanced at her. "I thought you'd better know."

Joan said: "I see."

Something in her tone pierced home and stung me up, and I said harshly: "All right. I know you think I'm messing up my life by marrying a girl like that. You needn't put it into words."

In the dim light I saw her looking up at me. "Well, old boy," she said, "whatever you do now you couldn't make it any worse, could you? Living alone, like you've been doing all these years."

I stared at her blankly. "You think I'm doing the right thing?" I asked slowly. I had not thought that she would take it quite like that.

She stood up from the balustrade. "Oh, Malcolm," she burst out, "you are so slow. I don't believe you know yet what you've got. I don't care where she comes from, or who her people are. You've got a girl in ten thousand. She simply adores you. She's learnt your ways—she knows you better than I do myself. She's even learning about boats and the sea, because that's what you like. Do you mean to say that you can't see it for yourself?"

I said: "I can see it for myself all right. But I didn't think it was so plain to other people."

She laughed. "My dear," she said, "you give the game away a fresh way every five minutes—both of you."

She threw her cigarette away and came a little closer to me. "Malcolm," she said, "I think she'll make you a good wife, and I think that you'll be happy. Don't worry about what people will say. The family won't like it, but that doesn't matter two hoots. I've had my share of that, and I do know."

"The times are changing," I said absently. "The family have got to learn."

She nodded in the dusk. "It's not such good fun teaching them, though," she said ruefully. She looked up at me. "You must be gentle with her, Malcolm. Sometimes she won't do things the way you like them done, sometimes she'll say the wrong thing and make you look a fool. But she'll only do it once. You'll find she never makes the same mistake again. And she'll be worth a little trouble on your part."

It was so dark that I could hardly see her as she stood beside me. "It's good of you to talk like that," I said. "I'd like to feel she had a friend in you."

She said: "Oh, Malcolm! Give me another cigarette." And when I had supplied a light for it she said: "You knew that you could count on me. We've never spoken of it, but didn't you do the same for me, when I married Philip? You know, you were the only one of the relations who ever made him feel at home. And I know about the time at Courton, just after we became engaged."

I laughed. "I didn't cut much ice for you down there," I said. "I'm not a hunting man, and that ended it."

"I know they're difficult," she said. "But you went, and months afterwards I heard that you'd been there, and standing up for us. You don't think I've forgotten that, do you?"

"No, Lady Stenning," I said whimsically, "I don't."

She laughed. "Poor Philip! They put his garage rent up half-a-crown when he became a knight—he was *furious*!" And then more seriously she said: "Class doesn't matter half so much these days. I wouldn't change if I could have my time again, and you won't want to either. Let me know as soon as she's accepted you, and I'll come down and see her, and we'll go and see the family together."

We moved towards the house. "I'll hold you to that promise," I remarked.

Joan and Stenning left next morning, after an early breakfast. Mollie and I went with them to the field and pulled the Moth out from its barn, and stood and watched while Stenning started it up and went all round it with a watchful eye. He ran it up and throttled back; then we packed all their gear into it and Joan got in. Stenning drew me on one side.

"I'm free any time after three o'clock today," he said. "Unless I let you know I'll be down here the day after tomorrow, in the afternoon. If you want me before that, give me a ring at the office, and I'll be with you any time."

He got into the cockpit and took off. The Moth slipped up into the air over the hedge, turned over the harbour, and dwindled away into a cloudy sky.

The day was overcast and clouding up, with a slowly falling barometer. It looked as if the fine weather was over for the time.

I turned and slipped an arm through Mollie's, and we went back to the house. After my absence I had business waiting for me at the yard; I left her at the house to look after herself for the morning, and went down to my office to get things squared up.

I found that nothing at the office wanted squaring up so much as did my personal affairs. I sat in my office staring at the calendar and absently polishing the telephone with a duster, and wondered how I was going to propose to Mollie. I had treated this part of the business as a detail up till now, but now that I was up against it it didn't look so easy after all.

I did very little work that morning beyond opening my letters, and went up to the house with an uneasy mind. We lunched together and I asked her what she had been doing; it seemed that she had spent the morning in the garden and down by the sea. It had grown too cold to bathe with any comfort, and she was no cold water bather at the best of times. I noticed when we went into the library that there was a gap where Mortimer's *Naval History* had been. So she had had another look at that. I found later that she had taken it upstairs to pore over.

It was while we were sitting in the library over coffee that the telephone bell rang. I lifted the receiver, and it was Fedden, speaking from his house.

He said: "I've just had a call from the Yard. It seems that they've had news from Gloucester."

"Oh," I said. "What's that?"

"The man called Palmer called on Gordon this morning, and gave him Friday night, the day after tomorrow, for the landing of the next batch of arms. Unfortunately, the man got away."

"Friday night?" I said. "That's earlier than was expected."

"Only a day or two. But the unfortunate part is that the man Palmer got away. The police weren't quick enough."

I asked: "Does he know that information has been laid?"

"I don't know," said Fedden. "I imagine that he does."

"Gordon must have protection, then," I said. "What's happening about that?"

"That's all right—that has been thought of. Gordon is on his way back to the Yard this afternoon. I think that Norman may bring him down with him tomorrow—we shall want him for identification if we get the boat."

"You're trying for the boat?" I asked.

"Oh, certainly. I am arranging that side of it here."

"Do you want any help from me?" I asked. "I've got that tug."

He considered. "Look here," he said, "could you come down and have a chat?"

"I'll come down now," I said.

## CHAPTER 11

I FOUND Fedden very busy with the local police officials. He broke off for a few minutes to have a talk with me, but he could not add much to what he had told me on the telephone. So far as he knew, Gordon had left Gloucester and was now at Scotland Yard. He expected Norman to come down on the next day to assist in the preparations for the arrest of the boat. He accepted my offer of the tug, and I promised to see that she was properly equipped for a long trip. He was not sure in what way he would use her, and would consult with Norman about this.

He was up to his eyes in work, and so I didn't keep him long. I went on to my yard, and gave instructions for the tug to be filled up with fuel oil and fitted out for a sea passage. Normally her crew consisted of the skipper and the engineer; I didn't quite know what to do about these men, and told them I would see them the next afternoon.

I was getting more than a little worried over this affair. Stenning's warning was troubling me a bit, though Billy seemed to be in safety from his associates. I was more concerned over the safety of my own men, the crew of my tug. I had offered the vessel for police use; one could hardly have refused that help. At the time I had not thought about the crew, but obviously the vessel was no use without her crew. If she were used for the arrest of a gun runner I might be sending my skipper and my engineer into some danger if I sent them out with her. I had not thought of that.

By the time that I reached home I had decided that I'd ring up Stenning and see if he could come. I called him up in London, and got through to him in a few minutes. He was free all the next day, and I fixed up with him that he would come down by the early train. I didn't want him to fly down; it seemed to me that the less attention that was directed to this part of the world the better for us all. I arranged to have the car to meet the train.

Then I rang up the yard and gave instructions that *Irene* should be got up on the slip at once. That would provide a reason for his visit.

I went to look for Mollie then, and found her with old Robertson in the garden. She had been with him all the afternoon, grubbing about in an old pair of gloves in the herbaceous border; she loved her flowers. As I came near she straightened up, and came and showed me what she'd done while I had been away.

I walked back with her towards the house, and as we went I told her about Billy. I don't think she was very greatly interested. Throughout the whole of this affair the politics of it made very little difference to her; she was pleased to hear that Billy's association with an apparently illegal business was coming to an end, but she had no interest in the business itself. She was far more interested in my garden and the traffic of the harbour mouth. She told me that she had seen two steamers coming in.

We went in and had tea together in the library. I was still worried and absorbed in this affair, and talked to her about it for a time, but not with much success. She told me that old Robertson had been telling her about gannets, how they eat so much fish that they can't fly and go scuttering off along the water when you come near them in a boat. And so I gave it up, content to watch her and to see that she enjoyed herself.

In any case, I was inclined to doubt if anything was going to happen after all. The glass was going slowly down; from a long knowledge of our local conditions it looked to me as if we were in for a spell of continuous bad weather, probably with a gale or two from the south-east. That would be no weather for landing anything upon a beach; it might quite well happen that the whole affair would come to nothing.

But after tea she said a thing that startled me. "I don't know what they'll be thinking of me at the Palais," she said, a little ruefully. "I ought to have gone back there on Sunday, but I can't till Billy gets right, can I?"

I fumbled mentally for my immature proposal, and put it back again. "I hadn't thought of that," I said. "Will they make a lot of bother if you stay a few days more?"

"I don't know," she said. "Things are generally pretty slack about this time of year. Of course, they might turn nasty and get somebody else in my place if I stay away."

I nodded slowly. "You'd have to stay on here if they did that," I said timidly.

But she said quickly: "Oh, I couldn't do that," and I hadn't the wit to take her up and ask: "Why not?" She added: "I could always get in at Birmingham. Mr Evans said he'd take me on any time if I was out of a job. He's ever so nice."

"You needn't really worry about that," I said. "We can probably fix up something between us when the time comes, both for you and Billy."

She looked up at me. "It's ever so good of you to take this trouble. But we wouldn't want any money. Only just to get started in a job again."

I smiled. "Get you a job all right," I said. "Even if I had to buy a Palais to do it."

She laughed, and said: "Oh, you are silly." And then she said: "Just an introduction, like, to somebody you know, would do."

And so we left it. I went off to write letters feeling I had been a coward. She spent a little of the time before dinner cutting and arranging the flowers she had picked, and for the rest she sat in the model room where I was writing, pretending to read a book but really looking out over the Range at the darkening sea. "It's ever so different," she said. "It looks all cold and grey like, now."

"It's like that all the winter," I said absently, from my desk. "You wouldn't like it down here then."

She said: "I think I should. It must be lovely when it's rough."

The dressing gong went soon after that and we went up to change. I had a fire in the library again that night for it had grown quite cold; when I came down Sixpence was standing before it, stretching out her bare arms to the blaze. She wore the same blue and silver frock that she had worn before. She had said that it was an old one, but as I came into the room and saw her standing there before the fire it seemed to me that she was most beautiful. To me that night she was the loveliest girl I had ever seen in all my life.

I said: "What about a drink?"

We had our cocktails and went in to dine. I had had a fire lit in the dining-room and we had the candles lit; outside in the grey evening the dusk was falling early. That was an intimate dinner that we had that night, and a good one; Rogers had done us well. I ordered up a bottle of the Château Yquem, and we dined merrily; we had nothing to be particularly pleased about, and yet we were very happy in the dining-room. I close my eyes and I can see the gleaming silver and the glass, and see the blue and silver of her frock.

We went through into the library, and sat before the fire with our coffee and liqueur. I suggested that she played a little on the piano, but she wanted to sit by the fire, and so we sat there talking all the evening. She wanted to know about the world, the foreign countries that she'd only seen upon the films. She wanted to know about my early life, about my time

166

in the United States and about the Amazon affair. She wanted to know about dogs and horses, and hunting; she had never ridden a horse.

I sat and told her about all these things, watching the play of the firelight upon her face and neck, and the slim grace of her arms. I told her all about my early life, the things that I had done when I was a boy, the places I had seen, the places that I meant to see before I died. As I sat there talking to her I seemed to slip back through the years; I was no longer a man of middle age, stuck in his own small groove of shipbuilding. I talked to her as if I was a young man starting out on life, wanting to see and to experience all that life could give. She made me feel like that.

She said, a little wistfully: "It would be wonderful to do all that."

"My dear," I said, "I want you to."

It had slipped out before I knew what I was saying, so easy is it when one isn't bothering. She sat there very quiet in her chair, staring at the fire. I rose and took her hand and drew her to her feet beside me in the firelight while I said my piece.

"I want you to stay here with me," I said as gently as I could. "This last fortnight has been the happiest I've ever had. My dear, I don't want you to go back to dancing. It was lonely enough down here before you came; God knows it would be lonelier if you went away." I drew her into my arms. "I mean, I love you, Mollie. That's a funny sort of thing for an old man like me to say. But it's true, dear. I want you to stay here for good with me."

She rubbed her face against my dinner-jacket coat. "Oh, my dear," she said, quite quietly. That was all.

Ten minutes later she looked up at me, and said: "You mean we'd live down here together, like? Just you and me?"

I bent and kissed her. "That's right," I replied. "I want you to stay and marry me as soon as this is all cleared up."

She said: "To marry you. . . ." And then she drew herself upright in my arms, and said: "Malcolm dear, I want to sit down and talk sensible."

I let her go, puzzled, and we sat down again upon the chesterfield. She took one of my hands in hers, and held it. "I couldn't marry you," she said simply. "It wouldn't do."

There was a little silence after she said that; I was attempting to collect myself. I fell to stroking the hand that was holding my own.

"Tell me what's the matter," I inquired. "Why wouldn't it do? I think it would do very well myself."

She shook her head. "It wouldn't do," she repeated, staring into the fire. "I know."

She turned to me. "I don't want you to think that this is a surprise to me," she said quietly, "or that I didn't know you wanted me. You don't have to have been in a Palais to know that. And I have thought of what I'd do if you told me, and if you wanted me to marry you."

I smiled. "So have I," I said. "This isn't any snap decision on my part. I've been thinking of it for some time. I'd like you to know that."

She nodded slowly. "Please," she said, "I want to tell you what I think."

"Of course," I said.

She turned away and stared into the fire, but she did not withdraw her hand. "Lots of the girls I've been with married fellows who came in to dance," she said. "And some didn't, but just went away, and in a year or so they'd be back again, but in some other Palais. And lots of the ones that married, married people in quite good positions, earning a thousand a year, some of them. And it didn't come out right, not for them. Not ever that I know."

She glanced at me. "And I always thought that whatever happened to me, I'd not do that."

I stirred. "You mean that the families made things uncomfortable for them?"

She nodded. "That's right. They didn't seem to settle right, and then the men would get going after someone else. . . ." She smiled at me, a little sadly. "Not that I think that you'd go doing that on me." She turned away again towards the fire. "Some of them just didn't want anything more than the money, and they got that so they didn't mind. But it never came out really right—not like one'd want it to be."

She said: "In the books, and the things you hear about men being dragged down by marrying wrong—they do happen. And the girls that get dragged up by marrying . . . I believe it's happier not to be married at all, when it's like that."

We sat for a little time in silence after she said that. I was

168

wondering how I could best get over this difficulty, which seemed to be so real to her. But she went on:

"I wouldn't know what to say to your friends, Colonel Fedden and the rest, and they'd not know what to say to me. They'd think you'd acted awfully funny, marrying like that."

I drew her to me on the chesterfield. "My dear," I said, "it wouldn't be like you think. You've met the only member of my family I care two hoots about, and there's nothing like that about Joan and Stenning, is there? And, my dear, I want you for my wife."

She sat there by me in the firelight, stroking my hand and looking down on it. "I know you do," she said at last. "That's what makes it so difficult."

She raised her eyes to mine. "I love to think of you wanting me that way," she said simply. "And what I thought we might do, we might just try it for a bit, and see how it went." She glanced around. "I don't mean here. It wouldn't do, with all your servants and that. But I thought we could go away somewhere for a month or two, where they didn't know you. . . .

"We could go to Torquay," she said hopefully, "for a sort of holiday together, like." She loved that place. She eyed me doubtfully. "Would you like that?"

I wondered absently if King Cophetua had had this sort of thing, and if so, what he did about it. I turned to her and smiled. "We'll go to Torquay for our honeymoon," I said, "or for the start of it. But it's going to be a proper honeymoon for us—no funny business." I thought about it for a minute. "I've never taken girls away for holidays, and I'm too old to learn. You can't teach an old dog new tricks."

She laughed. "I believe you'd learn that one all right," she said.

I shook my head. "Not me—you should start young for that. My dear, that isn't what I want at all. I want you to marry me in church, and be my wife."

She stared into the fire. "I don't know what to say."

We sat on like that for a long time, talking in little quiet sentences, with great pauses in between. She was distressed that I had turned down her solution to the difficulty, but not, I think, surprised. I could not bring her to agree to marry me. Perhaps if I had been rough with her I might have succeeded, but I couldn't do that. Each time I tried we came upon the same brick wall.

"Colonel Fedden would think you'd acted awfully funny, marrying like that." I cursed Fedden heartily that night. To her he represented all the old conservatism of my family. Rather curiously, she said something once about the pictures in the dining-room. I think she had been talking to the servants, or old Robertson: she knew a lot about my family.

We sat there for an hour, or longer it may be, but we got no further. There was something in her attitude which made me curiously humble in my arguments; I could not bully her with any he-man stuff. She had no other thought than for my interest. She was so conscious of the difference in our up-bringing, so certain that the marriage wouldn't do me any good. I could not get her to see my point of view. I could not make her see that for years I have had no friends, that I have lived so much alone that class means very little to me now. It's different when you're young and live in a clique of people of your own sort; you live narrow then. But when you get to my age and live by yourself, it's different. When you're as lonely as I've been you get to value friends for what they are; you get a little broader minded than you used to be.

At last:

"Let's have a cup of tea," I said, and rang the bell for Rogers.

She murmured composedly that that would be lovely. She was not upset, or noticeably so. Girls are so much stronger than men are in many ways; that night she sat and talked about this quietly, restrained. And her case was quite clear. She would not bind me with a marriage—that was how she looked at it—till we had lived together for a time.

"People don't see things right when they're in love," she said, a little sadly. "I know."

Rogers brought the tea, and we sat and drank it as if this evening had been ordinary. I could see no way out of this impasse except with time; in a few days I thought perhaps she'd change her mind, and I could bring her to my point of view. And so when we had drunk our tea I raised her to her feet, and said:

"My dear, I'm not going to worry you, or nag about this any more. Let's go to bed—and I mean go to bed alone, too." She smiled at that. "We'll argue this out later, when this other thing's all straightened up. But till then, I want you to know that I love you. That . . . that's all."

She took my hand and kissed the back of it. "I don't know what to say . . ." she said at last, very softly. And so we stood like that together for a minute till I sent her up to bed.

Next morning I reviewed the situation as I dressed. Stenning was coming down, and would be with me by the afternoon. By the afternoon I expected to hear something of Norman and Billy; I rang up Fedden after breakfast, and found that he did not know when they were likely to arrive. He thought not till nightfall perhaps. He had all arrangements in hand, so that there was plenty of time.

As regards Mollie, there was nothing I could do till this thing was cleared up. I did not think she would go back up North; we had this common ground, at any rate, that it was better for us both to be together. I thought that if I left things for a day or two till the immediate rush of this affair was over it would give her time to think about it, and I hoped that then I should be able to persuade her to my point of view.

If not—well, I should have to come to hers. At the end of our honeymoon, I thought, she'd probably agree to marry me. . . .

I went down to the yard that day and took Mollie with me in the car. They were getting *Irene* up on the patent slip when I got there; we stood and watched them till the vessel slowly slid up out of the water on the traveller. Mollie was amazed.

"She's ever such a size underneath the water, isn't she?" she remarked. "You'd never think!"

I gave instructions for them to start on scraping her; there was nothing the matter with her seams. Then I put Sixpence in a pram and she went paddling around the harbour, while I went into the office and went through my letters; an hour later I went round the yard and had a look at the *Sweet Anna*'s rudder with old Sammy Gore. His pintlets were all right, to his regret I think, but he succeeded in wheedling a lot of unnecessary running gear out of me, and a new stove for the galley.

That took me all the morning. Coming off on to the quay I looked about for Sixpence, and saw the pram alongside *Runagate*. I took the quay punt and went off to her; she put her head up from the forecastle hatch as I came up alongside. "I've been looking at the boat," she informed me. "It is funny in this little cooking place."

I dropped down through the hatch beside her in the forecastle. "There's plenty of room to cook sitting down," I said. "And anyway, you can reach everything."

She stared round. "It's sort of cosy," she remarked at last. "I never knew ships were like this inside." She stared through at the bulkheads of the saloon. "All this polished wood. . . ."

We went up through the forehatch and sat upon the bitts for a few minutes, smoking a cigarette. "It's ever so lovely here," she said at last. "The ships, and things."

I blew a cloud, and laughed at her. "You'd better stay here, then," I said. "It's up to you!"

She laughed with me. "You must think me ever so soft," she said.

I shook my head. "I don't."

She said: "Don't let's talk about it now." And a little later on she said: "It would be lovely to live here, with the ships and the seabirds, and all." She turned to me: "Do you know, I feel as if I'd lived here all my life, and my father and mother and all before. Just as if I'd been brought up here. . . ." She sat there staring up the river. "As if I knew what was up there, round the bend, with the river and the sea-shore in the middle of the land, like."

I nodded slowly. "I expect you do," I said absently. I knew just what she meant. Where a long estuary runs into the land, an estuary with a rocky bottom, you do get just what she had spoken of—the sea-shore in the middle of the land. Little sandy beaches all among the hayfields and the woods. She knew it all, and yet I had not taken her up there.

We went ashore and got into the car, and drove up to the house. And as we went indoors she said to me:

"Is Lady Stenning coming down this afternoon?"

I shook my head. "Just Philip. Why?"

She turned away. "I think I'd like to have a talk with her," she said quietly. "She was ever so nice to me."

I took her hand and smiled at her. "My dear," I said, "don't worry about it now. Leave it for a couple of days till this other thing has quieted down, and then we'll have a talk about it, and you can see her and hear what she has to say."

"All right," she said, "if that's the best."

I rang up Fedden after lunch and had a talk with him. He told me that Norman was coming down that night with Gordon, in readiness for the events of the following day. He said that they would not arrive till after dark—he thought about eleven o'clock at night. There were to be considerable movements of police in preparation for the landing, and it had been arranged that these movements should take place at night, to obviate the risk of a leakage of information. He asked if Gordon might remain in my house for the time being. He suggested that he should be brought straight there that night.

I said that that would be agreeable to me, and I mentioned to him that Stenning was coming down. I asked him what he wanted done about the tug.

He replied that he could not say definitely what the plans would be till he had had a talk with Norman. Could we arrange about the tug that night, after Norman came?

I frowned. "You mean tonight—after eleven o'clock?"

He said that they would probably be working all night. He had been up most of the previous night, and was going to snatch a little sleep after tea, if possible.

"All right," I said. "You'd better come up here with him when you send Gordon. You'd better all come up, and talk about it here. You've got to bring up Gordon, anyway."

"That's very good of you," he said.

"Not at all. I'll expect you about half-past eleven, or some time like that?"

He agreed that that would be about the time, and I rang off.

I remember glancing at the barograph as I set down the telephone. It had gone down again and this time rather sharply: in the Range an on-shore wind was getting up.

Stenning arrived a little later in the afternoon, and I took him down to see his vessel on the slip. That was the ostensible purpose of his visit, and I thought it was as well that it should be carried out in full. As we pottered about the yard I told him all that had been going on; I found him intensely interested. He was worried that I had asked the police up to my house, that I had offered to take in Gordon. I expostulated with him over that, and he listened patiently to what I had to say.

"I see your point," he said at last. "It's probably as well to have Gordon. But if the police have got to have a meeting they should have it in their own place. I don't see that you want them in your house particularly."

We went up to the house and dined with Mollie, changing into dinner jackets. She had been walking in the town that afternoon while we had been away, looking at the shops and exploring the streets and quays. She was especially intrigued by a crew of cadets that she had seen down on the water front, sailing a Navy cutter. She thought they looked ever such nice boys. . . .

And afterwards she sang to us. We sat in the darkened library, Stenning in a chair beside the fire, and Mollie at the piano in a little pool of light. I sat over by her as she played and sang the lyrics that she knew, the dance songs that were folk tunes of the young. We made no pretence. It must have been quite obvious to Stenning that we were deeply in love; he sat apart and puffed at his cigar, and took but little notice of us at the other end of the room. Joan had probably been talking to him and he accepted us for what we may have been —a pair of silly fools behaving as if this had been our first calf love.

Presently she was tired of singing, and we went over to him by the fire. I ordered the whisky and her tea, and we sat drinking this together, chatting of ships and of the flights that he had made, and ventures that he hoped to make. We sat there for a long time talking in that way, till at last we heard a car, and it was Fedden and his crowd.

I took them into the dining-room, as being more suitable for the meeting that we had to hold. I had had a few sandwiches and whisky placed upon the table, and a writing pad. The room was brightly lit. The curtains were drawn over the east window looking out over the harbour mouth, but the alcove with the oriel north window was uncurtained. That window looks out on to the north lawn.

There was Fedden and Norman and a police superintendent that they had brought with them, Gordon, and Mollie, and myself, and Stenning. We started the proceedings with a drink, standing beside the table before sitting down. I was with Stenning and Norman, talking to Fedden; Mollie and her brother were a little way apart.

Till Norman put his glass down, and remarked: "I think we'd better get to work."

## CHAPTER 12

THAT finishes the story that I set out to write when I began this book. I started on it so that I could keep the memory of what were very happy days for me; by writing so far I have satisfied myself, and that is all that I set out to do. There is nothing more that I would wish to tell or to remember. If I go on, it is because a job once started should be finished off; I would not leave the tag end of this story hanging in mid-air. In writing what remains I shall try to stick to facts and let the fancy go. Cold facts should not be difficult to put down.

Perhaps cold facts are harder than I thought. I have sat for a long time, and I am at a loss to convey in writing the great suddenness and violence of the shots. For they shot at us from the garden with an automatic gun, shot from the darkness into the bright radiance of the lighted room. We were so unprepared, so stupefied, when it began.

We were in the dining-room, all standing up and about to move forward to sit down round the table. Mollie and her brother were standing a little way apart from the rest of us, to our right as we stood facing the north window. It came so very suddenly. The first thing I can remember was the crash of broken glass, and the sharp clamour of the gun outside. In the frozen silence of the moment, broken only by the gun, I heard the bullets hit.

Eighteen bullets came into the room, not more than that, but in five seconds two of us were dying on the floor. I think the first shots missed. There was a low cry from Mollie as her brother threw her to the ground, and a sort of gasping as he spun around, tottering above her with the bullets pumping into him. Then as he fell they traversed; Stenning and I were down behind the table by that time, and Fedden went down with a bullet in the neck. The Superintendent was too slow, and fell, shot cleanly through the heart. A shot ripped Norman's sleeve, but he got down unhurt.

In the infinite, stunned silence when the firing stopped, I remember Stenning said:

"Get these damned lights out!" But the switches were high up upon the wall, and nobody was fool enough to stand upright to turn them off. I crawled across towards Mollie, and as I went I saw Norman wriggle out through the service door into the kitchen quarters, and I saw Stenning creeping forward by the wall towards the broken window. I got to her and found her conscious on the floor, her eyes filled with pain. Her left shoulder was a mass of blood. "My dear," I whispered, "is this all?"

She nodded slightly. "I do feel so sick." She had gone very white. "But it's all right. Please, see after Billy".

I turned and bent over him without much hope, for I had seen men fall that way before. And while I was examining him the door moved open and the lights went out; Norman had come in from the back and thrust his hand through, well protected by the door.

The room was very dark. A little light came filtering through the shattered window, and a little breeze came into the room; outside, the wind was strong. Billy was dead. I laid the body down and crawled towards the other two. Fedden was unconscious and bleeding a good bit from the neck wound; I found the Superintendent dead.

A shadow darkened the window and I looked up in alarm, but it was Stenning getting out into the garden. In the hall I heard Norman's voice upon the telephone, speaking quite quietly. "I want nine one, please—nine one. The police station. Will you hurry it? Yes."

I could not but admire the courage of the man. He was audible all over the house, which was in complete darkness; he had pulled out the master switch. He could not have known what enemy was lurking within hearing; he sat there, tied to the telephone, a sitting shot for anyone who cared to shoot at him. In a minute I heard him speaking to the police station. Crouching over Mollie in the darkness, I knew that help was on the way.

I got up and moved out of the door to him, saying as I went in the darkness: "It's Stevenson. Ring up eight two. That's Dr Dixon. Tell him to come here, and have the fire brigade ambulance brought up."

I heard him start that call and ran upstairs to get some shirts for bandages. And as I came down to the hall again someone else came from the dining-room. It was Stenning, and he said:

"I saw them go. There were two of them, carrying one gun, on the north lawn. They went down through the fuzzy to your bathing beach. They've gone right down. You can put the lights on now."

Norman said quickly: "Which way is that? There's landing for a boat?"

Outside, the wind howled dolefully; it was getting up in earnest. Stenning nodded. "You can get a boat in there, but it's a rotten night for it."

Norman hesitated for a moment. "Get down to the beginning of the path and watch they don't come up again," he said. "I'll join you when we get the men up here."

He moved away and suddenly the lights came on again. Stenning went out into the night. I went through into the dining-room and found Norman bending critically over Fedden. "Give me a pad here, quick," he said. "Have a look at the girl."

I stooped by Mollie and began to strip her shoulder. The bullet had gone through, breaking her shoulderblade; it was a clean wound in front and torn and ragged at the back. I remember that I thanked my stars that it was not more serious, and wondered, as I put a pad on it, whether or not old Fedden would pull through. It would be terrible if he died, I thought.

Mollie was quite awake, and in some pain. I moved her as little as I could, but I could not help hurting her a good deal. And when I had finished she whispered: "Please, Commander Stevenson. Is Billy dead?"

I remember that I thanked my stars I had not got to tell her that. "My dear," I said, "I'm afraid so."

She said no more, but lay there crying quietly. I glanced across at Norman working over Fedden, and asked him if he wanted help. He said he was all right, and where were those infernal police? And so I sat there holding her uninjured hand among the ruins of my blood-soaked dining-room, wiping away the tears that trickled from her eyes and doing what I could to comfort her.

And presently the room was full of people standing over

us, Dixon, alert and competent, with a fellow from the fire brigade, and very many police. "Have a look at Fedden first," I said. "He's bad."

Then there were stretchers and a clearing of the room; Norman had gone and there was a policeman at the door. And after what seemed many ages Dixon came across to me and said: "I think he'll do all right. Now for the young lady." And he stooped over her, undoing all my pads with his deft hands and talking in his best professional manner—he made a quick inspection—"That's not very bad," in cheerful manner, and began bandaging again with proper things. Finally he gave her a morphia injection, and they got her on to a stretcher and went out to the car. I followed it, and saw it move away.

Dixon lingered for a moment before following in his own car. "Fedden is serious, I'm afraid," he said. "I don't say critical, but serious. The girl is not so bad."

Freed from anxiety I felt the anger rising in me in a slow, cold tide. "This girl," I said bluntly. "She's all I've got. Ought I to stay near her?"

He looked at me curiously. "I don't think she's in any danger," he remarked; "although, of course, there'll be some pain. There will probably be a disability in some degree, more or less permanent. Why—are you thinking of going away?"

"I don't know," I said slowly. "I only know that two men have been murdered in my house tonight."

He turned briskly to the door. "The girl should be all right if things go normally," he said. "I am more concerned for Fedden than for her."

He went off in his car to follow up the ambulance, a fine, competent fellow and a man that one could trust. I turned back to the hall, and there was Norman with Stenning by his side, and a police official of some sort.

Stenning said: "They've got away. They've got a vessel in the Range. They went out in a dinghy, sculling." He said that a rift in the clouds had shown them that much from the top of the cliff.

Norman said grimly: "They've arrived a day before their time—and they were warned. That fellow Palmer has been wise to all that we've been doing here." He turned. "I must get off. We'll warn the ports all up and down the Channel. They can't get away."

"Don't talk such nonsense," I said angrily. "They can land anywhere they like. They aren't in charge of the *Olympic.*"

He turned on me. "What would you do, then?"

I laughed unpleasantly. "Me? I'm going for a sail in my tug." Outside, the wind howled noisily around the house; it was rising to a full gale. "It's a nice night for a pleasure trip," I said sarcastically.

"You'll never find them in the darkness, on a night like this," he replied. "They may be anywhere at sea."

"You bloody fool," I said. "What wind is it?"

Stenning answered: "It's about south-east."

I went on: "They're in a sailing vessel, possibly with an auxiliary. That's all the evidence. Where can they go to get away from here? They can't beat up against a gale like this. Even with an auxiliary they'll not lie seven points from the wind. God, man, you know that!"

"That's right," said Stenning. "I see what you're getting at."

Norman looked from one to the other. "I don't understand," he said.

"Oh, come in here," I said impatiently. I marched him into the model room and ripped a chart out of the drawer and laid it on the drawing board. Then with pencil and parallel rule I drew quick lines. "There's the wind. There's the most southerly course that he can lie, going east. He gets embayed with Portland—he can't help but go ashore if he goes that way, somewhere near Bridport. You'd better watch the coast from here to Portland, just in case he's a damn fool."

I paused, and drew rapidly. "That's the course that he can lie going west. He should be able just to scrape around the Start. Then he must bear up for the Lizard if he's going to get away. He can lie to in the Irish Sea till this blows out, and then go where he wants." I took a quick glance at the barograph, and at the isobar chart of the day before. "This wind may last for thirty hours or more. It'll move into the south a point or two at dawn; he'll have to keep close hauled for the Lizard. He'll have all that he can do to make it. You want to watch the coast from here down to Penzance."

Norman said: "You mean that you'd go westwards in the tug?"

I packed the chart and barometric chart together, and put in a rule, a pencil and protractor. "I do," I said. "He can no more change his road than if he had a motor car. I shall come up on him some time in the forenoon within sight of the Eddystone."

"I see," said Norman thoughtfully. "What then? Can you board him?"

I shook my head. "Not in this sea," I said. "He's armed, too. I can only hang on to him, and trust you to get in touch with me before nightfall. I shall have a signal lamp, but no wireless."

I turned to him. "Give me a sergeant and a constable. I think that I can find him and hang on to him, and I think you'll find us tomorrow afternoon between the Lizard and the Start, a bit towards the Lizard. I'll signal the Eddystone if I get near enough. Warn them."

"All right," he said at last. "I think you'd better go. Be careful, though. I'll let you have a sergeant and a man."

I turned to Stenning. "Will you come? I'll want a hand from time to time, I fancy, on a night like this."

There was no time to be lost. I went to the telephone and rang up the night watchman at the yard, and told him to go along and warn the tug's engineer that we were putting out in half an hour. He was to rouse him at his house, and tell him to bring down what food he had; we should be out all night and the next day. Then I went up with Stenning to my room and changed into sea-going kit. Coming down I found my sergeant and his constable waiting in the hall; the sergeant was a stranger to me, but I had seen the constable about the town from time to time. Neither of them had any arms, and I did not think we would need any. Our only function could be to find our quarry and hold on, mark where he went.

Then to the larder to collect what food there was, and to the stables in the rainy bluster of the rising gale. It was about half-past one when we were in the Bentley on our way down to the yard.

It was a filthy night. I drove in a cold, numbed sort of way. I do not think I was particularly excited: I only remember a slowly growing anger that was turning to cold hatred of the people who had done this violence in my house. I was not especially sorry for the victims, that I can remember, for the

Superintendent or for Billy or for Fedden. All these were in the game and subject to its chances. But as I drove down to the quay I think I knew that I was going to kill the people who had shot at Mollie, if God gave me strength.

The engineer was waiting for us at the tug; he had been quick enough. I swung out of the car upon the quay and turned to him. "Morning, Fleming. We're putting out at once." I turned to Stenning. "Tell him what it's about, and get on board and get her started up." Then to the policeman: "Give a hand, and get that stuff aboard." And I went down into the little cuddy of the tug, and pinned the chart down on the table, and laid off our course to clear the Start.

Behind the bulkhead a great heave and rumble told me that the port engine was alive. I went on deck and forward to the wheelhouse; as I passed the engine hatch I stopped and peered down. Stenning was there with Fleming, a lighted blowlamp in his hand; they were labouring to get the starboard engine under way. I went forward and uncast the lashing from the wheel and stripped the cover from the binnacle, lighted the binnacle light and saw that it was filled with oil. Then a low increase in the rumble told me that the starboard engine was alive; I rang Stand By and Stenning rang it back to me. Then he appeared on deck.

I leaned from the wheelhouse. "Cast off your stern rope now," I called; Stenning jumped aft and presently I heard him cry: "All gone!" The bow ropes were cast off and I rang Slow Ahead; the vessel stirred and slid quietly from the wharf into the main stream of the tide.

I worked her up to full speed as we went down the harbour, while Stenning and the police made all fast upon deck. I called up Stenning to the house and warned him to get everything secure and battened down, but Stenning knew as well as I did what we should find beyond the Range. He got her pretty well squared up, showed the police the cuddy and put them down there, and came up to the house with me.

For a summer gale it was a devil, that night. Out in the Range the wind was straight onshore, blowing the tops off the short waves and crashing them against the wheelhouse as we steered. It was pitch dark and difficult to see more than the bows. I held on till we took one green over the bows and Stenning stirred beside me, but he didn't speak. Then we took another rather worse; I put my hand down to the telegraph and rang Half Speed.

She took the sea more easily that way, and we went out to the open, rolling and pitching with a short, uneasy motion that was worse than anything I can remember in that way. She is rather an unusually short boat, with a good wide beam and little draught; in that heavy sea she got a screwing action on her every now and then that I would back to turn the strongest stomach up. Throughout that night and the next day we were all sick. The policemen were the worst; they lay for the majority of the time in coma in the cuddy, which got in a filthy state. Fleming stuck it like a man, coming up now and then out of his engine-room to vomit on the sea-swept deck. Stenning and I stuck by the wheel and did our stuff, soaked to the skin and trembling with cold, out of the lee-side window of the house. The vessel was a wonder in a seaway; when we slowed down she hardly took a drop on board, but I have never sailed in anything that had a motion like she had.

I took her out to give a wide berth of the land that night. When I judged Downend to be well abeam I turned and brought the sea on to her quarter, and set her on a course to pass some three miles off the Start. That took me well clear of the Skerries Bank and all the broken water that we should find there; whatever our quarry in the bawley might be going through, I had no fancy to get into any further trouble than we could avoid. The turn gave her a fresh set of motions in the wind-swept, screwing waves, and set us vomiting again.

All night we carried on like that, cold and alert, eating a little now and then and vomiting it up again. Dawn found us off Bolt Head with Salcombe on the beam, and on a straight course from the Lizard to the Start. As I expected, with the dawn the wind went round a bit; I judged that with the wind we had, about Force 8, their vessel would have all that she could do to lie the course, even assuming that they had a good big engine holding her nose up to the wind. So far as I could see, that course would take us four miles south of the Eddy-stone lighthouse.

We went rolling and screwing on our way. At seven o'clock I gave the wheel to Stenning and went aft. In the engine-room Fleming, white as a sheet, was trying to brew tea in the in-cessant motion of the ship; he smiled as I came down and said that he was quite all right, and wanted no relief. If he could make a drop of tea he would bring it up to the wheelhouse. I went aft to the cuddy and found both policemen on the floor, sunk in a sort of coma after vomiting. They were in a bad way and no good to us at all; I left them there, and went back forward to the house carefully, on the soaked and heaving deck. In general the visibility that morning was about two miles.

At about half-past eight, in a short lull between the squalls, I saw the vessel dead ahead.

She was about two miles away, close hauled and shrouded in the mist, lying sensibly the same course as ourselves. I judged her to be of about twenty tons; she had a trysail set and heavily reefed down. I only saw her for a minute or so; Stenning saw her first. Then she was covered in a rain squall, but we knew that we were on her track.

I judged that we were then about five miles south-east of the Eddystone. I was unwilling to close with the vessel to a range of less than half a mile; I had no wish to have a hail of machine-gun bullets flying at us through the scud, and that was pretty certainly what we should get if we went close. I carried on our course, and twenty minutes later, when the squall passed by, we saw her closer, little more than a mile off.

I had a good view of her then. She was a bawley, and I saw three men. They were crouched in a heap on deck about the stern; if she had any cockpit it was a shallow one. As I tried to keep her in the dancing field of my binoculars I got a strong impression of glasses staring back at me. Then the rain came again, and blotted her from view.

I held a discussion on her then, bawling to Stenning in the clamour of the gale. We decided to lie off and head a little to the north, aiming to pass within signal distance of the Eddystone and to pass the bawley some two miles to the north. Then we would lie to and intercept her course. I had in the back of my mind that we might head her off and make her bear away, and once she ran down wind I knew that she would never round the Lizard till the wind went down. We should have got her then imprisoned in the Bay, and we could take her when we wished.

I altered course more to the north. We saw her once for a few moments when she was abeam, and they probably saw us; a quarter of an hour later we picked up the Eddystone.

Stenning is better with the signal lamp than I, and he went aft to rig it in the cuddy.

I sent a short message for them to transmit to Norman, saying we were in touch, and got a short acknowledgment from that windswept tower. I did not dare to hang about for a reply but got the vessel on her course again, a course that would bring us out some three miles ahead of the bawley, by my figuring. We held on this one till about twelve o'clock, and then hove to upon the windswept waste to wait until the vessel came. I did not keep stationary, but slowly patrolled a two-mile line at right angles to her course.

We waited for two hours on that sickening, squalid beat, cold and wretched and soaked through to the skin. Fleming contrived to make soup and brought it up to us with sea biscuits to eat with it; I kept mine for an hour or two and felt the better for it, but Stenning was not so fortunate. We sent Fleming aft to do what he could for the policemen. He took them aft something to eat, but I don't know that it did them any good to speak of. Stenning and I stayed in the wheel-house taking turns at the helm and on the watch, and at about ten minutes to two we saw the bawley again.

She was coming up to us; we lay dead in her course. We saw her in a lull between the squalls, perhaps two miles away. I put the tug to slow and waited in her path; the rain came down again and blotted her from view. We lay there waiting, straining our wet eyes into the scud. In half an hour that squall let up a bit and visibility improved; we stared around, but she was nowhere to be seen. By all the rules she should have been somewhere close to us by then if she had held on to her course.

Then Stenning picked her up. She had squared right away and she was running to the north, making towards Fowey perhaps, or Looe. I turned to Stenning and grinned sourly, and Stenning grinned at me. "Turned him," I shouted, and he nodded back.

If the wind held we had him then. Already he was too far down the wind to hope to beat up round the Lizard, unless he had the luck of a good shift into the east. Rather than sail up close to us he had chosen to take his chance of dodging us inshore; I knew then that we were hounds, and we could put him where we liked. I turned the vessel and we wallowed after him in that unpleasant sea, the aft cabin battened down upon the police and trailing a little oil upon the water as we went to still the combers that slid under us. It was bad country, but the hounds were running heads up by that time.

I gave the wheel to Stenning and became immersed in mental calculations of the tides. I did not think that he would try to land. His object must be to attempt to put us off, to keep out of our way till night fall came, when he would try to beat away around the Lizard into safety. He had about seven hours of daylight left to do it in.

We came up on him and followed perhaps three miles away. Visibility improved throughout the afternoon; the rain got less, but there was no diminution in the wind. I kept as far from him as possible while keeping him in view; I meant that he should still feel free to dodge about. I knew that while he thought that he was free I could manœuvre him to where I wanted him to be.

He held on for the land, and by about three-thirty he was close inshore, between Fowey and Looe. He turned eastwards then as if to make Rame Head and Plymouth.

Stenning turned to me. "Just dodging about up and down the coast till dark," he shouted.

I nodded, and swung the vessel on a course for Plymouth that would bring us out ahead of him. "Slip downstairs and see what time high water is at Dover," I said to him.

He stared at me in astonishment, but went, and I stayed at the wheel, brooding over the murder in my house.

Stenning came back. "High water at Dover eleven-eighteen," he said.

I nodded. "Say five-thirty here." He nodded his assent, puzzled, and I glanced at my watch. Then after a little thought I turned the vessel a point more to the east; it would be time enough if our friend turned west again at four-fifteen.

And at four-twenty he did so. We were right in his path then and some three miles ahead of him, just off Rame Head. He put his vessel right around, and headed back the way that he had come; I laughed, and turned also, and followed him, heading four points to seaward of his course to convoy him along the coast again. "Dodging about," said Stenning. He glanced at me uneasily. "They'll get away as it gets dark, if someone doesn't come and give a hand."

I twisted my cracked lips into a smile. "Don't worry," I replied. "They'll all be dead by dark."

"What do you mean?" he asked, startled.

"Just that," I said, and fell to brooding over the doings of the night again.

He stared at me, but said no more, and we went wallowing upon our course in the late afternoon. "He's got to turn once more," I said presently. "Just once. Slip down and get the chart that covers Dodman and the Shackles, will you?"

He brought it, and I handed him the wheel and fell to studying the chart. The Dodman point lies between Fowey and Falmouth, and the Shackles Reef lies flung out from it like a scythe, eight cables long. The tide runs in a race around those rocks in the first hours of the ebb, a full two and a half knots. I studied the wind. I had gone back a point into the east; I turned to the rain-sodden chart and set the point where our good friend should turn again.

At five o'clock I altered course, and made as if to steer for Looe. That made me cross behind him, not much nearer than two miles, and gave him encouragement to carry on.

And then I started to close up. I followed in his wake along the coast till it was evident that he could lie the Dodman and get down to Falmouth; then I went out to sea and passed him, and lay to by the Thresher Rock that marks the seaward limit of the Shackles, and is buoyed. Through the blown scud the clamour of the bell came mournfully to us over the waves; in the blown drifts of rain we saw the bawley labouring to us. "This is the end of it," I said to Stenning; "if he turns. You'd better get those policemen up on deck for them to see."

Over a mile away we saw the bawley come up to the wind shiver in irons for a moment, and lay off on the other tack. "He's going back along the coast again," cried Stenning. "What do you mean by saying it's the end?"

I smiled against the beating of the gale. "He's got a three-knot tide now setting him upon the Shackles. No vessel ever built could beat against that in this wind. In half an hour he'll be ashore. Look at it for yourself."

He grasped the chart and stood there bending over it. "Good God!" he said. "He's embayed already, and he doesn't know it!"

"That's right," I said.

He raised his head and stood there staring at me. "You put him there."

I met his stare. "Yes," I replied, "I put him there. You'd better go and get those policemen up on deck."

He turned and went away aft, and I stood there watching the fading evening light. It was ten minutes before they realised the hole that they were in. Then they shook out two reefs and tried to drive her out in little tacks as their sea room got less and less.

At seven-twenty-five I closed right up and drifted down a lifebuoy to them, carrying a light line. I had no faith that anything that we could do would help them then, but it would please the coroner. The line broke when they got the buoy, before they could pull in the hawser that I had laid out.

At seven-forty-five she struck, about three cables from the land. I had the tug about a cable's length away; we lay there watching, helpless to do more than we had done. The mast fell as she struck, and she was swept at once by every wave. She went to pieces as we watched; I saw no sign of any men.

As it grew dark I drew away, and headed up for Plymouth. Off Rame Head, carrying a high sea on the quarter, we were badly pooped; the tug broached to and we were in a nasty mess. God sent us respite for a minute and a half, so that by the time the next one came we had things straightened up, and we passed the breakwater with the starboard engine dead and a foot of water sluicing in the engine-room. It was midnight when we anchored in the Cattewater.


CHAPTER 13

WE WERE dead tired when the anchor dropped. Stenning came stumbling aft down from the bows, walking like a drunken man and muttering about a riding light. I clambered stiffly from the wheelhouse and looked round; in the Cattewater it seemed immensely calm and quiet, and the ship was still. Fleming came up and sat upon his engine hatch, and for a few minutes we stood there together, watching the lights from the town reflected on the rippled, oily sea. We had been out for little more than twenty hours, but we were very, very tired. It was the seasickness that did it, I suppose—that and the short, uneasy motion of the tug, that gave no rest.

At last I stirred. "Got to go on shore," I muttered. I turned to Stenning: "See if you can get Mount Batten or the Citadel with that signal lamp, and ask them to send a boat, or have one sent. Say that it's urgent. I'm going aft to turn those policemen out."

I went down to the cuddy. They were sprawling on the bench seats, fast asleep; I stood there swaying in the fœtid, reeking air, fumbling to light the lamp that hangs upon the bulkhead. They must have had a rotten time of it. Most of the time they had been battened down below; I had not felt that I could trust them upon deck in the conditions we had had, and it had been impossible to keep the cuddy open in that sea. They lay on the benches sleeping, exhausted and ill. I bent over the sergeant and shook him into wakefulness.

"Wake your man and come on deck," I said. "We're anchored in the Cattewater—at Plymouth. It's about one o'clock, or getting on that way. We're going ashore in a few minutes now."

I went on deck again, glad to get out of the place, and found Stenning busy at the signal lamp. He had got a reply from the Mount Batten seaplane station, and he was talking to them in quick flashes of Morse code. At last he stood up and turned to me:

"I think they're sending out a launch."

We stood and waited in the cold, dark night, interminably. From the shore we heard the whistling of trains and the long clank of shunting in the goods yard. The police came up and joined us by the engine-room, walking unsteadily upon the deck. At last we heard the motor of the launch; it came alongside with a sergeant in charge, and we persuaded it to take us to the Citadel.

It was striking one o'clock when we got on shore. The policemen led the way, and Stenning and I followed in their wake, down the long, empty streets towards the police station.

They knew about us there, but they had heard nothing of the wreck out at the Shackles. Nobody had seen that vessel go on shore. "They went on the Shackles in trying to get away from us," I said. The police confirmed what I said, and that tale went, and has done till this day.

They got through on the telephone to Dartmouth and I spoke a little to Norman at the police station there. I told him briefly my version of what had occurred; that we had been sticking to their heels and waiting till some vessel came to help, and that in trying to shake off our pursuit they had gone ashore. I said that we had done everything that could be done, which was as true as made no matter. And then I said that I was coming back to Dartmouth as soon as I could get a car.

I asked how Mollie and Fedden were getting on. He said: "Both going on quite all right, I believe. To tell the truth, I've not had time to bother about them for the last few hours. That was at about six o'clock when I heard last. Fedden was the one they were concerned about—the shock, you know. The girl was getting on quite well."

I told him that I was going to try and get a car, and rang off. There was some business then with the police; the whole coast had to be patrolled for bodies or other evidence that might be washed ashore for fifteen miles each side of the Dodman, and it was evidently necessary that the watchers should be out by dawn. That took a bit of arranging, and it was nearly three o'clock when Stenning and I and the two policemen bundled sleepily into the car that was to drive us home.

That run seemed interminable. I do it in forty minutes in the Bentley; in that car it took an hour and a half. It was cold, too. By the time we crawled up the last hill to my house it was full dawn; Stenning and I got out on the gravel in front of my house and stared at each other in the clear, fresh morning light. It was about thirty hours since we had left the house.

"Bath," said Stenning sourly. "God, you want a shave."

We went into the house and he went on upstairs. I paused for a minute, and sat down to the telephone. I rang up the nursing home—the same that I had visited from time to time. The matron answered me.

"Commander Stevenson this end," I said. "I rang up to inquire how Colonel Fedden and Miss Gordon were getting on. I've just got back."

She said: "Oh, Colonel Fedden's through the worst of it.

We were a little worried this afternoon; the shock, you know. He's not a young man, is he? And it does tell, for all that he keeps himself so fit. But I think that's all over. He's having a lovely sleep now. I really don't think you need worry about him at all, Commander."

"That's fine," I said. "What about Miss Gordon?"

There was a momentary pause, and then she said: "Oh, well, I think she's going on as well as could be expected, you know." She repeated: "Oh, yes, as well as could be expected. Of course, you can't expect her to be quite the same as Colonel Fedden, can you?"

I said: "Do you mean she's ill?"

"Oh no. Just a little temperature, you know; nothing to worry about. She's rather restless——" She broke off. "Oh, there is Dr Dixon, just coming out of her room now. Would you like to have a word with him?"

I said: "I should."

Dixon came to the telephone. He asked where I was speaking from, and then:

"I think you'd better come down here," he said. "Yes; I rather want to see you. Yes; it's about the girl. I think it might be a good thing to have another opinion—things move so quickly in these cases, you know. Anyway, we'll have a talk about it when you come down."

I nodded slowly. "I'll be with you in ten minutes," I replied, and rang him off.

The sun was just rising as I went through to the stable yard; it came up behind a bank of watery clouds; the gale was dying with the dawn. I opened the stable gates and got the Bentley out, and ran down to the nursing home. I found Dixon in the surgery, and he got up to meet me as I came in.

I went straight to the point. "This girl," I said. "I take it that you mean there's something wrong."

He met my eyes. "I hope not," he replied. "The position is this. She was all right till nine o'clock last night. Then the temperature began, and the pulse went up in sympathy—you understand."

I nodded. "What's the temperature now?"

"A hundred and three point five."

"And the pulse?"

"About a hundred and forty."

I said: "And what is it you think she's got?"

He hesitated. "Provisionally, I am treating for septicæmia. That is—what I should be apprehensive of."

There was a little silence in the room. "Is there anything else that it could be?" I asked.

He said something a little diffidently about coincidences: I gathered that he was thinking of measles or something of that sort. Frankly, he did not think that that was very probable. And then he said that if in was septicæmia he would prefer to have some help. "Things change, you know—the treatments," he said, a little apologetically. "It's some time since I had a case like this. Now, Holderness over at Plymouth, I know he had three at least last year—he was dining with me the other night. I think it might be as well to have him over."

I nodded. "By all means. Get on to him at once."

He went out of the room to get the matron to put through the call for him, and when he came back I asked him: "Who's the authority on this thing at the present time?"

He glanced at me. "You mean in this part of the world?"

"In England. Harley Street."

He considered for a moment, and absently turned a pile of periodicals upon his desk. "I don't think Harley Street," he said at last. "I think you'd have to go to Liverpool, perhaps. Sir Donald McKenzie—he's the chap that writes so much about it, and he certainly has done wonderful work on it up there."

I nodded. "We'd better get him down," I said. "At once." I paused. "Get a call through to him, and tell him to fly down if he can. If not, to telegraph what time he can reach Exeter— I'll have the car to meet him there." I turned and stared him grimly in the eyes. "You understand? He's to drop everything, and come at once. He is to start within an hour from now."

"Well, of course," said Dixon, "if you do that you'll get the very best advice obtainable." He hesitated for a moment. "And, of course, you'll have to pay for it."

I asked: "How much?"

Dixon hesitated. "I really couldn't say. It is conceivable that if I ask him to drop everything as you suggest and fly down here, he might charge as much as two hundred guineas. I should not say it would be more."

I nodded slowly, and the room seemed to nod with me: I steadied myself by the table, for I was very tired. "Offer five hundred on the telephone," I said wearily. "Get him to come at any price he wants."

I sat down on a chair; Dixon stood eyeing me. And then he said: "I'm very sorry, Stevenson. You can depend upon us to do everything that can be done, regardless of expense."

I raised my heavy head. "You can have carte blanche up to ten thousand pounds," I said. "I'll give you that in writing, if you like. And after that as much more as you want."

He left me then to telephone, and I sat on there in the surgery for what seemed many hours, until he came again. "McKenzie arrives at Exeter at 2.15," he said. "That is the best that I could do. And Holderness is on his way here now."

I got on to my feet. "Good man," I said. And then I said, a little timidly: "Do you think I could look in and see her for a bit? Or wouldn't that be wise?"

"I think it would be excellent," he said. "She was asking for you all day yesterday. But you don't want to go in there like that."

"Like what?" I asked stupidly.

He laughed and swung a mirrored door till I could see myself. I was still in sea clothes, serge trousers and blue jersey, and an oilskin over all. I had a growth of stubble straggling across my face, and the features that looked back at me were lined and worn. Dixon laughed. "Get along back and have a bath and shave, and come down when you've had some breakfast," he said. "I'll expect you here at about eight o'clock."

Stenning had gone to bed, and was asleep when I got back. I left him there and went and had a bath, and shaved, and dressed carefully and neatly that disastrous day. When I had finished, I looked in the glass. Everything was neat and orderly except my face, which was all grey, the face of an old man. I went downstairs to my ruined dining-room and poured a whisky from the decanter which was still upon the table, and with that inside me I felt more myself.

Rogers brought me breakfast in the library, but I didn't fancy it. By eight o'clock I was down at the nursing home, and waiting in the surgery till Dixon came.

I heard him coming down the passage from her room, talking incisively to the matron, and I saw his face before he knew that I was there. He brightened when he saw me. "That's better," he remarked. He said that Holderness had been there and had seen the girl, and had gone away to have some breakfast. I gathered that he had not been of much help, and that the thing would have to run its course without much check, pending the arrival of the specialist.

"She's been asking after you again," said Dixon. "I think it might be a good thing if you went and sat with her a bit." He hesitated. "You'll realise, of course, that she has a high temperature," he said. "You won't excite her—she must be kept quite quiet. You may find her wandering a little, too. Still, I think perhaps it might be a good thing if you went and sat there for a bit."

In the pale room the blinds were still half drawn; a nurse was moving quietly about at the far end. She greeted me with a smile and moved a chair for me beside the bed, and I sat down to throw my weight into the fight. "Don't worry if she doesn't know you just at first," the nurse said quietly behind me. "She will later. She's been asking for you all the time."

I sat and stared at Mollie in the bed, flushed and uncomfortable, and most unlike the girl that I had known. I tried to think of something I could say to her as she lay turning restlessly, and staring through the place where I was sitting by her side. And finding nothing I could say, I took one of her hands in mine and sat there stroking it, and listening to the words that dropped from time to time from the hot lips.

And sitting there, I drifted back into another world. The odd phrases and the half sentences were all about her former life, the life that she had lived up in the north. Once came a stanza of a vaudeville song that I remembered seeing early in the war, and there was much about the stage, about soubrettes and leads. There was something of dancing, and of boys. All this came out in little bits and snatches between long, silent intervals of restlessness. Once the nurse came up and looked at her most critically, and felt the pulse. And then she turned to me and said: "She's ever so much quieter since you came." And that amazed me.

And presently, when I had been there for perhaps an hour, she suddenly lay quiet and stared at me with dull eyes, but awake. And then she said, quite quietly:

"Is that the Commander?"

"That's right," I said, "I've come to sit with you for a bit."
And I stroked the hand that I was holding.

She said: "It's ever so nice of you to come." And then in
explanation she added: "I've been such a long way."

"I know," I said. "But now you're home again."

They turned me out soon after that, telling her that I should
come back presently, and I was left to pace the surgery downstairs. Stenning turned up and I told him briefly what was on;
he was as powerless as I had been to help. All he could do
was to take the burden of negotiations with the police from
me, and he left me to go down to Norman to discuss what else
had to be done.

I went out at once into the town. At the entrance to the
nursing home a young man stopped me, and informed me,
a little hesitantly, that he represented the *Morning Herald*. I
told him that I owned thirty per cent of the shares in that
publication, that he'd be sacked before the week was out, and
he could burn in hell for all I cared. That settled him, but
there were others that I could not sack so easily. One took a
photograph of me as I went back into the home.

I did not see her again before lunch. Dixon came down and
said that I had done a bit of good, and that she was quieter
than she had been all the night. I had sent Adams with the
car to Exeter to meet McKenzie, and I walked up to my house
and snatched a little food, and walked down to the nursing
home again, blasting and cursing the reporters who accosted
me as I was walking down the street. The town seemed full
of them that day, and I walked through them, cursing as I
went.

McKenzie proved to be a little sandy-haired man with
pince-nez, by no means the great figure I had pictured him.
Dixon and Holderness were pleased with him, however, and
they took him into consultation in the surgery, and I left with
a dozen old copies of the *Tatler* and *Punch* that somebody had
given me to read. I heard them leave the surgery and go along
the passage to her room, and then there was a good deal of
movement of the nurses in the home, and passing in and out.
And presently, at rather after four o'clock, I heard them
coming down the passage. I heard Dixon say: "You might
have a word with him now, perhaps. He's in the other room."
I got up on my feet as they came in to me.

McKenzie started to tell me how ably his colleague, Dr Dixon, had been managing the case, as he was bound to do in etiquette. I cut him short when he was half-way through his piece. "You found a sick girl, I'm afraid," I said.

The little man shot a quick glance at me. "I'll not deny it. I'll not deny it at all. I found a very sick girl. Not that she won't pull through, mind you. Don't think it, but she'll want watching tonight, the while she's in the worst of it, and she'll do fine. I was just tellin' the doctor here, I'll bide with you tonight."

I cleared my throat. "That would be very kind of you. I was hoping that perhaps you'd stay the night."

He went into the details of the treatment in his dry Scots way—something to do with scarlet fever anti-toxin, which I have forgotten now. We stood there talking for a quarter of an hour, until he said:

"Well, now. Ye'll go and sit with her a bit?" He changed to a command. "Ye'll go away and have a bit of tea, and ye'll come back at five o'clock and sit with her a while. She likes to have you there, the doctor was telling me. And, man, it's what she wants she's got to have this night."

He eyed me narrowly, this little sandy man. "The doctor was telling me she thinks the world and all of you. Don't think because I've come from Liverpool that I'm the one that's going to get her through the night. It's you. Now, are you up to it?" He shot the question at me as a challenge, peering at me through his pince-nez.

I met his eyes. "Three nights ago I asked her if she would become my wife," I said. "I'll do all I can."

He turned away. "Weel, ye can't do more than that." He turned again. "Just stamina, that's a' she wants. Ye can't build up physique by dancing underground all afternoon and half the night, and lying abed all morn. And ye canna pump it in with an hypodermic squirt. Good food and exercise, and plenty sleep. That's all she's wanting. Ye'd better give it her when this thing's over."

"Just stamina," he said. "Losh, if you pump that into her I'll throw me anti-toxins down the sink!" And laughed at his own joke.

I made arrangements on the telephone for a room for him at my house, but it was evident he didn't contemplate much sleep that night. And then, obediently, I went and had my tea, and at five o'clock I went into her room to battle for her life.

She was awake and smiled to see me come, and I bent down and kissed her on the lips, regardless of the nurse. It seemed to me that she was less restless than she had been before, but every bit as hot; she was noticeably weaker than she had been in the morning. I sat down beside her bed and took her hand in mine, and I began to talk to her about the first things that came into my head.

If I were to try and put down all I said to her that night I should fill many volumes of this ledger, for I talked for hours. She said very little in reply; I sat there stroking her hand and arm, and every now and then she squeezed my hand a little, and smiled up at me. I started off with what we'd do as soon as she was fit to leave the nursing home. I told her that I'd get her moved back into her own room and bathroom in my house as soon as possible, and for that she smiled, and murmured: "I'd love to be there." And I told her how she could sit out in the sun in the garden all day till her shoulder healed, and read magazines and look out over the flowers at the harbour and the sea. And I told her that I'd get her a kitten to keep her company while I was away at the office in the mornings.

And then, without heeding that the nurse was there, I told her again that I loved her, and she lay there smiling at me with her eyes. I told her that I wanted her to marry me as soon as she felt she could, and if she felt she couldn't just at first we'd go away together as she wanted, and we'd get married when she liked. I told her that we'd go away and have a real holiday together, a holiday that would go on for as long as we wanted to. And that would be the first real holiday that I had taken since the war.

I told her that we'd start off at Torquay, and she smiled up at me, and whispered: "Lovely." I said I'd have the *Runagate* round there, and we'd live in a fine hotel just up above the harbour, in a double room, and we'd spend every day sailing and bathing together, and motoring upon the moors. And she could teach me to dance really properly at night, so that she could dance with me with pleasure all our lives. She said: "You'll learn ever so quick."

I told her that we'd stay there for as long as ever she liked, but that once or twice we'd just run up to town to buy her clothes. And I told her that she could have her frocks designed for her, but that I wanted one that would be like the silver and blue one she had worn in the evenings at my house; she must have one like that. And I said that Joan would help her and show her where to buy the things, and where to go for everything she wanted. And then we'd come back to Torquay and she could learn to drive a car, and I'd get her a little light saloon that she could drive herself.

And then I told her, as the autumn came, we'd slip across to the New World. Because once, so many years ago, I met an old merchant skipper—not one of my men—who told me that of all the places that he had seen all through the world there was one that was so supremely beautiful that it stood out like a mountain over all the lovely sights that he had ever seen.

That was the harbour at Halifax in the fall of the year. He pictured it to me as a wide inlet between wooded hills, and full of wooded islands on the water's face. And all these woods were maple woods, so that in the autumn they turned bright scarlet. With the calm water, the red woods, and the long, cloudless, pale blue autumn days it made a picture that that old man had carried with him all his life; he had longed to return to it again before he died. And it had bitten deep into me, too, so that I told her we would go and see it as the autumn drew on.

And then we'd go on to New York and see the greatest city of the century, so great that the foreigner is faintly homesick when he leaves. I told her that we'd stay there, possibly, till Christmas time, learning about America, and seeing how they lived. I told her, if she liked, we'd go across to Hollywood and see how films were made.

And then I told her that we'd come back home and go to Switzerland. Because by that time her arm would be quite strong again and she could learn to ski, and I told her about the snow and ski-ing and the skating, and the sitting in the blazing sun to eat your lunch on the veranda of the hotel above the snow. I told her about the joy of running on good snow in the sunshine, sweeping in stemming christies down the slopes to the inevitable drink of ice-cold milk in the châlet at the bottom. I told her about the hotels and the snow mountains, rose coloured in the sunset, and I told her about the people that she'd meet, and the dancing in the evenings, where nobody would be so good as her.

They came in then to do something to her, Dixon and McKenzie, and they sent me from the bed. After a quarter of an hour they went away, and I came back to her and took up my tale again where I had left it off. And I told her that in the spring we'd come back home and live at Dartmouth, with the sea and with my ships all summer, because that is home, and one cannot be travelling all the year through. And I told her that I'd teach her how to sail, and that I'd get a little sailing dinghy rigged for her so that she could take her friends out up the river bathing, because it's warmer up there. And all her friends would come and stay with us from time to time, girls on their one week's holiday from the grey cities of the north. And she whispered: "I'd have Edna first, if I may."

And then I told her that we would stay at home for all the summer months, close to the sea, and I would show her the fun of cruising in the English Channel and the West of Ireland. And perhaps, if she wanted to, we'd have one month of that away, and take the car to France, and run down to the south through Chartres and Arles and Avignon, until we reached the sea, to live the Lido life a little at some bathing place. And then back home again, to stay a week in Paris at a quiet place I know that overlooks the Bois, and she could get some shopping done. Then we'd go home, and be at home for August when her friends had holidays.

And in September we might go to Scotland for a little shooting, with some friends of mine.

Evening drew on, and she lay smiling at me there, seeming to drift into a doze, and then rousing again to squeeze my hand. McKenzie came in from time to time to see how she was getting on; the temperature showed no sign of going down. "Ye'll keep her interest," he ordered once in a soft tone. "Just keep her interest, and give me drugs a chance. . . ."

I went on talking to her, and I told her that we'd finish up our two-year honeymoon by going round the world. Because I never had seen India, and very little of the East at all, and I was longing to go there with her. I told her that we'd go there with no very settled plan, but that I wanted to go up into Kashmir to see a man who was at school with me, and that I wanted to work down into Ceylon to see the pilgrimage to

Adams Peak among the flowers. And then, I said, we'd go on over to Malay and on from Singapore to the South Seas. And there we'd charter a schooner to get off the beaten track, and we'd go cruising through the islands towards Honolulu at the end. Then we would cross to San Francisco and up into the Canadian summer in the Rockies, two years hence, and so to Montreal, where I have many friends. And so we'd come back home, after our honeymoon, to settle down to work again, to stay till we were tired and longed to see the world again beyond the sea.

She lay there quiet, in a sort of dream. And about nine o'clock I bent towards her lips, and heard her say: "I wish the others could have seen us, dear, just once. None of them ever had a gentleman friend like I've had."

I sat with her till far into the night. Then they made me come away, and Dixon took me home.

## CHAPTER 14

I DO NOT think I need put down the events of the succeeding week in any detail. A reliable account of the two inquests came out in *The Times*, and is available if I should want to look it up—a most improbable contingency. The other newspapers were only fit to burn.

They held the first at Dartmouth upon the two Gordons and the Superintendent. Norman gave evidence in a restricted sort of way. I think that he had had a conversation with the coroner before the case came on, for nothing came out that was of any consequence. They called me next and I swore by Almighty God that the evidence which I should give to that inquest should be the truth, the whole truth, and nothing but the truth; an oath which I took with every intention of committing perjury. But all the evidence they wanted from me was quite formal; I told them something of Mollie and her brother, and their lives. Only one question I remember clearly, when the coroner said delicately: "Are we to understand that these two were related to you in any way, Commander Stevenson?"

I raised my heavy head. "I had asked Miss Gordon if she would do me the honour to become my wife," I said. "I don't know if you call that a relationship or not."

That passed with a little buzz of interest in the court, and next morning I saw a placard close outside my own lodge gates:

### Q-BOAT CAPTAIN'S TRAGIC LOVE FOR MYSTERY DANCING GIRL

Stenning and Joan had wanted to come and stay with me to see it through, but I had told them, brutally perhaps, that I would rather be alone. And so they stayed down in the town, and I went back to build up my old life, working upon the drawings of the little cruiser I am building now, and working all day in my office at the yard.

The verdict in the first inquest was one of 'Wilful murder against some person or persons unknown'. It could not be fixed upon the people drowned in the wreck of the bawley, as neither Stenning nor I, nor anyone, could give more than presumptive evidence that the bawley we had come upon not far from the Eddystone had anything to do with the affair. So the thing rested till the inquest on the bodies from the wreck was held, over at Pentressan, some days afterwards.

And that produced little but identification. Three bodies were washed up within five miles of the coast, and it seems reasonable to suppose that that is all there were. The cause of death in every case was drowning.

The first was a young man called Peter Marston. He was twenty-three years of age, and had left Cambridge about ten months before. His father came down to identify the body, a grey-haired, venerable old man, from Colchester. He was much cut up. They were people of some means, and the boy, since leaving Cambridge, had followed no occupation. He was interested in the fishing industry. The bawley was his property, and he used to cruise in it a great deal, but his father knew little of the companions that he had upon these trips. The father had never before seen any of the other bodies.

The second body was that of a man between thirty-five and

forty years of age, dark haired, wearing a dark suit and boots of continental manufacture. There was no name upon the clothes, but in the pocket there was a love letter from a woman, addressed to Alexander Kurn, Poste Restante, Rotterdam. This letter was in a mixture of Russian and German, and bore no address. That was all, except that a small automatic pistol was found in the hip pocket.

The third was a man of about thirty, pale and thin. This man was known to the police, who identified him as an alien called Aukitch, who had been deported from this country for a case of robbery with violence. He was believed to be a Russian Jew.

This inquest was quite short, the verdict being 'Death from Misadventure', as I had supposed.

So those inquests passed, a little inconclusively perhaps, but no one had a shadow of a doubt that justice had been done. By that time I had lost interest in a great degree in the inner meaning of the business. I only wanted to be left alone, to get back to my rut and to forget the last six weeks. But I went down one day to the police station when Norman was there, and had a little talk with him about the business.

They had been to Trepwll, and had removed what they had found. They found a barn half full of munitions—thirty-two light machine guns, a number of cheap automatic pistols, a few bombs, and a great amount of ammunition. And they found a farmer who protested that he knew nothing of the contents of his barn, and they were forced to the conclusion that he spoke the truth. He had leased his barn to a man called Palmer for the warehousing of goods, and he knew nothing of the nature of the goods inside the packing cases. He knew that some of them were carpet sweepers, because he had seen the labels.

The police had removed what they had found, and had contrived to hide the matter from the Press.

And there the matter, Norman said, must rest till after the election, now only a fortnight off. There was no evidence at all of any destination of the arms; they had been brought to the barn and stored, and no one from the district had been near the place. At the Yard they suspected that the arms had come from Russia, and they were certain that the introducers of the arms were dead, drowned in the bawley. He agreed that there must be some local agent in the Glanferis district who had some knowledge of the business, but so far they had found no trace of him. And, acting on instructions from above, they did not intend to prosecute their search for him just at the moment.

"Frankly," he said, "I think this is the end of the affair."

I thought about it for a minute. "It may be," I said at last, "but I don't see how you come to that conclusion all the same. You've not discovered anything about the directing intelligence behind it all."

He smiled a little. "That depends on how you look at it," he said. "Do you doubt that the directing intelligence was Russian in its origin?"

I shook my head. "No."

"Well then," he replied, "there isn't any question of the origin, essentially. What you mean is that we haven't found the intermediate agents. I hope that we shall do so in due course. But the important thing is the discovery. For the time we have stopped the importation of the arms, simply because their secrecy has broken down. That gives us breathing space."

"Till after the election," I put in, a little cynically.

He shuffled with the papers on his desk. "I have no concern with that aspect of the matter, as you know."

I went away, and tried to concentrate upon my work for the next few days. Stenning and Joan had gone back to their place in town, tired, I suppose, of the treatment I had given them. And I went on living in my house alone, working all day and drinking rather heavily all night, dining alone in a black tie, and sitting after dinner in the library till I could feel that I could face my bed.

And after two or three days I came to the conclusion that I was not satisfied. The police might give this up, but I went over to Plymouth one fine afternoon, driving the Bentley faster than I might have done if I had had a little less to drink at lunch. I went to the accountant who handles my audit, and I said to him:

"See here. Isn't there some intelligence bureau that you people use? I mean, if you want to find out about anyone? For finding out their credit in hire-purchase matters, and that sort of thing?"

He nodded. "Certianly. I can get you a confidential report on anyone, if you like. It'll cost you one-and-sixpence in the ordinary way."

It seemed cheap to me. "That boy called Marston who was drowned the other day," I said, and I gave his address in Colchester. "I want to know about his women friends."

He wrinkled his brows. "That's a little out of the ordinary line," he objected. "The agency will handle it all right, but it may cost you a bit more. You want their names, social position and that sort of thing?"

I nodded. "That's exactly it. I want a list of all the women he knew well, who would have gone about with him alone. Their addresses, and what you can find out about each of them."

He mused a little. "It'll probably be one-and-sixpence each," he said. "Generally takes about two days. I'll telephone you when it comes to hand."

And three days later I had the report. There were only two of them, apparently: a waitress in a Cambridge restaurant, and his cousin, Adela Jennings, lately down from Girton. It did not seem to me that the waitress was the one I wanted, and so I concentrated upon Adela.

She lived at Esher, in her parents' house. I thought about it for a day, wondering if I should meet all Scotland Yard upon the doorstep of that house, and then I took the car and went to London.

I stayed at my club. Nobody I knew was there, and I was disinclined to go and look for anyone. And so I dined very well, alone, and sat alone in the top smoking-room with my cigar and with a magazine all evening, save once, when a waiter brought me whisky and I stopped him by my chair, and he told me about the Test matches, and we talked for a little time. Then he went away, and I sat on with the decanter by the fire, alone. At about three o'clock I went to bed.

Next morning I drove down to the house at Esher in the Bentley. It was a fair-sized place that stood in its own grounds; I drove up to the front door in my car, and rang the bell, and asked to see Miss Adela. They showed me into a morning-room and presently she came to me, an earnest-looking girl in a dark dress with a touch of black in it.

And when I saw her I knew that I had not gone wrong.

I rose to meet her as she came. "Good afternoon, Miss Jennings," I said grimly. "I've come up from Dartmouth to meet you. I want answers to one or two questions, about your cousin and yourself."

She stared at me, flaming, indignant at my tone. I was standing by the window in bright light, and suddenly she faltered, and the colour died out of her face. And then she whispered: "Oh. . . ."

I stood there eyeing her. "You seem to know my face."

She pulled herself together, and said quietly: "I don't. Who are you, and what are you doing here?"

I smiled, a little cruelly perhaps. "I'm a sojourner," I said, "as all my fathers were."

There was a long, restless pause after that. At last she said: "Have you come from the police?"

I stared her in the eyes. "I've come to get answers to my questions," I said harshly. "True answers, and none of your damn trickery. If you want to know, I've come to inquire into a murder."

She pulled herself together. "I don't know what you mean."

I smiled. "Then I'll explain. You've caused the death of five men and a girl, you and your precious friends. I know that much. If you go playing with me any more I shall disclose the whole affair, your part in it as well. You know what that means. Prison for you, and for a damn long spell."

She sank down on a chair beside the table. "We had considered this," she said, and as she spoke the tears fell slowly from her eyes. "We knew that if the thing went wrong there would be trouble. It seemed worth it, then. And it has gone most desperately wrong. . . ."

I laughed. "Then I hope it still seems worth it," I remarked. I turned serious. "You'd better answer my questions. If you don't, I shall tell all I know. I shall disclose your cousin Peter as the murderous scoundrel that he really was. I shall disclose your part in it." She had nothing apparently to say to that. "If you tell the truth I'll go away and leave things as they are, maybe, and you can square your conscience in whatever way you choose to kid yourself."

I paused. "I'm doing this because I think you saved my life, that night upon the beach. But for that fact I'd blast you up and down the country, in and out of gaol, until I had you dead. I'll give you this one chance."

She laid her head down on her arms. "You don't understand," she sobbed. "You don't understand at all."

"I'm dealing with a pack of murderers," I said. "I understand that part of it all right."

"You don't understand," she sobbed again. And then she said: "It was all for the election."

I have had many experiences in the life that I have lived, and sometimes I have been afraid. But I do not think that I have ever before experienced the feeling of sheer horror that came over me when she said that. She had said something utterly incredible. In that one swift moment there came to me all the manœuvrings of the hustings and the polling booths, the sordid trickey that froms a background to political affairs. I cannot describe in words the feelings that came over me as I stood there and listened to her sobbing at the table, the tense horror of this first hint that all that had been sacrificed and lost was staked upon some move in party politics.

I strode across and knocked her head up from the table. "Just listen here, young woman," I said angrily. "Now tell me what you mean."

She sobbed: "It's true, and now you've got it, and I wish that I was dead."

I said: "What's this about the election? By God, you'd better speak the truth!"

I held her head up from the table, and I held her tear-streaked eyes with mine. "The guns had to be hidden at Trepwll before the election. And then they were going to be discovered just before the polling day. It was the only way to save the country from the Socialists."

I let her head drop back upon the table, and she lay there sobbing unrestrainedly. I walked over to the window and stood there for a little time, staring out into the sunlit garden and the rhododendrons. Little by little in my mind the monstrous story fell into its place. Long ago the Zinovieff letter lost an election to the Labour Party; the incredible fact appeared to be that this affair had been conceived as such another. Guns had been brought into the country by some politician of the opposing group, and planted in a disaffected area. I could well see that if these arms had been discovered a few days before the poll and evidence supplied that they had come from Russia, the country would swing solid to Conservative.

One thing was evident; this girl had got to tell me all she knew. I crossed the room to her, and laid my hand upon her shoulder. "Come along," I said, perhaps a little more gently than I had done up till then. "This thing has gone awry. You tell me this thing is just a fake, a movement in some game of party politics. Six people have been killed in playing it, and now it's got to stop. More may be killed before it runs its course. Sit up, and tell me how it came about."

And with a little encouragement she dried her eyes, and told me everything. She had hardly said two sentences before I stopped her with a question.

"Who is the directing influence behind this thing? Who organised it, and paid for it?"

She hesitated.

"Come on, now," I said harshly. "Out with it. If not, I put it with the police."

The tears fell from her eyes again. "It was Professor Ormsby," she replied.

I pulled an envelope and pencil from my pocket to make notes. "Christian names, and address?"

"Charles Hemming Ormsby. He's a Professor of Political Economy. A Fellow of Nicholas—Cambridge."

I thought about this for a minute. "Who invented the name for the carpet sweepers—the Greek scholar? Was that him?"

She nodded tearfully. And then, little by little, out it came, until at last I had the whole affair.

I had been shocked by the revelation of the nature of the gun running. I do not know that I was less shocked at the high ideals that lay behind it all, and at the spirit in which it had been carried out. For the root of it lay in a real patriotism and a love of England, distorted but sincere. And here I may say at once that I found no villainy about the thing. Merely an overwhelming vanity, that could not brook another view of what was beneficial for this country that we live in now.

So far as I could understand, Professor Ormsby, the boy Marston, and this girl, his cousin, were the chief participants in the affair. It had no connexion with official Conservatism at all; it could have none, of course. It was a secret enterprise, conceived by Ormsby and carried out by young Marston in his bawley, whose object was to place a Conservative Government in power in England for the next five years. The whole affair had been most cleverly conceived. The guns had come, in fact, from Russian sources, and Russians had co-operated in the smuggling wholeheartedly. I did not hear the details of that part of it—all that had been manœuvred by Professor Ormsby, but the essence of it was that Communism had been invoked in this affair to bring about its own defeat.

In Marston Professor Ormsby had found a resolute young man, secretive and well suited to carry out the detail of his part. The girl had been introduced by Marston at a later date to help him in some business connected with the bawley; I could well imagine that it was a job that called for company of some description. I found strong evidence to lead me to believe that the man they knew as Palmer was Professor Ormsby himself; I do not think that there was anybody else in the affair at all.

If ever people played about with fire it was that little crowd.

Every trip they made they carried Russians to and from the country; almost immediately their smuggling became a means of introducing agents into England who could not get through the immigration barriers. They had been powerless to prevent this traffic, and contented themselves with the knowledge that it would not last for long. From the first their lives were carried in their hands. They served their country secretly, as criminals, and the reward that they were earning was a heavy burden to be carried to their graves. They were out to fool the country for the country's benefit, and no country takes that sort of trick too well.

The girl knew nothing of events for two or three days prior to the end, but from her knowledge she could reconstruct them well. It was impossible that Marston should have taken part in the murders at my house; he would have been down with the bawley at the entrance to the harbour mouth. I am inclined to doubt, in fact, if he had ever known that violence had been done; there was no occasion for the gunmen to have told him, and every reason why it should be kept from him if they desired to make a getaway. He was the only sailor among them, it is to be presumed.

At last it was all done. I had been there two hours, and for the last hour she had been talking collectedly, giving her evidence in a straightforward way. I had three envelopes of notes; I glanced them over and got to my feet. "That's all?" I inquired. "If there is anything else whatsoever you'd better tell me now."

She said that there was nothing more to tell. She asked, a little nervously, what I was going to do.

I stared at her. "God knows." And then I laughed quietly: "Getting a little bit afraid of your own skin, now, I suppose. Well, you needn't. If what you say is true, you're out of it. No worse can happen to you than publicity."

She faltered. "Will it get into the newspapers?"

"God knows," I said again. Her question sickened me; for the moment I had been back again in Dartmouth with a braver girl than this. I turned upon her viciously. "There were three of you," I said. "Between you you murdered two men and a harmless girl. That's what you've done, and you'll remember it."

There was a little pause. "One of you three is dead, and I shall see the other soon. And you'll be left alone to live your time out through the years, with all your memories." I took my hat from the table. "I must wish you joy of it."

I drove back up to town and garaged the car, and went back to my club to write. I settled down there in the reading-room, and because I was tired and feeling not so well the stream of tumblers came and went beside my elbow, for the bell was at my side. I wrote on steadily, page after page, and never paused till it was time to drain my glass and go and change for dinner, and then the writing was but half done. And I remember, as I crossed the landing to the stairs, I passed behind two men and heard one say:

"Can nothing be done about that fellow in the reading-room? The boy tells me he's had seven whiskies in the last two hours, and last night just the same. One doesn't expect to see that sort of soaking in a club like this."

I smiled a little and passed on. This was the England Ormsby had set out to fool. The task had not proved very difficult, perhaps.

I dressed with infinite exactitude, and went downstairs and dined alone. It seemed but a moment till I was sitting writing again, and yet I must have lingered over my dinner, for it was nine o'clock when I sat down again in the reading-room. I wrote on steadily into the night, and the little pile of manuscript grew steadily at my elbow, and from time to time the boy came to me again, and went.

At last it was finished. It was very still and silent in the reading-room, still with the silence of an empty London club at night, muffled in repose. I settled down to read my story through, and presently the swing doors parted and closed, and the night porter came to me.

"Will you be wanting anything further tonight, sir?"

I stared at him absently. "What's the time?"

"Five and twenty past one, sir."

I shook my head. "You might bring me a few biscuits and a double whisky. I shall be going up in a minute." And I settled down in the deserted room again.

At last I was finished. I addressed three envelopes: one to Jenkinson and one to Norman, and the third and bulkiest to the editor of the *Morning Herald*, a paper in which I had a holding at that time. I put all these in one large envelope and sealed them up, and addressed it to Jenkinson: "To be opened in the event of my death." Then I went to bed.

I suppose I slept that night, but it escapes my memory. I know I heard the clocks chime all the hours of the night, and as soon as it was dawn I pulled my curtains and lay back and tried to read a volume of essays that I had picked up downstairs. And so the night passed, till at last I heard the sound of movement, and I could get up and have my bath.

I put in a trunk call to Cambridge at about nine o'clock and talked for a few moments to the porter at Nicholas. Then I got through to Professor Ormsby, and heard a voice say: "Who is that?"

I smiled a little. "This is Commander Stevenson," I said, "speaking from London. I must introduce myself on the recommendation of a Miss Adela Jennings, of Esher. I had a most interesting talk with Miss Jennings yesterday over the matter of some carpet sweepers that I believe you are interested in, too. I was wondering if I might come down today —say this afternoon—and have a talk with you about them?"

He had guts, that fellow; there was only the slightest pause. "Certainly," he said; "I should be very pleased to see you. Shall we say half-past two, in my rooms here?"

"That's all right for me."

"Very well, Commander Stevenson," he replied; "I shall expect you then." And he rang off.

I had nothing to prepare. At about ten o'clock I left the Club and went and got the Bentley and drove down to Cambridge. It was a lovely day, high summer; in the country it was warm and fresh. I drove with a more contented mind than I had had for many days; looking back upon it now I think that I enjoyed that drive. I was going to a clean-cut issue, going unarmed to meet a man who might be dangerous, with no other weapon but my wits. I was inviolable, for I had nothing left to lose.

I lunched well in Cambridge and went on to Nicholas at the appointed time. The porter took me across the court to a staircase in the southern corner, up some dark stone stairs, and tapped at the door for me. A voice called to me to come in, and I went forward into the room.

He was alone. I found a tall, spare man with very pale blue eyes, a man of perhaps fifty years of age, going a little white about the temples and a little bald on top. It was the room that I had expected I should find, lined with bookshelves on all four walls, and with an oar slung up above the mantelpiece. It was all very quiet and peaceful on that summer afternoon. I close my eyes and I can see it now.

He greeted me cordially enough, and asked me to sit down. He indicated an easychair, but I drew up a chair to the table in the middle of the room and sat down there, resting my arms upon the table and facing him as he stood by the fireplace. "I think we can cut the preliminaries of this quite short," I said. "I had two hours with Miss Jennings yesterday. She told me a good deal about this gun running, that had not been quite clear to me before."

He did not deny or argue it; he was too good a man for that. "Exactly," he said quietly. And then he said: "Before we begin, I should like to know just where your interest lies, if I may inquire? Am I to take it that you represent the police?"

I shook my head. "I come in my own interest."

He raised his eyebrows a little. "Ah, as a private individual."

I stared at him grimly. "That is so. It is wiser to leave drunken men alone, you know. Once you start violence things begin to go wrong."

He nodded slowly. "I think that is so. From the first moment that I heard of that affair I was afraid that trouble might arise from it." He broke into a smile. "And now it has. I am sure that you will not accuse me of trying to disarm you if I offer my apologies for the treatment you received, in which I had no hand?"

I stared at him. "You are right in fearing that trouble might arise from me. It has. Bad trouble."

He met my eyes. "I think you had better tell me what you want," he said quietly.

I considered for a moment. "This is Wednesday," I said at last. "The country goes to the poll on Friday week, in ten day's time. On Saturday next, in three day's time, a story will appear in all the Labour Press which will bring certain charges against you, personally, together with Miss Jennings and the boy Marston, who was drowned. You know the story. You will be accused of having attempted to bias this election with a trick, to swindle the whole of England with faked propaganda in the Conservative interest. That story will be supported with concrete evidence which will bear examination, and it will be true."

He had gone very white.

I sat there staring at him from behind the table. "I have come to you now," I said in a hard voice, "because I am merciful. This story will appear on Saturday. I am giving you three days in which to cut the country before you are arrested on a criminal charge." I paused. "This thing is now in train," I said. "I mention that, in case you may be thinking of more violence."

There was a long slow silence in the room. Out in the court through the open window, I could hear a hum of voices, undergraduates going to and fro, and laughter now and then. There was a bee or two about a great bowl of wild flowers in the window seat, and the air was fragrant with the scent of them. And presently he moved forward and sat down at the table opposite me. "Let me explain a little, if I can," he said.

He thought for a minute, and then he began. And what he gave me was a clear-cut reasoning, as logical as a judgment in the High Court, of the motives which had led him to the action he had taken. He started in and took me, very simply and concisely, through the economic history of England since the war, and he drew parallels all through with the period that came after the Napoleonic wars. I sat there at his table in that summer afternoon and he talked to me as he would have expounded his knowledge to an undergraduate, showing me cause and effect in the kaleidoscope of politics and economic law.

And so he proved to me the essence of his creed. I call it a creed, for it was one to him; I had no doubt of that. On his premises, as he gave them me, it was inevitable that a further Labour Government would bring the country to an irretrievable disaster. He sketched the country as a blind man walking along the edge of a precipice, who follows the contour up and down in little slumps, and always straying nearer to the abyss. He proved this with economic logic that I could not controvert—upon his premises. And so he led me to the centre of his whole belief: that the one duty of a patriot who saw the country with unclouded eyes was to prevent this frightful thing—by fair means or by foul.

He told me that this had come to him a year or more before, and he had justified his implications in the intervening time. He sketched for me, very lucidly, the possible courses that could be taken if the country were to continue with a Labour Government, and he showed me in each case the irretrievable disaster which in each case lay ahead within ten years. And then he went on and told me, very briefly, of the steps which had led him to enlist the services of one of his pupils to prevent this thing, and how the enterprise had been conceived.

It would be idle to deny that he impressed me with his reasoning. He had a keen, clear mind, and much of what he said was pitifully true. I sat there motionless as he was talking, staring out of the window to the bright sunshine of the court. I had lost everything I had to lose in this affair. Had I been altogether wrong in my demand for justice, too severe?

I raised my head, and he was speaking of the course that I had told him I was going to take. "If you do this," he said, "these things will happen. You must not deceive yourself."

He smiled a little. "I can assure you that I am not thinking of myself, although the prospect of exposure is not . . . very palatable, I admit. But leave that out. If you expose this matter in the Press, you will be swinging the country solid to the Labour interests, and the consequences which I have outlined to you will occur. That is mere cause and effect."

He paused. "If on the other hand, you stop this Press campaign, the matter rests as it is. You tell me that no action is to be taken by the police till after the election has passed by. That means that the election will take place without bias in either way. I cannot swing it to Conservative, as I would have done. I am asking you not to swing it to the Labour interest, and I have told you why."

He stopped speaking, and there was a long silence in the sunlit room. "That lets you out of it all right," I said cynically. "I see that." He flushed but did not speak, and I moved over to the window and stood looking down upon the creeper-covered walls and the smooth turf.

And presently I turned to him. "Five men have been killed in this affair, and one girl. Three of the men were your agents, and as murderers of the others they deserved to die. Marston was one of those; if he had not been drowned he'd have been hanged. That is what you made of him." I paused. "One of the others was your lorry driver, and it may be that he was so involved as to be culpable in this affair."

I smiled at him, without mirth. "In fact, all your agents have received their punishment, and only you are left."

He did not speak.

I went on: "But it's about the last two that I am concerned. You've played your fancy game, and you've committed murder. You've murdered two quite innocent people. One was a police official, a married man with children. They'll be left pretty badly off. The other was a little dancing girl, from Leeds. She never did you any harm."

I paused. "I should like to know what you are going to do about these murders, first."

He inclined his head. "About those"—he hesitated for a moment—"murders, as you call them, nothing can be done, except financially. I should myself refer to them as accidents, in that they were not planned or willed by anyone. In this matter we were playing for a great stake. We were playing for the future of this country and this Empire. You run great hazards when you play for a great stake like that."

He turned on me. "You must keep a sense of proportion," he exclaimed. "These deaths are lamentable. But it is this country and this Empire we are dealing with. The issue is the place that Britain takes, the future of the Empire in the world. And you are putting in the scale against all that, a policeman and a dancing girl!

"Think of it, man," he cried. "A girl that you can pick up for a sovereign in the street! What does one girl of that description matter in a thing like this?"

## CHAPTER 15

THERE WAS a silence after he said that. Down in the court I heard the voices of the undergraduates talking and chaffing by the doorway of some staircase. They were talking about a round of golf, and dinner at some pub up river late that night. I remember that, because it was listening to them that helped me fight my anger down as I stood there. For the moment I was seeing red; it was as if he had slashed me in the face with a whip. And I think he saw that something had gone wrong, because he was very quiet when I came to answer him.

I moved across the room, and sat down again in my old position at the table, facing him. "I have listened to what you have to say," I said harshly, "especially the last part. And I regard it as a pack of nonsense. The whole thing is a figment of your own imagination, nurtured by your own conceit." And then I shot at him, suddenly: "Have you ever lived in Manchester?"

He shook his head.

"Or Newcastle, or Birmingham? Tell me, have you ever earned your living in any great industrial town?"

He said: "We have considerable industries here in Cambridgeshire. But I am a scientist of economics, as you might say. Not an industrialist."

I nodded slowly. "Leeds is a town as well as Cambridge,

but about thirty times as many Englishmen live there. And you know nothing of them, nor of Birmingham, nor Newcastle, nor Manchester. You've lived your life out in this little hole among your little class, and yet you've got the most disastrous conceit to legislate for them, the people that you do not know. How do you know what may be good for them or bad, or what they may do or they may not do?"

I stared at him. "Time you were out of this," I said. "You'd better pack your bag and get away. This matter will go on."

He had gone white again. "What do you mean to do?"

I rose to my feet and faced him across the table. "I mean to drive you out of this into the world, for the bloody murderer and scoundrel that you are. You've got three days in which to get away before I start this thing, and if you don't get out, on Sunday you will be arrested as a criminal. You will be tried for murder, and I think that you may hang. The Government and all the country will be crying for your death. But if you get off that, you won't get off a term of penal servitude. That means the end of everything for you." I stared around his delicately furnished, scholarly room. "You've done with all this."

"Yes," he said quietly.

I eyed him for a moment. "If I were you I should get off to South America."

He faced me, very white. "I want you to understand that I am not speaking for myself. But for the country. I believe that if you do this thing it means disaster, irretrievable. I would not have that happen, quite apart from what may happen to myself." He paused, and then said earnestly: "I want to explore every avenue. Is there nothing that will influence you to change your mind about this Press campaign?"

There was a heavy silence in the room. "Nothing whatever, while you are alive," I said evenly.

There was a long silence, broken only by the voices of the undergraduates below, and the low twittering of some bird among the creepers near his windowsill. "I thought that might be it," he said at last. A wintry smile appeared upon his face. "De mortuis nil nisi bonum. . . ."

"Exactly," I replied.

He moved across the room and came and sat down opposite

to me. "I see that you have all the power in this thing," he said, and it was as if we had been putting through some hard-fought business deal. "I want to be quite certain of your terms. Do I understand, then, that if anything should happen to me in the next few days, the general election would take place unbiased either way? The Press campaign you speak of, would that be withheld?"

"Certainly." I stared him in the eyes. "I am concerned with justice in this matter, not with politics."

He got up from the table, and I rose with him. He inclined his head. "I appreciate your position. Very well, Commander Stevenson. I will consider what you have said." He moved towards the door. "Perhaps you will hear from me in London."

I took up my hat and gloves. "There's one thing you should know, perhaps," I said.

"Yes?"

I smiled. "The dancing girl of whom you spoke so sympathetically," I replied. "She was going to become my wife." And with that I left him, and went blundering down the dark stone stairs into the sunlit court.

I must have driven back to town that afternoon, because I know I spent that evening in the club. I dined there alone, staring absently at the portraits of the benefactors that hung upon the walls, and mechanically eating what was put in front of me. I went up to the smoking-room after dinner, and sat there with my whisky before the fire, staring into the coals, and watching till they fell.

And presently, because I was very tired, and not so well, I went upstairs and went to bed. I lay for a long time in my bare, comfortable little room, reluctant to face the dark, listening to the rush and whirr of the taxis passing down Pall Mall in the summer night. Then I put out my light.

After a long time of wakefulness I raised my head, and stirred a little on the pillow. There was water trickling all down my face and salt upon my lips, and the bed that I was lying on was wallowing, so that I knew that the ship was in no good shape. I opened my eyes, and I was lying in a slop of blood and water that went streaming from me over the planking as the vessel rolled, and back to me again. I tried to sit up then, but somebody pressed me down from behind, and whispered: "Keep down, sir." And then I saw Osborne creeping towards me under the lee of the bulwarks with a pannikin of water in his hand.

They gave it to me to drink, and I asked: "How many of us are there now?"

And Osborne said: "There's only us."

I looked around the deck, and the thought came into my mind that we were done for, and that nobody would ever know how we had died. The little schooner was settling by the stern; it seemed to me that the whole stern must have been blown clean out of her by the explosion of the magazine, and most of the barrels in her hold stove in. I asked: "What's happening?"

And the snotty said: "They stopped the shelling ten minutes ago. They're practically dead ahead, sir. A little on the port bow."

I asked what had happened to the panic party, and he said: "They've been shelling the boat, sir. It's not playing the game. . . ."

I nodded slowly. "What armament have we got left?"

The leading seaman answered me. "The port six-pounder, and eight rounds, sir. I don't think there's any more ammunition. She'll want to be lying broad on the beam for it to bear, the way the ship is, but the gun's all right."

I could see it concealed on its mounting behind the bulwarks; it had not been touched. I lay for a little time, feeling the rotten, sogging movements of the vessel under us; she lay like a log, so that each swell sluiced down the bulwarks, pretty nearly swamping her, so that each time I thought that she would never rise again. Astern she was awash and in the house she was on fire, smouldering and smoking where the paint store had been. I thought of all my friends who had gone along this road in the last years.

I said: "This is the end of us. It's no good surrendering."

And then the snotty whispered to me from the hawse hole; "She's coming round on to the beam."

I dragged myself beside him, and looked out. The submarine was running slowly across our bows, submerged but for the conning tower and periscopes; from time to time the swell lifted her, and as the water sluiced away we could see the gun. Then she went down another five feet and was hidden but for the periscopes, and she began on a slow circle round us. We lay absolutely motionless upon the deck.

She passed astern of us and came up upon the starboard quarter, and passed up alongside, distant only fifty yards away, submerged all but the periscopes. Then she turned slowly across our bows and broke surface almost dead ahead, according to the snotty. And when next she came into my view she was running on the surface very slowly, perhaps two hundred yards away, and turning to pass down our port side again.

"Come up to finish us off, I reckon," said Wallis.

I said: "Stations for the port forrard gun. Be ready for it."

Her speed slowed to a crawl. A man appeared in the conning tower, and then an officer. And then in a moment there were men on her deck and round about the gun, and I said:

"Action stations. Get to it."

Then we were on our feet and racing for the gun. It swung up smoothly and the breech clanged home, and I laid her on the water line below the conning tower. The vessel rolled as I fired, and it was an over, and almost immediately there was a blinding crash as their first shell went home upon our forecastle. None of us were more than shaken by the blast; we pulled ourselves together, and I laid and fired again. And that went better, for I holed her on the water line and that shell burst inside. I laid my next shot carefully upon their gun and it burst just below; at that range there could be no missing, given time. With the fourth shot I holed her once again behind the conning tower, and I think I must have started fire inside that narrow hull, for smoke was coming out of her towards the end.

She began to blow her tanks, and the water came foaming up around her all white and creamy, and mingled with a little oil. She took a list to port, and then the hatches opened forward, and then aft, and men began to stream up on to her deck from the forward hatch, and one or two of them were waving white things at us, shirts perhaps.

With the fifth shot there came a hitch. I swung the breech wide and the case clanged out, but the next shell was not there, and instead of passing it the boy was yelling some infernal nonsense of his own. And then as I snarled at him he said: "Aren't they surrendering?"

I ripped out an oath and a command, and he slid the shell into the bore. I slammed the breech and swung the gun until it bore upon the forward hatch. And that damned boy was staring at me with a sort of horror, and I cursed at him and fired, and an inferno of flame shot up about the hatch, and I went on loading and firing like a man possessed. . . .

And so, with a cry of terror, I was fumbling at the door, and out into the silent, moonlit passage, and I went down it blundering from side to side towards something concrete that I knew, away from all the terrors of my bed, running as though all the devils in hell were at my heels. And by the stairs a light switched on ahead of me and checked me in my rush, and I was shivering and in a wringing sweat, and steadying myself against the wall. And there the night porter found me.

He said quickly: "Is anything the matter, sir? I thought I heard a crying out, downstairs."

I passed my hand over my eyes, and stared at him. "It's all right. I'm sorry. I must have had a bad dream, I think." And then I asked him: "What's the time?"

"Half-past three, sir."

I was dead cold, and wringing wet with sweat. I asked: "Is there a fire downstairs?"

He said: "I think there's still a little fire left in smoking room. I could make it up if you wanted it, sir."

I nodded. "That's best. You might bring me a double whisky down there. I shan't sleep again tonight." And so I fetched my dressing gown and went down to the empty, silent room and sat there in my chair before the fire till the dawn came, and long after that. Until a startled housemaid found me sitting there as she came in to do the room.

Then I went up and had a bath, and dressed, and came downstairs an hour later to my breakfast in the coffee-room. There was nothing in *The Times* that touched on my affair, for I went through it carefully. And then I settled down to plan my Press campaign. I made a list of the connections I could make in Fleet Street, and I spent a long time planning who should launch the matter first. That day was Thursday. On Friday afternoon, I thought, the matter should be put in train. I knew that it would go all right.

I had all that day to kill. I cannot remember where I went or what I did; I think that for the greater part of it I must have been wandering aimlessly around and looking at the shops. I know that late in the afternoon I was at the Round Pond in Kensington Gardens, and I sat there for a long time upon a chair, watching the birds and the children with their boats, and the swift rippling of the waves along the concrete verge.

And presently I left that place, cold and a little tired, and went back to the club. It was half-past six or so when I got back, and the evening papers had come in. And picking up the first that came to hand, I saw the news that I had been expecting all along.

It read: 'Sad fatality at Cambridge.' I knew the rest of it, but I read down the column carefully. It seemed that he had fallen from his window into the court during the night, a drop of forty feet. The theory was put forward that he had been opening the window, and had been seized with dizziness. It seemed quite reasonable, the way that it was put. A short obituary followed the account.

So it was over.

I stood there with the paper in my hand, re-reading the account, and a plump old man that I have sometimes spoken to came doddering to me and looked over my shoulder. "I see that you are reading about poor Ormsby," he remarked. "So dreadfully sad. Did you ever meet him?"

"No," I said shortly.

He went rambling on. "I used to know him slightly, just a little, you know, but I knew his cousin very much better. She married a connection of my own, a Colonel Wilkinson, in the Artillery, and they live down at Bognor now. Bognor Regis, we must call it. They used to live at Camberley, but now they live at Bognor—Bognor Regis. I feel very much for her. She will be broken hearted at this news—quite broken hearted."

At that moment something in me seemed to snap, and I turned viciously on him. "That's all nonsense," I said unevenly. I stared at him for a moment. "It must be. . . . Nobody ever yet died of a broken heart. That's not one of the killing diseases. . . ."

And with that I turned on my heel and went away to find some place where I could be alone. I believe he spoke to the Secretary about me.

And I went in and had my dinner in the enormous, silent

dining-room, where the food is the best in London and the wine without an equal in the country, I suppose. Where we all sit down at little separate tables by ourselves, our backs against the wall, eating alone and talking now and then to the ancient, friendly servants when the loneliness becomes intolerable. That night I was restless after dinner. I had my coffee and went wandering from room to room, picking up papers and reviews and putting them down again, longing for some occupation for the mind.

And presently I left the club and went walking slowly up Pall Mall, immersed in memories. Even at that time I was beginning to forget the details which I wanted to keep by my side, and it was then that I first thought that I must make a book of it. Which is what I have done. For I have so little to remind me of those summer days I had, when everything was gold and blue for me. I have not even a photograph that I could keep. Only a few of her clothes, which I have put away carefully in one of the wardrobes in my room, where they belong.

I turned into St James's Street, and walked slowly up towards the Piccadilly end. And near the top I turned and looked backwards down the empty street to the reserved, formal Palace at the end, a symbol of security beneath its moon-like clock. And standing there and looking down that street it seemed to me that there was the essence of England—stable, a little formal, and secure. And I thought that the election that was coming would be nothing but a phase in history, a milestone in the journey of a country which is capable of governing itself as competently in the future as it has done in the years gone past. The country would have a free, unbiased judgment for the choosing of its Government, and with that I was content.

On the next day I went back to work.

# Nevil Shute

'An honest, exciting adventure writer who blends narrative gift with a fine power of description'
DAILY TELEGRAPH

## A Town Like Alice 80p

A magnificent story of bravery, endurance and love in war and the aftermath of war.

## On the Beach 70p

The famous and controversial story of the final months in the lives of people living in an Australia doomed by radiation.

## Requiem for a Wren 70p

A deeply moving story of love between a young Wren and an Australian serviceman in the tension of England before D-Day.

## No Highway 70p

Breath-stopping suspense and mounting drama on a flight across the icy Atlantic.

## Ruined City 50p

A romantic but intensely realistic story of the last years of a businessman's life in the north country.

## So Disdained 50p

A thrilling novel of a great flier involved in espionage and treason.

## Marazan 50p

The first of Nevil Shute's many brilliant novels – a story of prison escape, murder and smuggling.

# Nicholas Monsarrat

## The Tribe That Lost Its Head 95p

Political crisis on the tropical island of Pharamaul erupts into
a ferment of intrigue and violence; a handful of white men
and women become hostages to fortune as events move
towards a barbaric climax . . .

'A splendidly exciting story' SUNDAY TIMES

## Richer Than All His Tribe 80p

A gripping successor to *The Tribe That Lost Its Head*. The
prime minister of newly independent Pharamaul has the best
of intentions; but his first faltering steps in statesmanship
leave him and his people tottering on the brink of hell . . .

'Not so much a novel, more a slab of dynamite'
SUNDAY MIRROR

## The Pillow Fight 80p

When a beautiful career girl marries an idealistic young writer,
she finds her former values questioned; but her husband
has tasted the sweet, corrupting fruits of success . . .

'Immensely readable' IRISH TIMES

## The Kappillan of Malta 95p

'In the figure of Father Salvatore who staunches the blood of
the wounded and runs his own church in the ancient catacombs,
Monsarrat has created one of the most memorable characters
of postwar fiction' DAILY EXPRESS

Farley Mowat
**The Serpent's Coil**  70p

The great sea saga of ships and men and the savage fury of
a North Atlantic hurricane . . . the crushing embrace of the
'serpent's coil'.

'The true story of the Liberty ship *Leicester* which sailed
for New York from England in the summer of 1948, ran into
a hurricane and was abandoned with the loss of six lives
in mid-Atlantic . . . and of the tug *Foundation Josephine*
which tracked the derelict over many thousands of miles . . .'
NEW YORKER

J. D. Gilman and John Clive
**KG 200**  95p

They flew Flying Fortresses. They wore American uniforms . . .
but they were Germans! KG 200 – the phantom arm of
Hitler's Luftwaffe. From a secret base in occupied Norway
these crack pilots plan their ultimate mission, the raid that
would bring Allied defeat crashing down from the
exploding skies . . .

Inspired by the best-kept secret of World War Two, this is
one of the most enthralling novels of air warfare,
espionage and manhunt ever written.

'Shattering' TELEGRAPH